DELTA SEARCH

DELTA SEARCH

QUEST FOR TOMORROW

WILLIAM SHATNER

HarperPrism

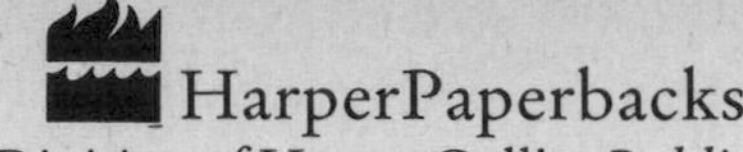

HarperPaperbacks
A Division of HarperCollins*Publishers*
10 East 53rd Street, New York, N.Y. 10022-5299

This is a work of fiction. The characters, incidents, and dialogues are products of the author's imagination and are not to be construed as real. Any resemblance to actual events or persons, living or dead, is entirely coincidental.

ISBN: 0-06-105274-4

Printed in the United States of America

First printing: February 1997

Designed by Lili Schwartz

Library of Congress Cataloging-in-Publication Data

Shatner, William.
Delta search: a novel / by William Shatner.
p. cm. -- (Quest for tomorrow)
ISBN 0-06-105274-4 (hard)
I. Title. II. Series: Shatner, William. Quest for tomorrow.
PS3569.H347D4 1997
813 '.54--dc20 96-35484
CIP

97 98 99 ❖ 10 9 8 7 6 5 4 3 2 1

Man must have bread and butter, but he
must also have something to lift his heart.
This program is clean. We are not spending
the money to kill people. We are not harming
the environment. We are helping the
spirit of man. We are unlocking
secrets billions of years old.

FAROUK EL BAZ
Skylab: Next Great Moment in Space

Advanced civilizations—if they exist—aren't
breaking their necks to save us before we
destroy ourselves. Personally, I think that
makes for a more interesting universe.

CARL SAGAN

So nigh is grandeur to our dust,
So near is God to man,
When duty whispers low, *Thou must,*
The youth replies, *I can.*

RALPH WALDO EMERSON

DEDICATION

Youth is not wasted, as some learned sage said, on the young. It is indeed a grace note on the slighly aging. I happen to know, for I am aging, slightly. But, into my life has walked, run, pummeled, and pounded a youth of such energy and beauty as to be extraordinary. And so, I dedicate this book to the woman who has brought me youth and energy, love and passion, inspiration and not some little perspiration, Nerine, The Beloved . . .

—also—

Along with that youthful theme, this book is dedicated to the young reading public of today. Hopefully some of the youthful members of the world will find in our hero inspiration, not only in terms of what Jim does, but also in discovering the magic of reading . . . weaning themselves away from the hypnosis of television to take a voyage into imagination.

ACKNOWLEDGMENTS

Bill Quick is a terrific writer and is, as I'm sure he's been told many times in his life, quick—to write, to think and to be creative. My debt to him for this book goes far beyond acknowledgment.

The wonderful editor, John Silbersack is the engine powering this vehicle.

Caitlin Blaisdell and Carmen LaVia.

PROLOGUE

1

The hunters had arrived even before Kate shouldered open the door to the dilapidated little Pleb-unit she'd illegally subleased from its rightful occupant in San Francisco's Hunter's Point district.

She glanced up at the sky as she juggled two bags of groceries and a large pack of disposable diapers through the doorway.

"I'm home." There was no reply, nor did she expect any—Carl was still at work, pretending to be a bartender, and Jimmy should still be sleeping—but she smiled at her moment of whimsy. The smile transfigured her tired features and made her seem young. She *was* young, though she hadn't looked it for a good while.

She had a strong, wiry frame, not tall, but condensed, sketched in the clear lines of her movements: sharp and controlled and, despite her exhaustion, vital. Her eyes punctuated her face, startlingly blue, intense, so that they seemed larger than they really were. Her hair was that sandy blond that made one think of lions; it was cut mid-length, wavy, springing up here and there in random curls.

Her mouth was strong and determined beneath a little nothing of a nose—the only nondescript feature on her foxy, high-cheekboned face. There was a spray of fine lines at the corners of her eyes, as if she'd spent a lot of time looking at distant horizons, and if those misty distances were as much imagined as real, who was to say? When she moved, she always managed to look as if she knew exactly where she was going.

She wore dirty sneakers, faded jeans, a man's blue denim shirt, and a heavy silver bracelet—a single hard circle, like punctuation—around her left wrist. If you were a mugger, you'd leave her alone. . . .

She crossed the shabby living room that smelled of stale cabbage and set her bags on the chipped counter in the kitchen.

An indeterminate sound from the bedroom brought her head up. It sounded strange—not a baby sound.

The movement electrified her with the air of a lioness sensing hidden danger. A terrible alertness burned in her fierce blue eyes as she pushed a wave of blond hair away from her face. Her purse was next to the groceries; she opened it and took out a black maser pistol so large it seemed ridiculous in her small hand, a joke or an unreal toy. But there was nothing childish in the way she cocked it with a deadly little buzz.

"Who's there?"

But in the wan yellow light of a cheap ceiling glowstrip there was only an unmade bed and the silent wide-eyed baby swaddled in his nest of sheets, staring greenly at her. Jimmy, awake now. No charming little bassinet or trendy cyberbuggy for him. Not when his life might depend on how quickly she could scoop him up and run.

She raked the little room with her fierce gaze, then went to the closet and flung it open. Nothing there. Slowly, her rigid muscles began to relax.

She exhaled, and it seemed all the strength flowed out of her with that breath. But his face, flowerlike, had turned to follow her movement, and now he offered her a toothless, trusting grin that made her want to weep. This was no life for him. Or her, either. As if anybody had a choice.

She picked him up and pulled him to her, marveling at the delicacy of his skull, the tiny perfection of the fingers he wrapped around her thumb with sudden amazing strength. She kissed the top of his head and whispered, "Strong little thing, aren't you? Sure didn't come from your daddy, did it? But you're special, yes, you are."

Then, a soft catch in her throat: "I love you, baby. If only your daddy wasn't such a pure-dee bastard, this would be a life, wouldn't it?"

After she put the diapers to good use and rocked him to sleep, she retrieved the maser pistol and switched off the light. Then she stood there a long moment, not knowing whether to cry or just blow her brains out. No, it was not a life, was it?

2

The battered black grav-van looked like a wirehead war wagon as it hovered silently above the curb on the opposite side of the street from the Pleb-unit. For several moments nothing happened. No movement was visible through the impenetrable mirror-windows, and no sound but the sigh of the hydrogen engine barely audible above the rising evening wind.

City repair crews no longer bothered to replace blasted-out lenses in the streetlights that floated randomly overhead, their once precise patterns shattered by computers no one bothered to maintain and program properly anymore. This was a ghetto, after all.

Darkness came early and hard here, pierced only by occasional hysterical laughter and the popcorn spatter and vicious buzzing of sporadic gunfire. A strange calm emanated from the vehicle; one yonderboy, lost in a wirehead daze, entered that zonal quiet, registered a befuddled stare, and staggered limply to the other side of the street.

He was long gone when the curbside doors of the van whispered open on frictionless bearings, and four shadows ghosted seamlessly into deeper shadow. Now the night took on a sweaty urgency, a musty scent of violence. A squirrel chittered sharply in protest, then fell silent. The lights in the window of the small house glowed steadily, brave against the darkness that seemed to press in against their feeble spark.

In the rusty dark, against the soft green glare of the instrument readouts, the tension was like tiny razors, scraping flesh, flaying nerves. It was always like this. They were used to it—as used to it as humans could get and still remain human. They were right on the edge of that, though, and sometimes they crossed over. Tonight might be such a time.

A voice whispered: "Lima Baker, this is Hitter One. We have target acquisition. Kill zone is optimal. I say again, kill zone is optimal. . . ."

After another beat of time, someone activated a helmet microphone, and said, "Go."

3

His name was Carl and his last name was whatever they were using this month. He automatically checked the crude little card taped to the doorframe, just as Kate had done, and saw that they were the Johnson family, at least for the time being. He did not notice the dusty black grav-van parked across the street and down the block, although he would spend years berating himself for that uncharacteristic lapse.

He closed the door and activated the electronic dead bolt. He glanced around the shabby living room as he tossed his backpack onto the sofa. "Kate, you here?"

"The bedroom."

He nodded to himself, walked over, and stuck his head around the corner. "I'm home."

She glanced up from where she sat on the edge of the bed and rocked little Jimmy in her arms. "Such as it is."

He sighed heavily. "I know, I know. We can't go on like this forever." He paused. "Kate? We've put it off long enough. You know what I mean. . . ."

She looked up at him, her blue eyes widening slowly. She stopped rocking the baby. "Carl . . . no."

He raised one hand. "I swear it, Kate. I can kill him. I wouldn't even think about it if I thought it would put you and Jimmy at risk. But it's been almost a year. He wouldn't be looking for me now. And nobody can protect themselves against an assassin who knows what he is doing."

She looked down at the sleeping child. "Yes," she said bitterly. "As long as that assassin doesn't mind getting himself killed in the process. Carl, I'm a selfish woman. I don't think there is a noble bone left in my body. I can live with the running and hiding as long as it's the three of us. But I won't have you sacrifice yourself on some masculine altar of vengeance—not for our sakes. You understand?"

He stared at her. "I'm not suicidal. And I was never noble. I won't deny the vengeance part, but I would never risk either of you for that."

She turned and carefully placed Jimmy on the mattress, and arranged the two pillows on either side of him as an improvised cradle.

She put her finger to her lips. "Let him sleep now."

He took her in his arms and squeezed. Then he began to dig his knuckles into the muscles of her upper back. She sighed with pleasure at the impromptu back rub. "You have exactly two hours to stop that, big boy."

"I know a few tricks I bet you'd like even better."

"Oh? And have I seen any of these tricks before?"

"Possibly."

"I'm not sure. Maybe you'd better show me again. Refresh my memory. Not in front of the baby, though."

He grinned, the smell of her hair filling his nostrils. "Kid's asleep."

She smiled. "Let's keep it that way."

4

Afterward, she curled her bare feet into the space between the sofa cushions piled on the sagging frame; the unit had long since lost its ability to shape itself to those who sat upon it. "That was a fun game. Do you know any others?"

He kissed the back of her neck lightly. For that moment, at least, he was able to forget the hopeless circumstances of their collective life. Even the decrepit living room took on a rich, warm glow in the lamp of their affection.

"Love is only half the illusion," he murmured into her ear.

She stretched and yawned. "Hm. George Santayana."

"Good. From what?"

"*The Life of Reason.*"

"What an educated woman I cohabit with," he said.

"Smart, too. Of course, to be in love is merely to be in a state of perceptual anesthesia."

He leaned back and stared at the ceiling. There was an ugly

orange water blotch up there that somehow reminded him of a map of Tasmania. "Ambrose Bierce."

She pinched his arm. "Nope. It wasn't Bierce. Try H.L. Mencken."

He reached over to the rickety little table at the end of the couch and hoisted the heavy book onto his chest. "*American Quotations*," he said. "The court of last resort." He turned to the indexes at the back: "Doesn't seem to be under Bierce. You're going to rub this in, I presume?"

"Hand me that rubber, pal."

"You are an evil woman," he told her. "Besides, we've already done that."

"So it is Mencken, eh? From *Prejudices*, I believe."

He shifted, nearly dumping her onto the floor. "Did I mention anything about your native evilness?"

She launched an assault against a particularly ticklish part of his anatomy, but before the mock battle could grow into anything seriously interesting, a soft wail issued from the bedroom.

"That sound like a diaper or a bottle call to you?"

"Doesn't matter," she told him. "You lost, you get to do the dirty work—which, from the sound of things, is what it is. Diapers on the kitchen counter, big fellow."

He stood up and stretched mightily. She stared up at him, inwardly amazed at his sheer physicalness. He exuded a masculine force so strong it was palpable. God, she loved him so much. Why did life have to be so unfair?

5

"Well, I've got good news and bad news. Which do you want first?"

She looked up from the extremely powerful little computer she was holding in her lap. He knew that, somewhere on a nanotech chip inside it, was the reason their lives had become the monstrosities they now endured.

"No news is good news, right?" she said.

"The diaper is changed—good news—but now he's wide awake. Bad news. How about if I take him with me? I've got to pick up some stuff at the mall."

She nodded absently. "Stick an extra diaper in your backpack. You never know."

He grinned. "Nope, if there's one thing you do know, it's that sooner or later an extra diaper is exactly what you're going to need."

He bent to kiss the top of her blond head, arranging Jimmy in his chest carrier as he leaned over. "I'll be about an hour, okay?"

"Be careful. Love you." She didn't raise her eyes from the small holographic screen that danced above her machine. He smiled fondly at the way she could sink into such a fog of concentration. But then, she was a genius—thank God. He knew what he was. He had given her something she needed desperately, but he was no genius.

He adjusted the straps of his backpack, opened the front door, and blew her a kiss. "Love you, Kate."

It was the last time he would ever see her alive.

6

Perhaps it was simply a case of nerves scraped by fear into a state of near-psychopathic awareness, or maybe there had been actual sounds: the soft scrape of leather, a nearly inaudible chink of metal. She had been dozing in a rump-sprung chair in the living room before a static-glazed holovision cube, but now she came up with the computer in one hand and the maser pistol in the other. Cords of muscle stood out in her neck. She looked first toward the door, then the window, frozen as a witch-woman caught in the moment of summoning.

Demons coming!

She took two impossibly long, loping steps that brought her into the bedroom. She turned, bringing the maser up in both hands. Her mouth opened and her lips drew back in a grimace that exposed her teeth. She pulled the trigger as an explosion blew in the front door. A harsh, improbably loud buzzing filled her ears. She was both lucky and good; her first shot knocked down the black figure that bounded out of the smoke. She never got off a second shot.

The tall, lanky woman with red lips who crashed through the window into the kitchen carried a scatter blaster. That shot slammed Kate in the back and nearly cut her in half.

"Jesus, Smith, are you okay?" the lanky woman said.

There were four of them, three men and the lanky woman, though it was almost impossible to tell which was which behind the opaque shields of their body armor. Only the blood-colored lipstick revealed the otherwise hidden femininity of the one who stooped next to the broken body of her victim and put gloved fingers on the silent throat. She glanced up: "This one's done."

Satisfied, she moved quickly to the one who had fallen just inside the door.

"Hey Smitty Smitty Smitty." She pushed back her faceplate to reveal unnaturally pale skin and straight black hair chopped off short—a face both beautiful and horrible, disfigured by death-lust.

"Okay, boy, you're okay, you hear me?" Her hands worked rapidly at the straps and catches of his armor. "Oh, all right, that's good, just a little bruise." She looked up. "His vest stopped it." And back down. "Now come on, damn it, wake up!"

The man groaned.

"That's it, baby, talk to mama. Yeah, that's good, you're gonna be fine."

She leaned back on her haunches and slapped her thighs. "Okay, gang, we got a schedule here. Let's finish it. This is for sure a crap-hole neighborhood, but these cannons make a bang. One of the yonderboys might actually call the cops." They shared a nervous chuckle over *that*.

The one called Smitty heaved himself up on his elbows. "What happened?"

"You took a hit, my man. Your armor stopped it, or we wouldn't be having this conversation. You okay?"

"I'm gonna live, I think." He grunted and grabbed her shoulder and began to haul himself to his feet. She took his weight easily, rising with him until he was upright.

"Smitty, get your ass back to the van. We'll be there as soon as we finish here."

Smitty pushed back his own faceplate. "No, I'm okay." He looked past the woman at the body sprawled in the bedroom door. "Jesus."

He had a large pack strapped to his back. He shrugged out of it and let it drop to the floor. The woman laughed. "That's right, you boom-boom boys kill me. Treat that stuff like it was a bag of bubble gum."

He opened the pack and rummaged inside.

"You've got four minutes."

He shook his head. "I won't need all of it. Go on."

He had to step over the woman's body to enter the bedroom. She lay in a wide pool of blood, her blue eyes open and empty.

"Jesus," he muttered. His nose twitched involuntarily at the acid-copper stench of her blood. But he moved quickly, slapping small packets of explosive against the doorjamb as he scanned the interior of the bedroom for the most effective places to turn this cottage into an indistinguishable funeral pyre.

The woman's mangled corpse repulsed him, and so, as he searched for the items he'd been told to look for, he did not turn her over. The computer she'd held lay beneath her, obscured by torn flesh and drying blood.

It took him thirty seconds less than the four minutes he'd promised. He left by the front door, looking neither right nor left. He climbed into the van. A moment later, the vehicle glided smoothly away from the curb. A block down, its red taillights began to glow, and it rose straight up into the air.

Forty-five seconds after that, the small cottage exploded into flames. By the time the fire squads arrived, nothing was left but ashes. Even with the latest DNA sniffers, it took the arson techs three days to find the bones. And they never found anything of the computer at all.

7

Fog stretched in a high gray wall about three hundred yards offshore along the San Francisco Bay, masking the glittering lights of the Greater Bay HyperMall. Carl boarded the monorail at the Hunter's Point terminal and leaned back again the railing to watch the approach of the huge man-made island floating on an unsinkable foam of high-tension bubbles.

Jimmy began to squirm against the straps that held him. Carl looked down at the top of the baby's head and the thick wisps of dark hair coiled damply there.

"What's the matter, big guy?" he whispered. "All cranky from making your mom's life a living hell? Did you fill up your pants for her several times today? Yes, I bet she liked that all right, yes I do."

Jimmy grinned and made soft grunting noises, as if in agreement with the incomprehensible ravings of the big man who carried him against his chest so gently.

8

Shouting chaos filled the frantic interior of the stealthed mother ship orbiting ten miles above the San Francisco Bay.

"*Where did he go? Damn it, I've lost—okay, hold it. Got him!*"

"*What? Give me coordinates, give me . . .* now!"

"Okay, I'm directing the backup teams. Gimme Team Baker and Team Charlie."

"Where *is* he?"

"Hang on—okay, he's headed for the HyperMall. Got it, the HyperMall!"

"Right. Team Leader Baker, Team Leader Charlie, stand by to download new mission coordinates. . . ."

9

Carl pushed his nose against the greasy, graffiti-etched window of the monorail car. He wished he could stick his head outside into the salt-laden air of the Bay, but he understood that if he could, the trans-Bay monorail would rival the Golden Gate Bridge as a magnet for suicides.

Hidden antigrav machinery emitted an audible hum as the car reached the top of its arc, jerked hard, and began to descend into the preposterous lighted warren of the mall.

He put one arm around the tiny figure at his chest, and said, "See that, kid? That's the world out there. Pretty, isn't it? Well, enjoy it while you can. Underneath, it isn't as pretty as it looks."

Yet despite the dire sentiment, in at least that moment Carl felt at peace, calm and relaxed, even hopeful. He sighed and watched the approach of the retail palaces coming up below, and allowed himself a thought:

We just might make it. Maybe.

It was hubris. He should have known better.

10

A large black troop carrier dropped straight down out of the night sky onto the emergency gravport atop the HyperMall. Doors slammed down into ramps. The guts of the carrier emptied as squads of men, their heavy lasers and slug guns held across their armored bodies at port arms, stormed onto the deck.

Last to exit was a group of six in plainclothes. Four men and two women. They moved quickly, the air about them scratchy with the sounds of their communicator implants. Their leader glanced around, then spoke into his throat mike, directing the deployment of the uniformed troops.

"Mother Hen, we are on site," he said.

Squawks of static, then—"Locate and terminate."

"Roger. Read and understood." He turned to the rest of the squad. "Location coordinates downloading . . . now. Okay, let's move on it!"

11

Slidewalks pulled torrents of gawkers past holographic towers where giant advertisements played out breathlessly upon thin air. Subliminal messages yanked at the subconscious, urging one and all to Buy! Buy Now! Buy A *Lot*! And fluttering in the air like abandoned flags, countless scraps of eyetugger advertising whistled, hummed, and moaned, demanding a moment of your time, just a moment, please and thank you.

In the huge windows of the big stores holographic dioramas and virtual-reality stage sets acted out tense scenarios wherein clothes, perfumes, leathers, drugs, food, and drink of all kinds made heroes and heroines out of everyday folks, even promised that life itself might be a thing of endless beauty and pleasure. If only you would buy.

Carl, like most of the throng, barely noticed the info overload. He drifted along, enjoying the sensation of movement. In the back of his mind was a short list: razor creme, thirty-day male birth control pills, a bottle of fat-depressant juice. Kate had been complaining about the extra five pounds she'd picked up somewhere.

But his old instincts were not entirely comatose. Here and there he spotted units of HyperMall's security force, mostly in plainclothes, on patrol. He couldn't explain just how he knew them, except that armed men and women held themselves differently than others.

It was a comforting sort of feeling. Big companies like HyperMall could afford far better protection than that offered by public police departments. Here in the mall itself, he wouldn't have to worry about a wirehead riot or a band of roving Pleb muggers spoiling his peaceful stroll. That interlude of complacency vanished when he saw a man and woman on the next level up, pretending to be just another couple as they leaned against the railing and watched him.

He was too much the professional to stare directly at them. He let his gaze slide on by, then watched them with his peripheral vision. He could no more explain how he recognized them for what they were than he could tell someone how he picked out the mall security forces. But this pair wasn't security although they shared something in common with the rent-a-cops: they were armed to the teeth.

Not obviously, but Carl recognized the bumps and lumps in odd places, and the strange thickenings caused by even the lightest of body armor. Professionals, hunters, killers—watching him.

And he knew what that sharp, cold regard meant: he was the mark. Their weapons were for him, and that meant only one thing. Maybe didn't work. Maybe wouldn't happen. Hubris was always punished. Only death, well dressed and inevitable, was coming here, coming now, coming for him and the *baby*.

He sped up a bit, weaving through the crowds, until he saw what he was looking for. Up ahead, a young technocrat couple eyeballed the sights, trailed by their cyberbuggy. He bent over as he reached the buggy, spilling Jimmy into the darkened interior before either of the couple saw him.

"Excuse me, mall security," he said quickly to the young man. "We've had a report of a child snatching. Would you activate your buggy's defense system?"

The young man stared at him, bug-eyed. Then he gulped, nodded, and quickly pressed a small button on the side of his expensive watch. The buggy made a warbling sound. An opaque black shield slipped over the top, and a red warning light began to blink, signifying that the buggy's automatic weapon system was armed.

"Should we leave?" the man asked.

"I would," Carl said. "Via China Basin Station looks safe enough."

Then he strode on, pausing only to impress the faces of the young couple on his memory. It wasn't much, but maybe it would be enough. He spotted the lighted entrance to a hotel up ahead and turned off the slidewalk. He could feel someone's stare boring into his back.

The young couple or a gaze less friendly? He didn't turn to look.

That would have been an amateur move, and, besides, he was about to be very busy. He just couldn't allow any more time for sightseeing.

12

"The mark has left the slidewalk," the heavyset, well-dressed man subvocalized into the microphone implanted in his throat.

"Roger, Number One. Has he spotted you?"

"Don't know. Doubt it. He talked to a young couple for a second, but then went on."

"Did he know the couple?"

"Can't tell. You want me to track them?"

"No. Follow the mark. We'll pick up stragglers later, if necessary."

Now armored figures were stopping, turning, heading in new directions all over the mall. Converging on the mark, who had vanished into the lobby of the HyperMall Imperial Toyota-Marriott.

"Base, I am inside the hotel," Number One reported.

"Have you located the mark?"

"Not yet," Number One said.

"Watch yourself. Full armor backup on the way."

"Good," Number One replied. He scanned the lobby but didn't see the mark. His briefing had included the mark's past history. If the mark had spotted him, this would not be easy. In the end, though, the mark couldn't escape. The only public ways off the island were via monorail or taxipod, and both those embarkation points were covered.

Number One allowed himself a moment to wonder what one guy had done to merit the commitment of an entire Class One forty-unit SWAT team. Ticked somebody off hard, no doubt about that. Hard enough to earn a premature funeral. Because that was the order of the day:

Locate and terminate.

13

Stiron und Ritter, the venerable German weapons firm, had been making superlative handguns for over 250 years. So when the government of Nouveau Québec came to them with a specific problem, they outdid themselves.

The specs had been simple; government police forces, tired of being outgunned by terrorists liberally supplied with weapons from sympathizers in the United States, wanted something that would knock down any human, no matter how shielded. A laser or maser wouldn't do: one big enough to cut through heavy armor would be far too large for a single soldier or cop to wield. But S&R knew that for sheer stopping power, the speeding bullet had never been equaled.

So they came up with the Stiron und Ritter Model .75 self-propelled mini rocket launcher—a very long name for a small gun. The Model .75 looked like a large automatic pistol. It held ten seventy-five-caliber rounds, each one a tiny rocket delivering an explosive warhead made of depleted uranium. This round was a miniaturized version of an old tank-killer round, though it was self-propelled at very high speeds, almost eliminating recoil and vastly increasing the force of impact.

Technical specs aside, an S&R .75 in the hands of someone who knew how to use it could destroy a good-sized reinforced concrete building with a single magazine. And 270 years after it had been created, the current incarnation of it was still the most powerful handgun ever made.

14

"Looking for a guy," Number One said.

He leaned across the bar and showed the bartender a fresh holocube, downloaded from the mother ship only moments before.

"Yes, sir," the bartender replied. "I haven't seen him, though. Sorry."

"Okay, listen, keep the cube. You spot him, call this number."

"Yes, sir. Are you a police officer?"

Number One flashed a holobadge that said he was part of a federal crime agency. He wasn't, although the ID had been made for him by a different federal agency—one the bartender had never heard of, and never would.

"Would you put it on my reader, sir?"

Number One nodded and set the small unit on the bar's credit reader. After a moment, when the little machine recognized the emergency government override, a green light flashed. The bartender handed it back.

"Thank you, Officer."

"Just call the number. And show the cube to the rest of your people, okay?"

The bartender nodded. "Shift change in a couple of minutes," he said. "I'll pass it on." He glanced up as another bartender appeared at the far end of the bar, wiping his hands on a bar towel.

Number One turned to look as well.

15

Carl walked directly across the lobby, searching for the sign he knew he would see somewhere. Yes, sure enough: *Employees Only*.

He pushed through the door and found himself in a room with six elevators. He opened one and saw that it went three levels below him. Hotels always put employee facilities in the lowest level of the building. He pressed the down button and waited.

The long hallway he entered thronged with people in various uniforms—housekeepers and bellmen, waitresses and housemen, bartenders and banquet waiters. Bartenders.

"Scuse me, I just got called in for banquets—bartending—and I need to pick up a uniform."

The young man nodded. "Turn right, go to the end, then right again. Ask at the counter."

"Thanks. Is it the same uniform as for front bartenders? I'm gonna train for that, too."

The kid grinned. "White shirt, black vest, black pants. Hasn't changed in three hundred years, I guess."

"Probably just feels that way. Thanks again." Carl waved and headed off. The attendant behind the counter looked him over, said, "Forty-four vest, right? And thirty-three waist on the pants?"

"You got a good eye."

"Ought to. Been doing it for twenty years."

"Where's the men's locker room?"

"Right behind you."

Carl changed, put his clothes into his backpack, and headed back the way he'd come.

He saw a manager. "Which way to the lounge? I'm supposed to cross-train tonight."

"Where's your name tag?"

"They said they'd have one there for me."

The manager nodded. "Be sure to wear it. Lounge is that way." He pointed. Carl followed the direction, pushed through a door, and found himself in a small room behind the bar. He took a deep breath and stepped through the curtained doorway, blinked, and caught his bearings.

A bartender stood about halfway down, holding a holocube. He was talking to a customer, a heavyset, well-dressed man. They both turned and stared at him as he entered. The bartender froze, then looked down at the cube and back up again. The customer slowly slipped his right hand inside his suit jacket.

Carl stepped closer and pulled back the bar towel a couple of inches, exposing the awesomely large snout of his weapon.

"Not one inch more," he said softly to the customer.

"What the—?" the bartender sputtered.

"Shut up," Carl said. He nodded at the customer. "Tell him."

Number One's eyes had gone wide in a face suddenly bleached the color of a freshly washed sheet. "That an S&R .75?"

Carl nodded. "Tell him," he repeated.

"Don't do nothing, buddy," Number One told the bartender. "Stay cool. I'll handle this."

Carl grinned tightly. "Yeah. You're doing a real good job right now. Just keep it up. You, bartender."

"Huh?"

"Don't touch anything, don't say anything, don't do anything. Just step over here to the back room, you, me, and mister guest here. All friends together, going to look at something, right?"

"Hey, buddy—"

"Do it," Number One said. "He won't hurt you."

"That's right," Carl agreed. "You either, unless you feel very stupid today."

Number One grunted. "I don't. Let's go."

Slowly, the three retreated toward the end of the bar. Number One stepped around and slipped into the back room, being careful to keep his hands in full view of Carl's watchful gaze. Number One had no moral compunction against using an innocent bystander as a shield. But a .75 would go through the bartender, his own body armor, himself, and three or four concrete walls behind him. No point in even thinking about it.

16

"What's going on? What the hell? Number One just dropped off the net!"

"Huh? Where is he? What happened?"

"Was in the Marriott. Lounge area, I think. Nothing now."

"Okay, okay. All team leaders, detach squads and converge on Marriott. Prepare to download revised maps. Penetration team take the lead, on my mark—*now*!"

17

Once they were safely out of view, Number One raised his hands slightly. "Now what? You want my piece?"

"Uh-huh. You know the drill. Careful."

"No problem." Number One gingerly reached beneath his jacket and pulled out an auto-stunner, commonly known as a buzz gun. He set it on the floor.

"Good." Carl glanced at the bartender, then back at Number One. "You got the standard field kit?"

"Like what?"

"Sleepy time."

"Yeah."

"Very good. Put the bartender down, please."

Number One took out a small kit and extracted a cube about an inch square. He adjusted a tiny dial on one side and said to the bartender: "It's a hypospray. Shoots a dose right through your clothes. This will put you to sleep, no problem, you won't even have a headache."

"Hey," the bartender said.

"Your choice, pal. Me or that big damned gun there. This way is less permanent, I guarantee it."

The bartender gulped and closed his eyes. Number one stepped closer and touched his upper arm. There was a sharp hissing noise. The bartender sank noiselessly to the floor.

"Now what?" Number One asked. "We got a Class One team aboard. You don't seriously think—?"

Carl shrugged. "Why not? What have I got to lose?"

"Beats me," Number One replied. "You get smart, maybe we all walk out of here alive." He glanced at Carl's pistol. "If not, then maybe we don't."

"You're awfully calm, aren't you?"

Number One shrugged.

"A Class One team. So that means—" He stepped closer and touched the side of Number One's voice box lightly. "You're wired."

Number One grinned. An explosion blew out the far end of the small room, knocking both men down.

A huge, booming electronic voice thundered: "*Carl Johnson, you are surrounded. Release your hostages and come out now.*"

But Carl was already moving, rolling. He triggered two quick shots through the gaping hole at the shadowy armored figures he saw beyond. The noise the .75 made was enormous: a sharp whooshing sound, then a ringing explosion, like somebody setting off a hand grenade beneath a gigantic cathedral bell.

He kept on rolling until he was out of the room and in the hallway behind. He'd already come this way. The hall emptied past the service bar into the huge kitchen of the hotel. He dashed on through, then quickly slowed when he reached the kitchen proper.

Employees ran past him, heading for the bar to see what the commotion was all about. Red fire lights flashed in the ceilings. Carl walked quickly to one of the deep-fat fryers, grabbed a pan, scooped up some of the hot grease, and tossed it onto a nearby stove.

Flames roared up, setting off the kitchen fire extinguisher system. He felt a wash of heat across his skull, smelled the distinctive stink of burning hair. Impenetrable billows of white powder blasted from a dozen outlets, filling the kitchen with fog. The fire alarm began to bleat.

Carl kept on going. Near the back of the kitchen was the waste-recycling room. He ducked inside, reached down, and opened a hatch. A slowly flowing, turgid stream of waste and garbage flowed beneath, bound for underwater pipes that fed an onshore reprocessing plant.

"Ugh," he said.

He went back to the kitchen doorway, aimed, and triggered off several blasts. Twenty yards away, the ceiling began to collapse.

Without another glance, Carl turned, took a deep breath, and dropped down into the tube passage. A moment later, he was gone.

18

A hundred yards offshore, just out from the China Basin recycling plant, a muffled explosion roiled the calm waters. Noxious goop and fetid odors bubbled to the surface, followed by Carl Johnson. He took a deep breath, then struck out for shore.

19

Teresa and Patrick Kendall stared out the window as their monorail car paused at the China Basin Station. They were going farther, on to Russian Hill, but the view here was so nice.

"I think we must be okay by now," Teresa said. "Surely it's safe to turn off the buggy?"

Patrick, who still looked upset, glanced around. They were alone. "Okay," he said, and touched his watch.

The black shield slid away as Teresa bent over the buggy. She stopped. "Patrick!"

"What! What's wrong?"

But before she could tell him, a tall dark man, hair burned off on one side of his head, soaked to the skin and smelling of sewers, pushed onto the car.

"Sorry, folks, one of them is mine." He scooped up Jimmy, nodded, and vanished into the night.

20

He came in low profile and fast—at least as low and fast as he could with an infant strapped to his chest and half his hair burned off.

He knew. But he didn't know, not with the blood-deep knowledge that came of getting a good bear hug on disaster. And he needed that, to sustain himself in the years to come, needed to see and smell and taste the bitter dregs of failure.

There was a crowd, of course. The stench of ancient, fire-seared wood and cheap, melted plastic filled the flashing night. A hundred separate communication channels scratched on the busy darkness. The night was electrified with death.

He pulled the blue knit watch cap down low over his skull, masking the burn that disfigured his scalp. The cap had rested in his backpack for nearly a year, along with the Stiron und Ritter rocket gun, extra ammo, ten thousand dollars in gold coins, a folding combat knife, and three sets of false identification. He had been prepared—just not prepared enough. His own ruthlessness had more than met its match.

Now his nostrils twitched at an old and horribly familiar stink—the rich, greasy aroma of burned flesh. Human flesh. He couldn't get any closer without giving up the protection of the crowd that surrounded him. There was a police line, of course; armored and shielded men and women, heavily armed, their voices buzzing and inhuman, filtered through vocoders so their identities could never be analyzed.

"Stay back. It's all over," one of them growled. "Go on home."

Good advice. *Except if home is where the heart is*, he thought to himself, *then that's my home over there, that steaming charnel pit still glowing over whatever shreds remain of the only woman I ever loved.*

And just in that moment, but for the tiny bit of humanity sheltering next to his heart, Carl would have thrown himself against that line and joined her, yes, and taken a few of the bastards with him to light his way to hell.

But Jimmy squirmed, and Carl's foot bumped against something heavy on the street. He looked down, then slowly squatted. The force of the explosions had burned off its covers and blown it this far, and the water from the fire sprays had soaked it and swollen it into something puffy and malignant. Nevertheless, he picked it up carefully. In the uncertain strobing light he could still make out the words: *American Quotations*, by Gorton Carruth and Eugene Ehrlich, published by Wings Books in the long-forgotten year of 1992.

With trembling fingers he placed the book in his backpack. Then he turned and stared at the barren hole and the wasted embers that still burned in its heart.

He whispered, "She's labored long in my vineyard. And she's tired—She's weary—Go down, Death, and bring her to me."

And he could hear her voice as he turned to trudge away from her forever:

"Henry Wadsworth Longfellow. *Go Down, Death.*"

Almost as if she spoke from beyond the grave. And in some chill, awful way he almost envied her. She was gone, but he remained, and would have to go on.

He vowed that his vengeance would be terrible, and in the end, it was—though not the way he expected.

CHAPTER ONE

1

The space cruiser grew slowly larger against the vast sweep of stars; shining, white, overwhelming in its power. Jimmy Endicott hung in the virtual dark, in utter silence, his heart pounding at the approach of the great ship. He could smell the tang of his own nervous sweat, almost feel the vacuum strain against the imponderable mass of the vessel. It was a perfect meshing of man and machine that, for him, embodied the highest hopes and deepest dreams of all humankind.

Someday I will be a part of you, and you of me. Someday you will call me Captain.

The splendor of endless space was breathtaking. Jimmy felt a momentary vertigo, as if he were actually falling forward into the approaching maw of the cruiser. Reflexively he put his hands forward to shield himself from the impact—

"Jimmy! Turn that thing off. Dinner's on the table, birthday boyo. Eat it now or I'm throwing it to the hogs."

The ship began to break up before his eyes; long cracks snaked across its perfect surface, showing fading stars beneath. Then, as he reached up and gently tugged the cyberjack from its socket beneath his right ear, the entire virtual vision vanished, and he found himself staring at the mundane walls of his room.

Jimmy blinked and glanced at the doorway. "Hogs? Where'd you find a hog, Mom? Can I have five minutes?"

"Five minutes? You sure that's all?" Tabitha Endicott said.

"Sure, Mom. Just one little thing . . ."

"Okay. Wash your hands first."

"Uh-huh."

He swung his swivel chair until it faced his desk. "Computer, generate file 'academy application' and print it."

Obligingly, his "axe"—the name everybody used for Universal Access Units, the miraculously small machines that allowed access to the InterWorldWeb, also called the Wobbly for reasons nobody remembered anymore—responded by printing out a copy of his preliminary application for entrance into the Solis Space Academy.

He closed his eyes as he visualized that legendary military space school on distant Terra, thirty light-years from his small room in a house in Prima City, the capital of Wolfbane, the first interstellar human colony. What a leap, of both distance and imagination. But he would make it, he promised himself. He *would* become part of the quest, as humanity took its first steps into the far reaches of the universe. Or, he thought, feeling embarrassed at his own melodrama, he would die trying.

He checked over the application a final time, making sure that everything was filled out correctly. It was just a preliminary application, but Solis Academy took only the best of the best, and the entrance process was long and grueling. Small mistakes counted. The earlier he started, the better his chances would be.

Name, James No-Middle-Initial Endicott. Age, sixteen. As of today, at least . . . Height, five feet, eleven inches. Weight, 165 pounds. Hair, dark brown. Eyes, green.

Interests: Weight training, tae kwan do martial arts, track and field, computers, theater, exobiology, personal weapons training. He stared at this litany. His life had always been a busy one. But did this look too much like the lifestyle of a boy unhealthily obsessed? Striving a little bit too hard for perfection, maybe? He shook his head. Ask Dad about it, see what he says.

Parents. Carl and Tabitha Endicott. What a banal entry for the two people who meant more than anything in the world to him. What could he say? Mom and Dad, and that was it. All and everything.

"Supply complete genotype records for applicant and parents." That would be the subject of the conversation at dinner. Part of his little surprise.

Today was his birthday. He knew they would plan something special for him tonight, and now he would do the same. He tried to imagine how his dad would feel when he showed him the application. He had always told him, "Son, do your best. You might as well aim as high as you can, and put everything you have into it. There is no shame in failure, only in never having tried at all."

Jimmy Endicott nodded to himself. It was good advice, and now, with this scrap of intelligent paper, he took the first step down the long road of fulfilling it.

He stood, folded the paper and stuck it in his shirt pocket, then headed for the bathroom to wash his hands. He was sixteen. He still did what his mom told him to do.

He hummed softly while the fresher sprayed water and odorless disinfectant on his palms. There might be no shame in failure, but he didn't care. He had no intention of discovering whether that was true or not. Failure?

Failure was for other people.

2

Their small house was not the most modern in the Terran Colony on Wolfbane—nor was Wolfbane, as far as it went, as modern as far-off Terra itself. But for a sixteen-year-old boy, both the house and the world were just about as okay as they could be.

He came out into the main room and saw that it was already configured as a meal room. Usually that was his chore, to instruct the house computer as to how to arrange the self-constructing furniture, the scent of the air, the temperature, the holographic decorations. He nodded with approval at the fire that crackled in the fireplace, and inhaled deeply of the piquant woodsy smoke. Not real smoke, of course. Humanity had learned its lessons from the Terran ecocollapse of two centuries before.

His father glanced up from where he sat at the dinner table, poring over a chip reader. More business, no doubt, Jimmy thought. Carl Endicott ran a small security service, and worked far harder than Jimmy thought was good for him. Part of that opinion, Jimmy knew, was simple selfishness. He loved his father and wanted more time with him.

"You wash your hands, son?" Carl asked.

Jimmy grinned and raised the appendages in question. "Clean as a baby's behind."

His father laughed. "You haven't had much experience along those lines, son, or you'd never use an example like that."

Jimmy pulled out a chair and slid into his place. As he settled himself, he heard his mother's soft, clear voice behind him in the traditional refrain:

"*Happy birthday to you, happy birthday to you, happy birthday, dear Jimmy, happy birthday to you.*"

His father, whose singing voice was notoriously awful, smiled and hummed along, then clapped his hands at the finale, and said, "And many more, son."

His mom placed a small birthday cake on the table. "I baked this, not a machine," she told everybody. "I hope it's edible."

Jimmy pointed at the candles. "Sixteen candles. When do we light them?"

"After I turn off the smoke detectors," his father said with a straight face.

Jimmy turned. "You mean you learned your lesson from your last birthday? What was it? A hundred candles, something like that?"

Tabitha Endicott brought a large platter to the table. "All your favorites, Jimmy. Fried chicken, biscuits, gravy, corn on the cob—and chocolate chip cookie dough ice cream to go with your cake!"

She seated herself at the end of the table and began to serve food onto the plates. "Carl, I think your work can wait a little while, can't it? It *is* a special night, after all."

Her husband glanced up, a faint frown curving his lips and creasing his forehead. He seemed about to say something, but caught the anxious look in her eyes and nodded instead. "You're right, Tab. Sometimes I don't know when enough is enough." He snapped shut his reader and slipped it into his shirt pocket.

"Well," he said, rubbing his hands together. "This smells wonderful!"

After a while, Jimmy said, "That was great, Mom. Is it time for ice cream and cake yet?"

"You finished your veggies, buddy?" his dad asked.

"I love corn on the cob. Now if it had been spinach . . ."

"Spinach on your birthday? What kind of monster do you think I am?" his mother asked.

"The best, Mom. You're the best."

"Hey. What about me?" his dad asked.

"Uh, you're okay too, Dad." Jimmy grinned.

"Okay? Is that all? Just okay?"

"Well, maybe a little better than okay."

"Hmph. Well, if that's the case, maybe I ought to find somebody else to give this to . . ." Carl reached down and retrieved a brightly wrapped package and placed it on the table.

It was about the right size. Jimmy's eyes widened. "Dad! You're the best. Really, I'm serious, you are."

"Your sudden fervor wouldn't have anything to do with this package, would it? I mean, not that I'm a cynical old dog or anything."

"Dad! How could you think such a thing? You know I love you just for what you are. Really. Now can I open it? Huh? Please?"

"I don't know. You don't sound sufficiently sincere to me. Tab, how about you? Does he sound sincere?"

"Carl, quit teasing him." She turned to face Jimmy. "Son, I agreed to this because you've always shown me you have good sense. And because I think you are mature enough for the responsibility. But I just want you to remember to be careful, and keep in mind everything you've learned."

Jimmy felt a surge of joy. This was a familiar enough mom lecture, mild but concerned, but in this context, it meant the box could contain only one thing. A huge smile began to stretch across his features.

"Dad? Mom? Can I open it now?"

Carl nodded with mock sternness. "I guess so. Here you go." He handed the package across the table. Jimmy took it eagerly, his hands dropping only slightly at the deceptively heavy weight of the box and its contents. His fingers flew at the bow, the tape. He lifted away the top and breathed softly: "Jeez, it is. Oh, you guys, *thank* you!"

"You will be careful?" his mom repeated.

"Oh, Mom, of course. Something like this, you have to be." And for an instant, Jimmy's innate seriousness shone through his normally cheerful mien. Carefully, he lifted it out of its fitted case and hefted it lightly.

"An S&R .75, just like yours, Dad," he breathed. "Oh, thank you both. I've been wanting one like this forever!"

His dad glanced at his mom. Both smiled, although Tabitha still showed thin creases of worry at the bridge of her nose.

"I figured you had just about outgrown that little twenty-two laser pistol simulator you've been practicing with all these years. Maybe you didn't notice, but there's more."

Jimmy placed the heavy, gleaming weapon on the tabletop and picked up the box. A slip of paper fluttered out. He picked it up and read it.

"Dad! You okayed me for the adult training range! Oh, man, this is just perfect! This is the best birthday *ever*!"

Which was the thought still running through his glow of happiness as his mother brought out heaping bowls of ice cream. Everybody applauded when he blew out his candles with a single puff. Perfect, indeed.

And it stayed that way for almost an hour longer.

3

"So, Dad, why is it we rejoice at a birth and grieve at a funeral?"

Carl grinned. "Cause we aren't the person involved. Mark Twain said it."

"Good," Jimmy replied. "Where?"

"*Pudd'nhead Wilson.*"

"Smart guy that you are," Jimmy told him. "Your turn."

"Turn?" Carl replied. "The rascals out, you mean?" He grinned expectantly.

"Um. Tricky. Oh, *turn* the rascals out. Got it. Greeley's Liberal Republican Party slogan. Eighteen seventy-two, I think it was."

"Check the book?" Carl glanced at the ancient volume, its charred covers now encased in unbreakable plastic, that rested on the coffee table.

"Nope, I'm right."

Carl thought about it. "Yeah, I think you are. Okay, now you."

"You know, I can't always be right," Jimmy said softly, almost musing. "So my struggle is to do my best; to keep my brain and conscience clear; never to be swayed by unworthy motives or inconsequential reasons, but to strive to unearth the basic factors involved and then do my duty . . ."

"That's a mouthful, son, even in paraphrase—and so it was back when Dwight David Eisenhower first said it, over three centuries ago, in 1943."

Jimmy nodded. "Duty. You know how it is. When duty whispers low, *Thou must*, the youth replies, *I can.*"

Carl stared at him. Even Tabitha had put down her reading—she didn't like to play the game as seriously as her two men did—and now watched the byplay with a questioning gaze.

"Ralph Waldo Emerson," Carl told him absently. "*The Voluntaries*, in 1863. A strange and terrible time for the United States, Jimmy. Is there something you're trying to tell me?"

Jimmy's cheeks flushed. Wordlessly he fished in his shirt pocket and took out the folded application. "Duty calls, Dad," he said quietly, and handed the scrap over.

Forehead wrinkled, Carl Endicott scanned the paper. He exhaled slowly as he read and puffed his lips in and out. Once, he shook his head, as if something pained him. When he finished, he returned the application.

"You haven't filed this, have you?"

Jimmy shook his head, puzzled. "No, not yet. I need your genotype and Mom's, too. Is something wrong?"

Carl's icy blue eyes fixed on him. "Well, yes, I imagine there is, Jimmy. You can't transmit this in."

A nonplussed expression spread across Jimmy's features. "Well, not right away. I still need to get—"

Carl shook his head. "No, that's not what I mean. You can't apply for the Space Academy at all. Ever. It's just not something you will ever be able to do."

He watched his son's expression crumble, but his tone never wavered. "I'm sorry," he said. "It's—I'm sorry."

4

Jimmy could hear his father talking in low tones out in the living room with his mom. There was worry in the sound, but he couldn't make out the individual words.

He rolled over on his stomach and pounded his fist into his pillow. What in the heck was going on? There were many things about his father he did not understand; but he had never considered him to be an arbitrary or unreasonable man.

True, Jimmy did not always understand exactly what his father's intentions were, nor why Carl might wish him to do or learn certain things in certain ways. But he had always trusted his father to have his son's best interests at heart. More important, he had always taken it for granted that Carl loved him.

All of which made it nearly impossible for him to comprehend his father's actions now. Carl had offered no explanations, nor had he said anything beyond his first flat refusal. But that was not the worst; the most damaging, the most inexplicable thing—and by far the most intolerable—was the idea that he must somehow choose between his father's wishes and the one ruling passion of his young life—to enter the Space Academy and, ultimately, command one of the great white ships of Terra.

He closed his eyes, but the vision of his father's gaze, cold and impenetrable, would not leave him. And the worst thing was that other thing he thought he saw in his father's eyes, something he'd never seen before, and never expected to see.

The expression that frightened him beyond even his own anger.

It was fear. His father was afraid.

But of what?

5

Carl Endicott leaned forward till his face was inches from Tabitha's and whispered intently, "Honest to god, Tab, anything but this."

She shook her head back and forth. "Carl, I don't understand. What is the big deal? We've both known for years that Jimmy is starstruck. He certainly hasn't made any secret of it. So why the big surprise now?"

"But the Academy."

"Do you know any other way to make starship captain?"

He rolled his eyes. "I thought it was just a kid thing, a phase. Like wanting to grow up to be a cowboy or something."

"Carl, Jimmy is sixteen. A little old for that kind of daydreaming, don't you think?"

His voice was sad. "Yeah. I guess he grew up when I wasn't looking."

"No, you were looking, all right. But sometimes, Carl, I think you only see what you want to see."

"What's that supposed to mean?"

She made an exasperated clicking sound in her throat. "You can be a pretty straight-ahead guy, Carl. Don't worry, it's one of the things I married you for, but maybe for Jimmy it can be a little confusing."

"Tab, he can't apply to the Academy."

"Why? Why not?"

"Because of the genotypes."

"Genotypes? What in the world does that have to do with anything?"

But he wouldn't tell her. He just shook his head, stood up, and said, "I guess I'd better go talk to him. No point in putting it off any longer."

She nodded. "He's been waiting almost an hour."

"No," he replied. "I've been waiting sixteen years."

6

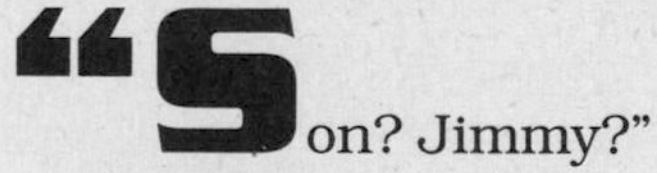on? Jimmy?"

The lights were low, the small room plunged into shadow. Jimmy was a darker lump sprawled across the bedspread. Carl squinted, trying to make him out. "A little light, maybe?" he said.

"Whatever you want, Dad."

So it's going to be like that, Carl thought. "Talk a little?"

"I thought you already said everything you had to say. Sounded pretty final."

Carl Endicott seated himself on the edge of the bed, touched Jimmy's shoulder, then withdrew his hand as the boy flinched angrily away.

"I understand how you feel, son," Carl said softly. "Do you want to talk about why you can't submit that application?"

Jimmy grunted. "It sounds like there isn't any way to change your mind—and if that's so, then why are we talking about it at all?"

"Because I'm . . . I'm your father, son. I'd do anything in the world not to hurt you—and I know how much this *does* hurt. But sometimes you have to take the things your father tells you to do on faith, simply because he is your father."

Jimmy flopped over on his side, angry gaze aimed at Carl's face. "Really? Do it because I say so? Don't think, just obey? I'm sorry, Dad, but that doesn't sound like anything you've ever taught me to do. If you ever taught me anything, it was to use my brain, to think for myself. Is that what this is? Doesn't feel much like it."

Carl winced. "I know, son. It doesn't fit very well, does it?"

"No, not at all. So why can't you talk to me? At least give me a reason?"

But, pain still evident on his drawn features, Carl only shook his head. "I . . . I just can't, son. For your own good. Even for my good. You'll just have to accept that, and trust me, Jimmy."

The boy heaved himself back the other way, away from his father's anguished gaze. He was silent for a long moment. Then he sighed, a long, drawn-out shuddery sound that might almost have been a sob.

"All . . . all right, Dad. If that's all you can say, I guess I'll have to accept it. You're my dad, after all. But would you do me a favor?"

"What?"

"Would you call me Jim from now on? I guess what you're telling me is that I'm all grown-up now, able to take orders like a man. So if I'm grown-up, I'm not Jimmy anymore. Call me Jim."

Carl stood up and stared down at the boy, understanding that some tremendously important moment in both their lives had just occurred, but unable to define it exactly, or deal with it in any effective manner. In the end he just shook his head and sighed.

"I love you . . . Jim."

"I love you too, Dad. But this is hard. Real hard," Jim Endicott said. He exhaled softly. "I'll try, though. I really will try."

Carl leaned over and patted him awkwardly on the shoulder. "That's all I can ask, son."

But as he stared into his son's eyes, he knew it was a lie. He was asking more than that. One hell of a lot more.

7

The night was soft and breezy as Jim clambered out the window of his room. He had long before gimmicked the house computer not to notice his departure in this manner.

Overhead, Wolfbane's twin moons bounced like golden pinballs across a sky crowded with stars. Prima City was a far different proposition than what Jim might have known centuries earlier; it had been planned from the beginning to respect its environment and to enhance its niche in Wolfbane's ecology. Prima emitted no noxious fumes, polluted no water tables, hogged no nonreplaceable resources. It was lighted pleasingly, and silent enough that the sound of the wind was what Jim heard most as he jogged silently down empty gravlanes toward the ancient museum near the edge of town.

Even for a teenager, Jim was in excellent shape, thanks to the rigorous conditioning programs he'd followed since he was ten years old. His breathing was unchanged, and he'd barely broken a sweat by the time he reached the crumbling wall that marked the outer boundary of the museum.

It was but a moment's effort to clamber over the broken stones of the fence, and then he began to walk slowly toward the small ferroconcrete building in the center of the compound, and the flag that drifted in the wind and the eternal flame before that building.

He stopped when he came to the bowl of living fire on the narrow plaza which held the flag, and bowed his head. After a moment he opened his eyes and read, as he had many times before, the names on the primitive bronze plaque that stood on a tripod above the dancing flame.

His lips moved as he whispered softly, "Captain Delevard Johimba. Lieutenant Sheila Finch. Commander Jason Mohammadan. Corporal . . ."

It took him ten minutes to finish the litany, though he had memorized those holy names years ago. Mankind's first push into interstellar space had not come without a terrible price—and these were the many names of that ongoing payment. It was this memorial, now nearly forgotten by the local residents, that the starfaring ones still came to visit.

Jim had watched them many times—the men and women of Terra's space forces, from the lowliest deckhand to the most exalted admiral: they came here with no fuss, and stood for a moment with their heads bowed in silent tribute to those who had gone before.

It was this that Jim thought of now, as he stood with his own head bowed, the litany of names rolling down the thunder of history into his mind and heart.

Give up the Space Academy and his dreams? Betray these men and women who had given their lives in blazing the trail of his own, and mankind's, future?

He stood for a long time, his face twisted with pain. Finally he uttered a single sob, shook his head, and turned away.

His father was his father, but he was Jim, no longer Jimmy, no longer a child. He would make his own decisions now.

The plaque said that even heroes died, but that was okay. Families grew up and apart, children matured, the links between father and son changed, became different. Heroes passed away, and it was all okay, it was life.

As long as the dream still lived.

Jim stared blindly into the shivering, wind-whipped flame at his feet.

I love him more than anybody in the whole universe, but what he asks is too hard. Father or not, the dream lives. My dream, which is only a spark of humanity's greater dream.

He could do almost anything for his father. Anything but let that dream die. He loved Carl Endicott, but in the end, he loved the dream more. He thought of the quotation game he and his parents had played for years. What had Julius Caesar said?

Iacta alea est: The die is cast.

He turned his eyes up, to where the eternal stars burned, and saw himself going out in the great white ships of Earth.

He would not let the dream die.

CHAPTER TWO

1

Jim worked up a good sweat on his morning run. He was glad. The normality of his usual routines helped to cleanse the rancid memories of the night before from his turbulent thoughts. He needed a clear head. He had decisions to make.

Prima was a deceptive city. Much of it was underground, especially the grittier parts, so that the urban area was an attractive blend of well-trimmed forest and carefully maintained gravlanes, traced through neighborhoods where single-family units snuggled behind leafy screens. The only indication that this was a high-density region was the large number of gravcars rushing silently along the lanes as he stepped up his pace near the end of his run.

He pounded to a halt at the edge of the public recreation center. Sweat dripped from his thick brown hair into his green eyes, stinging a bit. He bent over, put his hands on his knees, shook his head, and sent a spray of perspiration flying. Then he straightened up and checked the link bracelet at his wrist. Heart rate, ninety-one. Not bad, after completing an eight-mile run.

The Prima Recreation Center was across the central gravlane from the planetary administration building, and got a lot of use. Jim glanced across a wide stretch of neatly cropped grass and saw several men and women, all ages and sizes, wearing the traditional white coat and pants of the ancient Terran martial arts.

They were part of his class. He was almost late. He sucked in a deep breath, swiped hair out of his face, put his head down, and took off at a dead run.

An hour later, showered and freshly combed, feeling cheerfully drained and, to his relief, much better than he had the night before, Jim stepped out of the main doors of the rec center and squinted at the bloated orb of Krager One, the somewhat elderly and mildly fading star around which Wolfbane orbited.

He checked his wristlink again, then whispered, "Schedule?"

Obediently, the link beeped once, then spoke in a tinny whine: "You have forty-five minutes free. Then your first class of the day, advanced calculus with Doctor Bernau. Doctor Bernau has transmitted a message to all his students: 'Today is a meeting day. Please go to the physical classroom in person, rather than the virtual schoolroom.'" The little unit clicked. "Would you like me to construct a holographic map with verbal directions?"

Jim shook his head. His wristlink was an old model, and tended to take things very literally. Sometimes it sounded more than a little stupid. But it was an utterly reliable connection to his axe, his access box, and he saw no need to replace it with a newer, fancier model. Such decisions were a kind of hardheaded practicality he'd picked up from his father without really noticing he had done so.

"No," he told it. "I know the way." And, as it happened, his destination was only about two minutes from this very spot. So he had forty-five minutes of freedom in his otherwise usually nonstop schedule.

He loped across the wide lawn, his open, cheerful expression drawing friendly waves from folks walking or sitting beneath tall trees and chatting. He found his own tree and plopped himself down in its welcome shade. It looked something like an oak, but smelled very much like a pine; as a species it had been created ninety years before in the genetics lab of the colony-class spaceship Wolfbane, just prior to planetfall.

He closed his eyes and leaned back against its silken amber bark, relishing the soft breeze on his cheeks and the scent of springtime tulips in his nostrils. For a moment he let his thoughts drift, but then, sighing, he focused his attention once again upon the matter at hand.

On the face of it, everything he had ever learned told him to do it one way: if his father said he must trust him, then that must be true. His father loved him and would not harm him and had only his best interests at heart. And, in his innermost thoughts, he did believe that. But . . .

His father was wrong. Or, rather, he could not accept that his father was right, not this time. So what could he do about it?

He sat and chewed on the inside of his cheek and watched the slow passage of Horus, the daytime moon, a red coin drifting across a blue-green sky. After a time he understood the problem. Somehow, in some way, his father misunderstood the situation. He did not comprehend just how much going to the Space Academy meant to his only son. So, while he was not—could not—be wrong, it was possible for him to be . . . mistaken.

As he concluded this torturous bit of analysis with so happy a result, he looked up and smiled at the sky. He felt suddenly light as a soap bubble, as if he might float off into the blue-green vastness overhead. Not wrong. Mistaken. And mistakes could be handled. Could be *rectified.*

The answer seemed simple enough. Prove it to him. *Show* him how much the Academy meant. And there was only one way to do that.

Jim raised his watch to his lips. "Axe," he said, "upload file 'academy application' to TerraNet, address currently linked to file."

Just like that, that quickly and easily, it was done. A very wise man had once, long before, remarked upon the ease of the computer-aided world by noting that one could now make mistakes one hundred times faster than before, thus opening limitless new vistas in mankind's ever-expanding search for progress.

Jim waited until a soft buzzing told him the application, with his father's genotype—though not his mother's—had been mailed. He had spent the late hours the night before hacking into his parent's private files, which was the principal cause of today's guilty feelings. Because it was missing his mom's data, the application would be returned for amendment. Or so he hoped. In the meantime, he would do his best to be a perfect, obedient son. And when the application was returned with the request for further information—he could not believe it would be rejected out of hand—then he would show his father by his own actions how unfair it was to banish the dream. For by returning the application with a request for further data, the Academy would be telling Carl Endicott that, no matter how mistaken his ideas were, his son had at least a chance of being admitted into its hallowed halls.

He felt the tiniest flash of unease and grimly pushed it from his thoughts. He had never disobeyed his father in any meaningful way. Only by convincing himself that he had *not* disobeyed him in this matter, not really, had he been able to do what he had just done. Yet he was still young enough to know the smell of his own bullshit when it filled his mental nostrils.

He knew that he had crossed yet another threshold. Unfortunately, he had no idea how great a step it had been—nor that it had been far greater than he'd imagined.

2

"Carl, what is it? Jimmy?"

Carl sipped his coffee, put it down, and knuckled his red eyes. He looked as if he hadn't slept at all. There were dark shadows beneath his eyes. His skin look raw and tender.

"I think his name is Jim now."

Tabitha Endicott had already heard an abridged version of the story, late the night before, while her husband tossed and turned beside her in their bed. Now she shook her head. "Don't take that too much to heart, Carl. I think it's just the hurt and surprise talking."

He glanced across his coffee at her. "Do you think I'm a monster, too, Tab?"

She shook her head, mildly exasperated at this melodramatic turn in her usually stodgy husband. Her short blond hair caught the light, revealing strands of silver. Carl saw, and for some reason this saddened him. Time went on, children grew up, wives grew older, the world changed, even love grew dull and comfortable. If only it were true! But it wasn't. Some things never changed at all. Some burdens you carried forever.

"Monster? Of course he doesn't think you're a monster. Like I said, he's just hurt. And confused. He doesn't understand. And I can't say that's so strange. I don't really understand either."

"I haven't been what you'd call a good provider, have I?"

Her expression grew more concerned. "Don't be silly. This self-pity doesn't suit you, Carl. We live well enough. We don't go hungry. Anything that boy wants, any lesson, any piece of equipment, any tool, he gets it. And I've certainly never felt . . . deprived."

She paused, eyes thoughtful, searching for the right words. "Carl, I know there are things you think you can't tell me. We've been together a long time. I knew what kind of bed I was making for myself when I married you, and I did it willingly! You're a good man, Carl Endicott, even if you are too hard on yourself." She shook her head. "I didn't want a hero. Only a man. A good man."

He raised his eyes to her face. "You think I'm a good man, Tab?"

"Of course I do. Do you think I would willingly marry a bad man? Or stay with him, if he'd managed to fool me in the first place?"

He shrugged. "Do you want to know why I'm doing this?"

She shook her head. "Not unless you want to tell me."

"You know there is only one reason I *don't* tell you . . ."

"That it would hurt me, or put me in danger somehow."

"You do understand, then."

"Yes, Carl, I do. Jimmy loves you, but don't forget—I do, too."

He grinned faintly. "Even when we've moved half a dozen times? Changed jobs, even changed planets? We changed *names* once, when he was three and didn't notice the difference, remember?"

"We've talked about it. I asked if you were a criminal, if we were running from the law."

"No, I told you then. I've done nothing wrong."

"Well, then." She patted the back of his hand. "He'll be better, once he calms down and thinks about it."

"I wish it didn't have to be this way."

She smiled. "There are worse things could happen to the boy."

He only nodded glumly. In his mind's eye, he saw the burning wreckage of a cottage, imagined the laughing chatter of murderers.

"I know," he told her. *And to us, too.*

3

In the darkness of Jim's bedroom the little tattletale fluttered like a tiny red flag a few inches above his axe. He slid into the chair before his desk, and whispered, "What is it?"

Obligingly the machine replied at the same nearly inaudible level. "Confirmation received from TerraNet: 'Application delivered, SSA-remote local, time 21:04. Forwarded 21:05 local.' Do you want the details?"

Jim shook his head. He didn't want the details. Already he felt the greasy lump of guilt curdling in his stomach, burning behind his breastbone. But it was too late now, wasn't it? He'd already done it, disobeyed his father.

For only the best, most honorable of reasons, of course.

He was surprised to find this didn't seem to make any difference in how awful he felt. He was not old enough to have much practice in self-deception, even if his native honesty had been so spurious as to allow it.

"Jim?"

It sounded strange, hearing his mom, who had always called him Jimmy, now call him Jim. "Are you home?"

"I'm here, Mom." They must have talked, his mom and dad. He would have liked to have been a fly on the wall for that. Then he shook his head. Add eavesdropping to his other crimes of disobedience, disloyalty, betrayal? Sure. No doubt that would make him feel better.

He had occupied most of the day in thought about what he'd done, and as a consequence the day had not gone pleasantly. Now, sitting in the brooding silence of his room, he felt more wretched than he had ever felt before. It was an adult feeling, he thought to himself, and now he was learning the terrible bite of that adult lament: *if only*!

He'd thought this caveat an arcane bit of adult blather, but now that he found himself living with the slow, corrosive drip of his own guilt, it no longer seemed so trivial. Instead, it made him ache with that curiously unchildlike emotion of regret.

Call me Jim, he'd told them. I'm an adult now. How brave. How . . . childish.

"No," he whispered at last. "I did it, but he has to know. There is no other way. I have to tell him."

As soon as he whispered this to himself, the word pushed him to the deed—although the deed felt better, more honest, more *correct* than the one he had done this morning.

He glanced at his axe as he left the room, and for a moment regretted how easily, in the modern age, the will might become the action, not just in this moment of decision, but earlier. He had barely thought of sending the application, and it was done. Now he had to think of the consequences, and take further action.

There is, he thought, *a valuable lesson to be learned from this.* He resolved to discern exactly what it might be.

Adulthood. How complicated it is.

But confession, he thought, remembering something from a half-forgotten lesson, *is good for the soul.*

I hope.

4

In a *vireo*, a virtual reality video, it might have been some vast room or hive, swarming with busy technicians, black-clad warriors abuzz with frantic purpose. In the reality it was mundane, almost boring. After a chain of machines had done their work and shifted the results one from the other, the extracted product was copied to the electronic inbox of a highly placed executive assistant. The assistant sat in a small, gray-walled cubicle where both obtrusive sounds and the higher ethical perceptions were decently muffled.

This woman, who functioned more or less as a barely permeable membrane, was long accustomed to straining gold from dross. The tiny nugget attracted her attention immediately, and she opened it up like a bit of the most exquisite origami, the better to examine its implications.

This process took 1.3 minutes. At the end of it she rose and walked purposefully through the door behind her desk, then across ten yards of velvety black carpet to the front of a desk that had been carved out of a solid block of onyx. Had anybody watched her progress, that one might have thought of cats.

"Yes?"

"There has been a possible match on one of the probable genomes," she said. "The results are on your machine."

A holoscreen appeared, glowed, vanished.

"I see. The Space Academy." A pause. "Very well. Please have Commander Steele report to me."

She did not have to check anything. The whereabouts of Commander Steele were something she kept herself current on at all times.

"Commander Steele is in the Singaporean Empire, at Kuala Lumpur, dealing with certain, ah, aspects of the rebellion. It will take half a day to extract her and bring her here."

"Then do it."

"Yes," she said. "Right away."

5

"You what?" Carl said.

Jim recoiled. He'd seen the quickly repressed reflex in his father's right arm, the hand half-raised, then dropped again. He knew what it meant. He'd had enough martial arts training to interpret such physical markers. For the first time in both their lives, his father had come very close to striking him. And on Jim, his young mind already churning with doubt and guilt, the impact of intention was as heavy as any actual blow.

"Dad . . . my God, I'm sorry."

"Oh, Jimmy . . ." Tabitha said.

Jim looked at his father, amazed at the transformation in the man he'd thought he knew so well. A psychic aura of danger seemed to tremble around him, causing the familiar confines of the Endicott living room to appear harsh and brutal as a frozen hologram.

Carl's jaw quivered as he struggled to master himself, to hide from his family the true gravity of what his son had done. Yet this battle could not be entirely concealed, written on his features as it was. Jim saw it, of course. All Jim's training had been designed to help him see such things—how could he not?

Jim felt sick, horrified at the nakedness of his father's features. What he had done—or at least what his father evidently believed he had done—was far worse than his own worst imaginings: for in his father's face he saw the fear of death.

Jim felt a sudden urge to talk, to babble, to fill the yawning void between them with words. Words would somehow make things right again.

"Dad . . ."

But Carl shook his head. He stood up, his features closed and hard. "All right. You did it, son, and now we all have to live with it. So be it."

He turned to his wife. "Tab, pack what we will need for an extended trip, but not too much. We may have to do a lot of moving in a very short time."

"Dad, what . . . ?"

"Son, we'll talk about it later. If there is a later. I can't explain what you have done, but I wish you hadn't done it. If you had only trusted me—"

He shook his head sharply. "Well, that's in the past. Now you go and do the same as your mother. Pack what you need, enough to keep you going, but only enough to carry easily. Just your backpack would be about right. We will be leaving in"—he checked his own bracelet link—"two hours. I'm sorry, but that's all the time I can give you."

"Dad . . ." Jim tried a third time, misery as thick as bile choking his throat.

"Son, this time, please do as I ask. Can you do that?"

"Yes," Jim said. "What—"

"Don't pack the S&R .75," Carl said.

Jim's eyes widened.

"You'll be wearing it."

CHAPTER 3

1

The storm over city central blew up late that night, hard black clouds spitting thunder and lightning, sheets of rain flogging the whiplashed trees.

Carl Endicott unpolarized the big window in the living room and stared out into the night. Behind him, Tabitha cinched tight the straps on a large carryall she'd just finished packing. "Bad weather," she remarked.

Carl shook his head. "No, good weather. They'll have the latest detectors, the hottest spyeyes, the newest everything, but nature still throws a monkey wrench into stuff like that."

"Dad, who is they?"

Carl turned. "Jim? What would you say if I said I couldn't tell you? Would you accept that?"

Jim faced him squarely. A lock of brown hair trailed down across his broad forehead, but his green eyes focused steadily on his father's face. "No, Dad, I wouldn't. I know you think I betrayed you—I probably did. At the least, I disobeyed you. I should not have sent that application without your permission. Or at least I should have told you before I did it."

"Yes, you should have. I would have forbidden it more strongly."

Jim shook his head. "I have to be honest, Dad. It wouldn't have mattered, not without a reason. I would have disobeyed you anyway." He spoke calmly, steadily, but the determination in his voice was so strong his father blinked.

"You have a very strong opinion of yourself. Strong enough that you are willing to put not just yourself, or even me, but your mom in danger as well."

Now Jim blinked. "I wouldn't have done it, Dad, if you had explained that was what I was doing. But you didn't explain, so I couldn't know. And because of that, evidently I made a bad mistake. But you made it first, by not trusting me. And you are making the same mistake again, right now, by not telling me what is going on."

For the first time in the course of the evening, the hard shell of Carl's expression slipped a bit. He paused, glanced over at Tabitha, then back at his son. He sighed.

"You've got me. You are exactly right. That doesn't make what you did any better, but if I expect you to take responsibility for your own actions, then I guess I'd better take responsibility for mine. Are you willing to admit you disobeyed me?"

"Sure, Dad. I did disobey you. I'm just saying that, given the same circumstances, I would do it again. I won't be sixteen forever—and some decisions have to be mine to make right now. Like the ones that concern the rest of my life."

Carl nodded. "Okay, I accept that. But I want you to understand. What you may have caused is not a game. It's a matter of life and death. Our lives."

"Then will you tell me what I need to know now? Man to man, so I don't do anything else stupid?"

The two, man and boy, faced each other. Carl shivered slightly, then stepped forward and wrapped his big arms around the boy in a crushing bear hug. Jim returned the gesture. After several moments they broke apart.

"All right," Carl said. "Here's the deal. The chances are very high that by putting your genotype and mine out on the public nets, especially by sending it to a *government* agency, you have attracted the attention of someone who means us great harm." He stopped, considering. "I'll be honest, Jim. Somebody who will kill us all without a second thought."

2

"Stuffy," Steele remarked. "I hate these little packet ships. It's like being tossed across a bunch of light-years in a tin can."

Molly Harrison leaned against Heck Campbell's huge frame. Campbell grinned, a spectacle of white teeth in black skin. "You said it was a rush job."

"I don't like rush jobs," Steele grumbled. "And it's the only kind we seem to get anymore. It's like nobody can do anything right from the beginning, but who gives a damn, just call Steele's people to pull your bacon out of the fire . . ."

"Well, who you gonna call any better than us?"

Steele shrugged. Her straight, neck-length black hair now showed a startling wing of white that crossed the top of her round skull and streaked across her chopped-off bangs. Her lips, as always, glistened the color of fresh blood. "Nobody, I guess. But it's sloppy. Sloppy thinking, sloppy planning. We ought to be a last resort, not the first thing they reach for."

"Hey, Marty. 'S true this comes right from the top?"

Steele didn't answer directly. She glanced down at her bracelet link, muttered a scrap of code, and watched the holocolumn build. "Carl Endicott and happy family," she said as the figures solidified. "Hello there, folks. See you soon . . ."

"Seems a shame," Campbell rumbled. "The guy, sure, but waste a young kid and woman like that."

Steele looked at him. "Job's a job," she said. "Let everybody else get sloppy if they want, but we won't. We'll do it right." She raised one thin, raven-colored eyebrow. "Right?"

Campbell sighed and nodded. "Right, boss."

3

The cabin was far enough to the north it had missed the storms which drenched the capital region. They disembarked at the Tula Point tube station in gauzy, star-shot darkness. Overhead, Wolfbane's two moons, Mutt and Jeff, chased each other in slow-motion arabesques; at the end of the station's platform, a single lamp glowed against chrome railings. It was very quiet. Jim's nostrils widened at the thick, mountainous scent of pine and dark earth that filled the air.

"Smells good," he remarked. "Wish I'd known it was here before. Would have been a nice place to come visit in the summer."

"Right," Carl agreed. "And would have been neatly listed on any dossier put together on the Endicott family. 'Visits mountain cabin every summer. Location as follows.'" He snorted.

"Well, let's get a move on. This won't last forever, but it may hold till we can figure out what to do next."

He glanced both ways before he led them across the platform. Only Jim noticed that his father kept one hand in the pocket of his jacket. He'd seen Carl put his aged .75 in that pocket before they left the house . . . for the last time?

What, Jim wondered, *have I done?*

4

"All right, people, it took a superluminal beamcast from Big Daddy on Terra to get the info here this quick. Enough to pay your salaries for twenty years, so listen up." Steele, wearing black leather, her armor shell hanging unstrapped and loose from her skeletal shoulders, opened the hasty briefing session. Campbell and Harrison squatted before her, similarly garbed, in the silent emptiness of the Endicott living room.

"Wonder how they knew we were coming?" Campbell said.

"Who cares. The thing is, it looks like we have a line on where they *went.*"

"Where's that?" Harrison wondered.

Steele keyed her bracelet link. A tridimensional picture began to form: a small wooden cabin, primitive-looking, in the shadow of tall mountains.

"There," Steele said. "Right there. . . ."

5

She knew some things. Other things she didn't know. But she had to tell the boy anyway. Sometimes even Carl was just plain wrong.

Tabitha Endicott pushed the old-fashioned lace curtain away from the equally old-fashioned plate-glass window, looked outside, sighed, and let the curtain drop again.

Jim watched her. *She's as upset by all of this as I am,* he thought to himself. *I wonder if she blames me? I don't think Dad does, not exactly—well, he knows it's my fault, but I guess he understands why I did it.*

"The sunset's pretty," Tab said.

"I like it up here," Jim told her. "It's too bad—"

They stared at each other. Neither of them wanted to discuss what was too bad.

"Jim—"

"Mom—"

They both stopped again, took breaths at the same time, looked at each other. And burst out laughing.

"You first, Mom," Jim finally got out.

She nodded, then went sober. "Jim, there are some things I want to say to you—and I don't want you to take this wrong, but I wanted to wait until your dad wasn't here. It will be . . . easier. But if it makes you feel disloyal, we can wait till he comes back. Either way, it's your call."

A murmur of fear whispered up his spine. All at once he felt far too young for all of this, way out of his depth. He didn't want to be the repository of secrets, his mom's, his dad's, anybody's. But there was a lot his father had not yet told him, and Jim could sense it, those secrets, lurking just beneath the deceptive calm of their new relationship.

"Mom? Is it okay?"

She exhaled, rubbed her elbow, glanced away, then back. "I honestly don't know. I may be doing the wrong thing. But I think you need to understand what your father—what Carl—is worried about. Beyond the obvious, I mean."

Jim nodded slowly. "Okay. Tell me, then."

She turned back to the window. "You were barely a year old when I met Carl." She stopped and waited for it to sink in.

What? Jim thought. *But that can't be right. If it is, then it means she isn't my mother—*

"Mom! I mean . . . uh, no . . ." His voice trailed off helplessly.

She came over and put her arm across the back of his neck. She bent over and peered directly into his eyes. "Listen to me, Jim. I *am* your mother, legally and everything." Then, without turning away, she took a deep breath and dropped the real bombshell.

"It's legal, because I adopted you the same day that Carl did—which was the same day we got married. One week after your second birthday."

He stared into her ice blue eyes. At first he didn't get it. Then, like a hard kick in the belly, it hit him. The day his *father* adopted him. But why would his dad adopt him, unless his dad wasn't really his . . .

"*Mom!*" Only that single word exploded out of him, out of his very core, but she heard the immeasurable anguish that filled the one syllable. She hugged him close, rocked him back and forth.

After a few moments his silent shuddering began to subside.

"The truth is, son, I don't know for sure," Tab said. "Your father won't talk about it. He may actually be your real father, I don't know. But he did go through the motions of adopting you. Something happened with the two of you, happened before Carl and I met. I've known we were hiding from somebody, something, all these years. I didn't know what it was, and I still don't."

He spread his hands helplessly. "All that stuff that he talked about, Mom. That somebody wants to kill us all. Is it true, do you think?"

She stepped back, her face suddenly stern. "Your father said it was, and he isn't a liar. Surely you know that."

But Jim felt as if his skull was full of raging sheets of white light, great silent detonations of blinding pain. "A *liar*? Mom, *lying is all he's ever done to me*!"

6

Three of them came up onto the main platform of the Tula Point Station. To the unpracticed eye, they looked like any other party of recreational hunters. But to Carl Endicott's very practiced gaze, there was nothing recreational about them at all.

"Gotcha," he murmured.

He put the binoculars back to his face, noting the way the big one hefted the large pack to his shoulders. There were two women, both with their backs to him. One blond, the other taller—wait, turning now . . .

Oh, my God! Her!

In his shock he involuntarily jerked his binoculars and her distinctive, red-lipped face vanished for a moment. By the time he got refocused, it was almost as if she were looking straight at him. Impossible, of course, but—

He reached for the small radio detonator next to him, picked it up, squeezed the plunger home.

7

Steele said, "Well, so far it's been easy enough. Maybe our boy has lost his edge. It's been a long time." But even as she said it, she felt the twinge of hubris in her words, winced, and looked around uneasily. Carl had taught her much of what she knew, and one of the things he'd taught her was not to underestimate the enemy. At least not out loud where the Gods of Payback could hear you.

"Nice weather here. Pretty white clouds," Molly Harrison said. Heck Campbell only grunted softly as he hoisted the pack with their heavy weapons and other, more specialized equipment, to his shoulders.

Steele walked to the edge of the platform and stared out at the rising wall of greenery that marched up toward the distant peaks. Unspoiled-looking . . .

She knew what the telltale pinpoint burst of light meant, almost before it had registered in her brain.

Binocular flash!

She was moving toward the platform railing even as she shouted, "*He's got us taped. Get off the platform now*!" And tucked herself into a tight ball as she launched herself out into empty space.

8

The distance, almost half a mile, made it eerie.

Carl Endicott saw the line of puffy gray explosions well before he heard them. One moment he was looking at three people standing on a deserted tube station platform. Then the carefully patterned antipersonnel bomblets he'd concealed all over the station exploded, covering the squat structure in a billowing wreath of dirty white smoke. Another long beat, and the high-pitched crack of the explosions reached him.

"Come on," he muttered, pounding on his thigh.

Finally the mountain winds began to rip away the smoky veil. He strained forward, squinting into the binoculars. Smoke, smoke, now the station . . .

Nothing.

No dead hunters. Somehow she'd sensed what he was doing and beaten him. Well, he'd always known she was good. He just hadn't expected ever to see her again. But now he knew better. Maybe it would make a difference when they met the next time.

Soon, no doubt.

He stood up and vanished into the trackless woods.

9

Steele shook her head as she sat up and gingerly checked her arms and legs. Nothing seemed to be broken.

"Ugh. What the hell . . ." Heck Campbell, several yards over, struggled to his hands and knees. Blood leaked from a long slash in his forehead. "Got us good, damn it," he mumbled, and shook his head. Blood splattered brightly.

He would live, Steele decided. "Molly? Where you at, Harrison?"

"Yo. Over here, boss."

Steele turned to see a dust-covered Molly limping toward her. But there was no blood in evidence.

"You okay?"

Molly shrugged. "Turned my ankle. Tape it up, I think it'll be okay."

"Good. Check out Heck, would you?"

"Right, boss."

Slowly, Steele pulled herself to her feet, slapped her big hands against her fake hunter's garb to remove the film of white powder that covered everything.

She wrinkled her nose at the sharp, ammonia smell that filled the air. Some kind of plastic explosive, though she couldn't quite pin down the type simply from its residual odor. Well, it didn't matter. He'd missed.

She turned to the others. "Heck? You gonna live?"

Molly finished pressing a medicated fleshpad over Heck's wound. "Boy got it in the head. Can't hurt him there."

Heck grinned.

Steele nodded. Carl whatever-he-was-calling-himself-these-days had missed. Bad mistake.

Now it was personal. Now she would show him just how bad a mistake it could be.

"Okay, people," Steele said. "Let's move on out."

10

Carl Endicott burst through the cabin door, slammed out of the living area into the bedroom, and skidded to a dead halt as he looked right down the yawning barrel of an S&R .75.

"*Jim, no*!"

Slowly, Jim Endicott lowered the heavy pistol. His face was white, his green eyes shot with thin red traceries. He looked as if he had been crying.

"Son, first rule," Carl said, speaking carefully. "Make sure you know what you are pointing that pistol at. Because the second rule is, when you point it at a human, pull the trigger. Now, what's been going on here?"

Jim stared at his father, a welter of thoughts clogging his brain. He could see that Carl was under enormous stress—something had obviously just happened—but still he wanted nothing more than to grab the older man by his shoulders and shake him until the truth came out. All the truth.

"Dad," he said. "You've got to tell me the truth."

Carl paused, stared at him sharply. "What?" His gaze slid toward Tab, who stood behind her adopted son.

She nodded. "Carl, I told him. I thought he needed to know."

"Told him? About what?"

"The . . . adoption proceedings. And our marriage."

Carl groaned. "Oh, Tab. I wish you hadn't."

"Dad, can we talk now?"

Carl turned back to his son, anguish creasing his worn features. "No. Because some people are coming here to kill us. I tried to kill them and missed. If we set it up right, we won't miss the next time."

He took a deep breath, then let it out slowly.

"After that, son, we'll talk. I promise."

11

"Okay, this is far enough." Steele brought them to a halt in a narrow clearing in the underbrush beneath the big trees. Late-afternoon winds roared softly through the shivering leaves overhead, cut though their heavy clothing.

"Colder'n a witch's—"

"Shut up, Molly." Steele squatted. "Campbell, give me the downlink tablet."

Wordlessly, the big man fished in his heavy pack, found the flat tablet, no larger than an old-fashioned book, and handed it over.

She flipped open the top of the little machine, exposing an old-style nonholographic screen. This was battlefield equipment, built for rugged dependability. She spoke the proper codes; a moment later, the tablet made contact with an overhead satellite and began to draw an extremely detailed real-time picture of the area surrounding the cabin.

"Um," Steele said. "Okay, there have been some changes since we looked the last time. Campbell, take a look . . . here . . . and here. See these spots where it looks like the earth has been disturbed, the heat signatures?"

Heck grunted agreement. "More booby traps, looks like to me." He grinned faintly. "That man sure don't have the welcome mat out." He nudged Molly. "Scuttlebutt says he taught the boss everything she knows."

Steele glared up at him. "You got a mouth on you, you know that, Campbell? Two things: First, back then, maybe he did. Second, I've learned a lot since then."

"So what's the problem?" Molly asked.

"I don't think he taught me everything *he* knew." Steele hefted the little computer and sighed. "Well, maybe he hasn't kept up with the equipment as well as he should have. We'll find out. Gather round. Here's what we'll do."

12

"Gather round," Carl Endicott said. "Here's what we'll do. If we're lucky."

Jim pushed next to the holographic map shimmering over the top of his axe. He licked his lips, suddenly oppressed by the smallness of the primitive little room. From here the presence of the vast forests outside the cabin pressed down on him with vast green psychic weight. Anything could be out there. Coming to kill them all.

Jim felt his mind creak dangerously, as if things might begin slowly to tip away, leave him floating helpless in the blank and the black. He shook his head. "I'm sorry," he said. "What did you say, Dad?"

Carl looked up. "Pay attention, Jim. This is important. There are three of them, two women and a man. I know one of the women. Long ago—before you were born, Jim—I trained her. She is their leader, and she is very good. I know her, and she knows me. So she will try to anticipate what I will do. That's why I've tried to do several things much differently than I might have once done them."

Jim nodded, his head spinning painfully. *Dad, training a killer woman before I was born? What*—He bit down on his tongue, and for a moment the pain blew the endless questions away.

Finally Carl finished. "So here's how we handle it. Tab, you don't have the skills, so you go outside, and you wear this jacket. I'll show you where to go."

He turned to Jim. "Son, you and I will be right here." He gestured to an area in the holographic map, then stopped.

"A lot depends on you, Jim. You are far too young to face this, but I have to know. Can you kill a human? Man or woman? Because if you can't, I have to make different plans, you understand?"

Jim thought that Carl looked very tired just then, deep lines carved in his cheeks and around his eyes. Almost like an old man. It was a frightening effect.

"Sure, Dad, I can—"

"Son, *think*! This isn't holovideos, this isn't some game. It's reality. That .75 of yours will blow a hole in a human body big enough to put your fist through. Blood and bone everywhere, and you can see right through the wound. Nobody gets up, puts on a bandage, and keeps on going after that. Can you do that to another person, son? In cold blood?"

Slowly, Jim thought about it. He licked his lips. "I . . . think so, Dad. It's not really in cold blood, is it? They are coming to kill us. You and me—and Mom." His eyes flicked in Tab's direction. "I think I can kill to stop that."

His father stared at him hard, then nodded. "Okay. I hate this, Jim. I hope you understand that."

"Dad, I don't understand anything."

Carl Endicott nodded. "You will, son. I promise. But first things first."

They made their preparations.

13

"Okay, Molly, light them off."

Steele spoke into her throat mike. Her voice was as calm as if she were ordering out for pizza.

Overhead, the stars wheeled past like God's own jewelry box, stirred by the passage of the pinball moons. She glanced up, her helmet shield depolarized, and wondered if she'd guessed it right. Carl was not a man to fool around with. There were some people dead on the San Francisco HyperMall fifteen years ago to testify to that. Some of them had even been almost friends.

"Payback time, Carl," she promised herself softly, then slapped one armored thigh as, overhead, two bright flares suddenly exploded into hard actinic light.

"Blast off," she said into her mike, then she did.

14

Carl Endicott looked up, a quick, bitter smile twisting his lips. "Gotcha again," he said, and pressed the button.

15

Their man-portable liftpacks tossed them like thrown stones through the mountain night. Tiny computers minutely adjusted the thrust according to the terrain below. Steele and Molly made pinpoint landings on the roof of the small cabin, pointed their weapons down, and prepared to blast their way in through the shingles.

"Oh, damn it!" Steele screeched as she saw the deadly little Easter eggs that littered the roof. She reached for her battle belt.

The roof blew up.

16

The force of the shaped charges lifted the entire roof off its rafters, and slashed a deadly sheet of shrapnel straight up, but the charges had been prepared so carefully Carl Endicott only felt a momentary downward pressure before his vision cleared and he began to search for targets.

Guessed I'd try to take you on the ground, didn't you? he thought with savage satisfaction. *Good thing even the best spy sats can't tell fake booby traps from real ones.*

Nothing overhead but stars and settling dust. He snap-rolled through the open front door and came to his knees. Saw a shadow moving slowly and put two .75 slugs through it. Good hits, he didn't wait. Whatever armor, it was dead meat. One down. Where were the other two?

He leaped just in time to avoid the sizzling beam of a power laser out of the forest that turned a chunk of the cabin behind him into blazing ruin. In the darkness, someone screamed.

17

Frantically, Steele righted herself. The liftpack had already begun to move her away from the blast. The explosion itself only sped up the process. Nevertheless, as she bounced to her feet, her entire body felt as if she'd just been the main dancing partner in a three-gravcar wreck.

It took a moment to orient herself in the darkness. The cabin was over . . . there.

She took off at a lumbering gallop, burst into the front yard just in time to see Molly's head vanish in a tremendous burst of blood and bone.

He has a .75, her mind told her coldly.

She began to roll away from the source of the shot. A laser beam sizzled out of the woods. Somebody screamed.

18

Heck Campbell raised the heavy laser rifle again. He'd moved the guy, but doubted he'd hit him. Quickly he scanned for more targets, saw a shadow slide into the front clearing, and then something screamed and landed on his head, clawing and scratching.

He reached up and grappled with his attacker, quickly realized it was a woman. Could only be the Endicott wife. Fine and dandy; she was a target, too.

He grabbed with both hands and heaved. She flew through the air, landed with a dull thud, and uttered a sharp moan.

Heck grinned and leveled his laser.

19

Jim heard his mother scream from the general area where they had concealed her in a coat hand-lined with tinfoil to mask her infrared signature.

What was she doing? She should have been perfectly fine if she'd kept herself concealed. He lunged through the underbrush, the heavy .75 in his right hand leading the way.

There, up ahead! A large figure, struggling with a much smaller shape. With huge effort, the big one peeled the smaller one away and heaved. Then he bent over, a long, weaponlike object cradled in his arms, as if searching for something to shoot with it. He was far too big to be Jim's father or mother. In other words, a target.

Jim skidded to a stop and raised his pistol. The movement felt smooth, automatic after all his years of practice. He settled the front sight on the center of the big shape and—

Could not do it! Couldn't pull the trigger!

Sweat burst on his brow. He began to shake. The pistol barrel wavered as he envisioned the heavy slug, launched by his conscious and cold-blooded act, tearing apart the human in front of him . . .

And the human turned, almost as if he could sense Jim standing there, locked in his silent internal struggle. Jim got a glimpse of the long weapon wavering toward him. Another shape rose off the ground and threw itself at the big man.

20

Carl Endicott flung himself into the scrub, homing in on the sound of his wife's scream. Threw himself down when he saw the big one, the man, level his laser rifle and trigger off a blast. Then, inexplicably, the big man turned, sweeping his aim off toward his left. Something launched itself out of the night at the big man.

Too late, Carl thought, and snapped off another pair of shots. They hit the big man in the chest and punched him backward.

Carl waited a moment, trying to locate the other shadow, but couldn't see anything. Torn, he risked a short cry.

"Tab? Jim?"

The night exploded around him.

21

Steele hammered through the woods, bouncing off trees, trampling brush under her heavy boots, seeking the source of the scream.

She came in from the rear, so that the source was between her and the burning pyre of the cabin. She gritted her teeth. Anybody wanted to get away from this, they'd have to go through her first.

Now where—? Oh, there! She whirled, just in time to see Heck slammed off his big feet by the force of another brace of .75 slugs. A part of her mind whispered calmly, *Gotta be Carl.* Too professional. Two shot patterns. One to stop, one to make sure.

Silence. She raised her head.

Somebody called softly, "Tab? Jim?"

She whirled on the voice and let loose.

22

Nausea gagged in Jim's throat as he realized what had happened. It had been his *mom* on that big man—and he hadn't been able to pull the trigger, even to save her. What kind of a man was he? What did all his brave promises, his shining ideals, mean when he couldn't even save his own mother?

But before he could think any further, he heard his father's voice call softly, "Tab? Jim?"

He started to reply, but lightning rolled out of the forest beyond, blinding him. He heard his dad cry hoarsely, and tried to blink the mask from his vision, his own weapon waving wildly.

Something moved. He gasped, straightened, and pulled the trigger just as he'd been taught, a clean, snapping two-shot. Then raw panic clutched him, and, convulsively, he emptied his entire magazine into the dazzling, star-shot night.

With that, everything went silent.

For a long moment, nothing. Jim felt numb. His brain didn't seem to want to work. Then, with disorienting clarity, the world burst back into his consciousness. His ears rang with the recent explosions, screams, cries.

His nose burned with the stench of explosive powders and laser-lighted fires. His stomach was a cold and curdled knot of fear. Gradually his vision cleared. In the background, the cabin burned with a lively crackle, casting weird shadows.

The night throbbed with menace. He could feel his teeth chattering in his jawbone. And all he wanted to do was burst into tears, run to his father and mother, and have them hold him and tell him it was all right.

"Jim . . ."

"Dad?"

"Over here," came the choked reply.

23

In the ghastly light of the cabin's destruction, Jim knelt by his father, a few feet from Heck Campbell's mutilated corpse.

Something sticky and black was leaking from his father's chest. A strange, whistling sound came from the wound. Something from an old first aid class came to him: sucking chest wound. There was a hole in his dad's lung.

"Oh, Dad! We gotta get you—"

"Where's your mom!"

He paused. "I dunno. But you're wounded, Dad, hurt bad it looks like. We gotta—"

"No! Jim, just listen to me. Listen carefully, and memorize it, okay?"

"Dad . . ."

"Jim, just *do it*!" His passion seemed to drain something essential from him, and Carl fell back into his son's arms. He licked his lips, shuddered, and tried again. "1992—217—4," he whispered.

"Dad, I don't understand."

"Say it."

"1992—217—4," Jim replied. He possessed what is known as a verbal eidetic memory—fancy words that meant he could remember everything he heard. Perfectly and forever.

Handy little talent. In that moment he would have traded it and everything else he had to be able to take back that Space Academy application. Oh, yes, he'd been right. But you could be right and wrong at the same time. Horribly wrong.

"Oh, Dad . . ." Tears leaked down his cheeks as he felt his father's body slump in ominous relaxation. He looked down and saw his father's eyes gaze up at him, frighteningly bright in the wavering moonlight.

His father's fingers, smeared with blood, rose to brush Jim's cheek.

"No matter what happened, son, I love you more than life itself," Carl Endicott murmured. "I always have. You believe that, don't you?"

"I believe it, Dad," Jim choked out.

A faint smile ghosted across Carl's lips. "Good," he whispered.

Then he died.

24

Steele groaned as she levered herself to her feet. That last wild burst—she hadn't expected it, had walked right into it. Now she was missing a large chunk of her left knee, and though her armor had partially deflected it, she guessed a pretty good piece of her left arm wasn't around anymore, either.

The pain was incredible. She whispered to her battle medpack, waited, then felt a jolt of painkiller flood into her veins. Heavy-duty stuff. She could even walk, though her ruined knee would pay a heavy price later.

Grunting softly, she dragged herself forward, using her laser rifle as a makeshift crutch. She heard voices whisper several yards away, thought about it, then decided the odds were too great. Wounded as she was, she could not come silently, and Carl, if he was still alive, was too good to hand that kind of advantage to.

She bent over the crumpled body of the woman, considered, then slapped another injection into her own veins. She couldn't remember the technical name of the drug, but everybody called it Superman. Unnatural strength roared through her limbs. She hoisted the woman to her shoulders. Tabitha Endicott's breathing seemed steady enough. Part of her mission had been to kill this one, but Carl had been too good.

There would be another time. Maybe this one could be bait—for Carl and for the brat.

One way or another, she intended to find out.

Grinding her teeth to keep the involuntary gasps of agony choked inside, Steele limped off into the night.

25

Jim thought he heard some rustling noises back in the brush, turned, peered vacantly, then turned back. Gently, he lowered his father's body to the soft earth.

The wound in Carl's chest had ceased to make those hideous sucking noises. Jim bent over, hoping even for the horror of that sound, any sound that might mean life.

Nothing. He stared at the wound. No burn marks, no blackening. But whoever had fired that other weapon had used a laser. A laser wound would have charred edges. There was no way to avoid it. But this wound didn't.

Carl had not been killed by a laser.

Jim remembered his father's words. The hole in his chest looked *big enough to put your fist through . . .*

Jim Endicott realized what he'd done with his last wild burst of shots. His throat locked in horror for an instant, but finally it tore open and he began to scream.

He didn't stop for a long time.

26

Heck Campbell's body lay unmoving ten feet away from where Jim remained locked in his endless shrieking stasis of suffering. Sound, though, could not raise the dead, no matter how anguished. Two tiny LEDs on Heck's massive chest seemed to blink in response to Jim's mindless noise, though.

Blink and blink, blink again, blink.

Almost like eyes.

CHAPTER 4

1

He would never remember precisely how he got from the cabin to where he was.

The morning sun slashed scalpels of hard red light into his aching eyes. It had been three days since Jim had shaved or bathed. He found himself standing next to a dilapidated gravlane protective railing near the heart of Plebtown, his hair hanging in greasy tangles across his forehead and his teeth feeling as if someone had planted a moss garden across their surfaces. And he had no real idea how he'd gotten there.

Now, finally, his brain began to dissipate the hormones and protein clusters of panic and guilt and shame in which it had been marinating ever since his father's death. Much of what had transpired then was becoming hazy, fading into the kinds of waking dreams the mind will always spin to protect itself.

Only a few fire-shot moments remained: his father, slumping into the final relaxation of death in his arms. The way he thought his own chest would explode when he'd realized it was *his* bullets that had slaughtered Carl Endicott. And, finally, the utterly hopeless sense of guilt when he discovered that his mother had vanished. He had no idea if she was alive or dead.

That had been the straw that had broken him, sent him shambling aimlessly into the empty forest for almost a day until at last, mercifully, he'd collapsed into exhausted sleep.

He sighed and glanced up at the position of the sun. Coming on noon, the sky a clear pale emerald, not a cloud in sight. Hot. Sweat on his upper lip. He ran the tip of his tongue over the scraggly mustache there and tasted salt. He felt grimy, gritty, and bruised over every inch of his body.

The pack full of things he'd salvaged from the burned wreck of the cabin dug into his spine, and he shifted it a little; he had absolutely no idea what he would do next.

Plebtown. He looked around at the few ancient gravcars that trundled along the local lanes, the faded and peeling plastic skins on the walls of ill-tended storefronts. In the air drifted the twin smells of decay and despair. Those solitary folks who took any notice of him at all shuffled past with only sideways glances, older people with the expressions of whipped dogs on their sagging faces.

Why in the world had he come here? His own house, safe and warm, was no more than ten minutes from this very spot, if he was lucky with tube connections. He shook his head. That house might still be warm, but it wasn't safe. For his purposes, it might as well be ten light-years away, instead of ten minutes.

He hoisted his butt up on the creaking safety railing and began to pick at the crop of pimples forming at the base of his nose. It would be a major eruption, no doubt, thanks to the fact he'd forgotten his antiacne pills. In light of all that had happened, he knew it was ridiculous, but the sudden pimple bloom bothered him almost as much as all the rest of his change of fortune. Maybe because he could at least get his mind around something as mundane as pimples. Was it only a few days ago that pimples had been one of his main concerns in life? He snorted bitterly.

For a long time he sat motionless, grateful for the warmth, grateful that nobody seemed to notice him. Somewhere in the back of his mind a little record had begun to play, but he managed to ignore it: *out of the light, out of the light, hide, hide, hide—*

It was the music of paranoia, except that Jim had learned one of the sad truths of adulthood. Even paranoid people might have enemies. Sometimes they *were* coming to kill you.

After a time the sun began to feel too hot, and, almost without thinking, he slid off the railing and ambled aimlessly off down one of the pedestrian walkways. You actually had to walk, here in Plebtown—if these pedwalks had ever moved, their mechanisms were long since broken. In a citizen neighborhood like the one where he used to live, slidewalks got fixed as a matter of course. In Plebtowns, they didn't. He knew that, although it had never been of much concern. Idly, he wondered what new things would concern him now.

The black funk hit him like a hammer. He closed his eyes, waiting for the swirling mental clouds to pass, but for two or three seconds he stood as immobile as a statue.

"Hey, citizen, you get lost some way?"

Something punched him hard on the shoulder. He turned and saw three young men, adults no doubt, but not much older, he guessed, than he was.

"Hey," he replied. "What's the hops?" But one glance told him what was about to happen, and his stomach clenched in weary anticipation—and then, suddenly, rage.

After everything that had already happened, now *this*?

Three young men, all as greasy and disreputable as he, except their clothing was even more ragged, all of them showing the brassy gleam of wirehead sockets behind their right ears. Right-brain wireheaders, the worst kind. Prone to spasms of random violence, if his reading of the news webs was anything close to correct.

Two short, stocky, blond-haired boys, close enough to be brothers, flanked their obvious leader: black hair and eyes, a scar running across one cheek barely missing his bloodshot eye, yellow teeth cracked in a nasty grin.

"What's the hops?" this one said. "The hops, citizen, is you got yourself into a place you shouldn't be. Not your neighborhood, know what I mean? So you gotta pay a toll. And the rest of the hops, brother? Those hops is we're the toll takers."

He snickered, and was echoed by his flankers, whom Jim immediately dubbed Mutt and Jeff, in honor of the moons. This pair looked about as bright as Wolfbane's two tiny night satellites.

Their leader, naturally enough, he dubbed Wolfman—his yellow teeth and mop of matted black hair seemed tag enough for that.

"Sorry," Jim said, raising his hands and shaking his head. "I'm flat broke, guys." Imperceptibly he moved back from them.

He'd learned in his martial arts training that sometimes potentially violent situations could be defused with body language. Nor did he notice how his brain plucked up that nugget of knowledge as, for the first time in days, he consciously began to control his own actions.

But Wolfman wasn't having any. He was obviously practiced in the arcane arts of street intimidation, and as Jim moved backward, he pressed right into the resulting space, filling it both with his physical presence and the psychological blackmail of his ominous grin. His two sidekicks, equally adept, moved right along with him. With dismay, Jim realized they were herding him toward something, but he was afraid to risk a glance to his rear.

"Oh, hell, citizen. We aren't fancy-dancy highties like you. We're just poor Plebs, y'know? Money don't mean anything to us. Hell, we'll be happy to take whatever you got. Ain't that right, friends?"

Once again, Mutt and Jeff offered choruses of sniggering agreement. Wolfman nodded, pleased with himself and, almost as an extension of that movement, pushed suddenly forward. The heels of his hands popped off Jim's chest. The double blow wasn't particularly heavy, but it was enough to move him backward, where Mutt, on his right, neatly tripped him up.

He fell, his pack further altering his balance, so that when his reflexes tucked him into a snap roll he barely noticed that they'd adroitly thrust him right through a man-sized hole in the rusty fence beyond the slidewalk.

He landed on his butt, hard, kept on rolling, and bounced to his feet in a garbage-strewn vacant lot, golden brown weeds pushing through chunks of crumbled architectural concrete, brushing at his knees. They piled through after him with the sort of practiced ease that announced they were no strangers to this particular ambush scene.

"Now we're all private, see," Wolfman purred. "For our little transaction, citizen. So why don't you just toss that pack over here and let us get on our way, huh? Otherwise—"

Wolfman's hand moved, and something shiny dripped into his palm. Jim heard a metallic snick! and felt his stomach muscles clench even tighter as he recognized the long molyknife in Wolfman's hands.

Molyknife, his obligingly perfect memory prompted him. *Blade fashioned from an unbreakable strand of monomolecular wire. Only a single molecule thick, the sharpest edge known to man. Able to slice through high-alloy steel or six inches of plate glass.*

Or me, Jim thought.

2

She heard the soft, familiar, breathy sounds of physical aggression as she walked along the fence. Only Plebtown, she thought, a wash of self-disgust coloring her thoughts. But she took a peek anyway, in much the same way ancient motorists would slow to watch any passing mayhem along their antique freeways.

Three on one, she thought, even more disgusted. *My people, we can't even be brave robbers. Grave robbers is more our speed. Or three full-grown men on a boy.*

Make that three grown men and a molyknife.

She ducked down and climbed on through.

3

Jim kept his attention focused, not on the knife, but on Wolfman's belt buckle. Amateurs watched the weapon. People who knew what they were doing watched the body and its center of gravity. That told what the weapon would do.

But it was Jeff who made the first move, sliding farther to the side, then launching himself in a clumsy tackle at Jim's knees.

Jim had just turned sixteen years old. For ten of those years he had been going, three times a week, to his martial arts classes. Ten years was more than enough time to transform the stylized, almost artistic movements of aikido and tae kwan do into something more brutal and practical: reflexes.

Jim's hands lowered just a bit, along with his own center of gravity. He never took his eyes from Wolfman's belt buckle, until the force of the wheel kick he launched from his left leg spun him halfway around, and the heel of his right shoe cracked sharply into Jeff's naked forehead.

Jeff dropped, air belching from his slack mouth. Wolfman lunged forward, but stopped himself as Jim came easily back into a defensive stance.

"Some kinda fancy stuff, huh?" Wolfman's eyes flickered. Mutt began a slow circling movement.

"Don't think you can get us both, fancy boy. Now that we know." Wolfman tossed the knife from one hand to the other, a move designed to appear threatening, but to Jim's experienced gaze, only amateurish.

Damn it, Jim thought. *Why me? I don't want to hurt these jerks. But this guy is gonna start to think about killing me pretty soon. And Mutt's making those funny snuffling sounds, like he thinks he's some kind of attack dog—*

Once again without conscious thought Jim pivoted, this time swinging low, then bringing all his weight up behind a two-handed crossing blow his *sensei* called "the killing fan."

He knew he hadn't killed Mutt, but he'd felt cartilage in the boy's nose shatter beneath the heel of one palm, as the callused edge of his other hand hammered Mutt's jaw halfway into his collarbone. The blow itself wasn't the fan, but, properly executed, it was supposed to set up an extremely painful conflict between the bunch of nerves buried beneath the jaw, and another fan of nerves along the bridge of the nose. In theory, the victim felt as if his face were being ripped off. From the sounds Mutt was making, Jim decided he had performed the movement correctly.

"Now," Jim said. "I only have to get *you.*"

But if he'd hoped Wolfman would succumb to this onslaught of bravado, he'd underestimated the twin goads of fear and rage on a brain already addled by years of wireheading.

Wolfman shrieked once and launched himself forward, knife swinging wildly. Jim parried the blow easily, took the force of Wolfman's rush on one shoulder, let the force of it move him along as he lifted Wolfman off his feet and threw him six feet away.

Wolfman hit the ground hard, a graceless tangle, and Jim was on him while he was still shaking the cobwebs from his skull. Jim twisted the knife from his fingers.

Wolfman snarled and slashed out with his yellowed fangs and cracked fingernails. "Fatherless bastard," he growled. "I'll kill you."

And Jim Endicott lurched back over the edge, into the blank and the black.

4

Transfixed in smoke darkness: the sound of screams. Sheet lightning flickers. In endless judgment night he flounders, engulfed and engorged; time's liquid weight of blood. Father blood, mother blood, guilty blood, shame: no man endures here and lives.

Reveries and rivers of blood, time and treachery, betrayal. Father I love you. Father I kill you.

Fatherless bastard!

5

He woke from his bloody fever with absolutely no memory of the nameless and terrible place his mind had visited. His left hand was tangled in Wolfman's greasy hair, his right held the edge of the molyknife against a softly throbbing blue vein at the side of the Wolfman's darkly stubbled throat.

So easy, he thought dreamily. Just a hint more pressure, and watch the lips of flesh split apart, see the pink muscle and white tendons beneath, smell the hot, red, upwelling gush—

His hand began to shake. The tiny movement was enough to open a thread of gore against Wolfman's skin. He stared blankly at the thin stream until his hand twitched. Then he shuddered, tossed the blade away, stood quickly. Dumped Wolfman like a bag of flour.

Turned, shaking his head, his eyes blurred with tears. "Can't do it," he gagged through the bile that burned his throat. "Couldn't when I had to, can't now. Ah, I want to die."

Behind him, Wolfman screamed. Jim knew what was coming. He could hear the heavy thud of pounding feet, sense the narrowing of the distance between Wolfman's unbridled killing rage and his own defenseless back. But so what? What did he have left to live for?

He'd killed his own father.

Two sharp cracks—his first thought was, ridiculously, of firecrackers—took him completely by surprise. He jerked his head back as something hot and quick sliced past his right ear, a deadly little gnat.

"Ugh!" Wolfman said.

Jim turned, saw the taller boy falling, a burst of sticky red on his shoulder; another crack snapped the upraised molyknife from Wolfman's hand. Jim kept on spinning, his heart whacking in his rib cage, till he'd come all the way back around and—

"Hey!"

From the rear he heard the flap-slap of scrambling shoe soles, gulping gasps of panic as Mutt and Jeff made their escape.

She smiled at him as she lowered the small slug-thrower in her right hand. "The name's Cat," she said. "Cat Thibaudeaux. Pleased to meet you."

She paused, then stuck her left hand out for a shake. "Just wondering, but aren't you awfully young for suicide?"

CHAPTER 5

1

He'd seen those eyes before. Maybe that's why he took her hand.

Eyes like ice. What a stupid description, a cliché, really, Jim thought. *Do eyes really look like ice? Of course not,* he told himself, and yet they still pulled him forward, pale, pale, blue, into their chilly, sparkling depths.

Her hand felt small, dry, and competent. She squeezed his fingers lightly, then took her hand away as if she didn't trust him to hold it for long.

"Cat . . ." he said. "What a great name." He knew he sounded stupid. He didn't care.

"Well, my parents didn't think so," she told him dryly. "They sorta liked Catherine, but I didn't. Are you going to tell me yours, or do I have to guess?"

His new life was still much too new—he didn't have the reflexes yet, the automatic defenses of dishonesty and deception. "Jim," he said eagerly. "Jim . . . uh . . ."

So maybe it wasn't such a good idea to blurt out who he was to every passing stranger, no matter if the stranger had just saved his life and had ice blue eyes. And hair like strands of golden corn silk. Was that another cliché? He didn't care. He could improve his literary descriptions later.

She grinned. "Well, hey, Jim Uh, pleased to meet you. Did I interrupt anything important, or do you let jagged wireheads work on your back with molyknives every day?"

There was a bubbling brightness to her voice that matched the sudden new brightness in the sky overhead. And abruptly Jim found himself noticing how smelly and dirty he was. He felt his cheeks grow hot with embarrassment. "I'm sorry for the way I look . . . and stink, probably. Haven't been able to get into a refresher closet in a while."

She cocked her head. "Really? Listen, Jim Uh, a little bird is telling me you aren't from the neighborhood, am I right?"

He grinned and shrugged his shoulders sheepishly.

"And I'm even willing to make a small bet—say a minicredit—that your name isn't really Jim Uh."

"Uh . . . well. How about Smith? Jim Smith?"

Now she shrugged. "If it suits you, it suits me fine. So, okay, Jim Smith, what's next? I gotta warn you, I don't buy that ancient Asian stuff about how saving your bacon makes me responsible for you the rest of my life. You want, I can turn right around and walk away from you forever."

"No!" He breathed. "I mean . . . wait, okay?"

"Sure. Actually, that's probably not a good idea. Waiting, I mean. Curlylocks down there is gonna wake up and start making a fair amount of noise pretty soon. Or his two bumpkin friends are going to come back with the cavalry. I can shut this one up permanently, though, if you want me to," she said thoughtfully. She started to raise her little gun again.

Jim pushed her hand aside. As he did so, his fingers brushed across her velvety skin. He felt a sudden electric tingle and inhaled sharply. "That's okay. Can we get out of here? Have you got someplace we could go?"

She stepped back and eyed him appraisingly. Once again he felt himself blushing. What right did he have to ask her such a thing? He didn't even know her. He waited, feeling his blood pump, while she considered.

"As a matter of fact, I do," she told him. But as she stared at him, a sudden shriek rent the air . . . the source unseen, but close.

Her eyes went wide. "Oh, no . . ."

"What, Cat? What is it?"

She shook her head. "Pleb Psychosis," she replied. She seemed suddenly terrified. "Come on, we gotta get under cover, before—"

A pair of sharp cracks, then a louder explosion, distant and muffled. More cries, floating thin on the air, growing closer . . .

"I said *hurry*," she shouted, and grabbed his hand, tugging him along with frantic urgency.

They almost made it.

2

Together, they ducked back through the fence, Cat dragging him down the shattered concrete. A thin, acrid haze of smoke now drifted in the air, stinging his eyes. But he could still see well enough. The street, which he'd thought empty, began to change before his eyes. What he'd barely noticed before, a pile of refuse, a clump of shadows, now disgorged tattered figures.

A man leaped up before them, hands clasped to the side of his head, screaming. A quick mind-picture as they rushed past: the beggar's eyes impossibly wide, but empty of all sanity; drool sliming a whiskery chin, yellowed teeth grinding, purple tongue distended, clogging a mouth trying, and failing, to open farther.

The man fell away behind them, but now more figures appeared, staggering, shrieking, falling, and rising again.

The smoke grew thicker and sirens began to wail. Overhead, police floaters began to swarm, swooping low, a distinctive chatter sounding as they fired tanglefoot guns again and again.

And still the rushing, shrieking Plebs appeared. It was as if a light suddenly flashed in a darkened room, and an army of cockroaches, suddenly exposed, began to scurry about. Except these pitiful human insects were bleeding.

They scrambled past a bizarre tableau. One woman lay on the ground, arms and legs twitching in bone-breaking spasms. Over her prone form, a man and woman grappled with each other. The woman, small and gray-haired, might have been somebody's old grandmother. But her face was covered with blood, and her right arm worked like a metronome, thrusting again and again into the man's belly.

He caught a glimpse of her crimson scissors as the man howled. Suddenly a bright, glistening tangle of wet worms erupted from the man's stomach and spilled out, twisting, upon the pavement. But the worst thing was, he didn't seem to notice. His hands were wrapped around his assailant's thin neck and, oblivious to his own ruin, he kept on throttling her. Together, slowly, they sank down on the third figure, and then were gone, leaving nothing but horror behind.

"I . . ." Jim said, turning aside, his palm rising to his mouth.

"*Come on, damn it!*"

He couldn't help it. He bent over and vomited the few bits in his stomach, a thin, stinking stream, his gut clenching and clenching with terror.

She finally got him going again. The street was crowded now, the air full of enraged howling, gibbering laughter, sirens, the metallic thunder of police orders from the circling floaters.

Jim ducked as gunshots began to crack. He heard the heavy buzz of an illegal ripper; the rich, greasy odor of charred pork filled his nostrils, and his gut contracted again.

The smoke was now so thick he could barely see, but Cat was still yanking him forward. A huge explosion shook the pavement, almost knocking him off his feet. Then everything went out from under him, and he tumbled pell-mell down a short flight of steps.

A doorway loomed as he picked himself up and staggered through. She slammed the door behind them and stood with her back against it while he sprawled on his butt, looking up at her.

Her face was twisted with an anguish so deep he feared she'd gone as mad as the insanity on the other side of the door.

"What . . . ?" he managed weakly.

"Pleb Psychosis," she said. "Now you know."

He took a breath. "God . . ."

She shook her head. "No. Not God. God doesn't have anything to do with it at all."

3

Steele clamped her teeth together as the realdoc probed into the mostly healed mess of her knee.

"Mmm. Autodoc did a nice job for an emergency," the realdoc muttered. He was a short man with what Steele thought of as roving eyes, and his hands were both too soft and too familiar.

She consoled herself with the thought that, unlike most of his other female patients, if it came to it, she could snap his pudgy little neck like a chicken.

"Yeah, yeah," she told him. "So what's the bottom line?"

He shrugged. "I put in a brand-new joint and replaced a lot of tendon with new stuff. You may notice a small limp, or maybe not, if you rehabilitate hard enough."

Steele nodded and mentally doubled the hours she planned to spend in physical rehab. A small limp might not bother most people, but in her line of business . . .

"Anything else?" she asked.

"I'm curious," he said. "What did you do to the other woman?"

"Hmm? Oh, her? Nothing, not a damn thing. Why? Is something wrong?"

"She's mute. Physically she checks out just fine, and she seems responsive enough, but she can't say a word. Oh. Can't read or write, either. It's . . . odd."

"She's faking," Steele said.

The doctor shook his head. "I don't think so. Our tests were very thorough."

"She doesn't need tests," Steele told him. "Give me ten minutes alone with her, and she'll be chirping like the birds in the trees."

Now the doctor drew back, a faint expression of distaste on his doughy features. "What department did you say you worked for again?"

But her gaze had wandered from him, become somewhat unfocused. "I didn't," she told him. "What about the others? The rest of my team?"

He pursed his lips and tried to look sad. It didn't work very well. He thought there was already enough violence in the worlds, and he'd seen what something extremely violent had done to Molly Harrison and Heck Campbell and the third, unnamed body that had been retrieved from the mountain cabin. The only thing that came immediately to mind was that if you lived by the sword, your chances of dying by one were fairly high.

He was chief surgeon on a Terran Navy cruiser. He understood all about keeping his mouth shut and keeping his judgments to himself. And twenty years of such experience came to his aid now.

"Succumbed to their various traumas. We were too late for even the most heroic measures to do any good."

Various traumas. Fair enough description for what was not much more than hamburger by the time we got to them.

"Couldn't raise 'em from the dead, huh?" Steele's shoulders

moved dismissively. "Well, if they'd been a little faster, it wouldn't have happened."

"A little faster?"

Steele slid off the examining table and headed for the door. Her limp was more than slight. "See you later, Doc. You need me, I'll be in rehab."

He watched the door close behind her, stood still for a long moment, then gave a little start.

Did it seem warmer in the room, now that she was gone?

4

"Another one of your mysterious errands?" he asked her.

He sat up and shaded his eyes against the sun that flooded through the foggy window over the mattress on which he lay, still wrapped in a yellowed sheet almost thin enough to see through, blinking sleep from his eyes. He combed his tousled hair with his fingers, smelling the coffee she'd made, thinking it was going to be a fine day. Already hot, though. His memories of the nightmare of the Pleb Psychosis had faded, for which he was profoundly grateful.

She paused by the door, turned, smiled. "You know what? Your rent isn't high enough. You've been here what—almost a week now? Okay, buddy. See that cook unit? Hasn't worked since I came here. You say you're some kind of electronics genius? Fix that puppy." She glanced down at her bracelink, her bracelet computer link. In her case, Jim knew she wasn't linked to a private axe, but to the Public Web available to anybody, but used mostly by Plebs because it was free.

"I'll be back before lunchtime. I found a neat little place." She grinned. "My treat, of course."

Jim grinned back, but uneasily. He couldn't recall what had been going though his mind as he'd picked through the wreckage of the cabin while he stocked his bag, but one thing he sure hadn't brought: cash money. But then, why should he have? It was such an . . . archaic . . . thing to consider.

He wasn't broke, of course. Not technically. In fact, his credit account, which he could access simply by speaking his codes into his own bracelink, was pretty plump. He'd been stuffing it for years with the proceeds of his part-time, freelance data-sniffing business.

He wondered how many would come to kill him this time, if he so much as tried to lay a finger on that money.

"We gotta talk, Cat," he told her. "This isn't right, me freeloading on you this way."

"When I get tired of it, you'll be the first to know. I promise." She squinched her right eye and tapped her cheek in mock concentration. "Just fix the cook unit, and try to stay out of trouble till I get back. Then we'll talk, okay?"

He nodded. She closed the door carefully behind her. It locked with an audible click, and Jim wondered what she'd done to the normally flimsy lock. Well, he was certainly in no position to pry, but there was without a doubt something awfully odd about Ms. Cat Thibaudeaux, lately arrived from someplace else she wouldn't talk about.

A mystery in search of an enigma. As if he didn't have a full plate of that kind of stuff already. He flopped back and stretched, then swept the sheet off his naked body, did a half flip that put him on his feet, and padded softly over to the pot of still-steaming coffee.

Another mystery. It wasn't synthetic coffee, but the real thing. A *lot* of money . . .

Well, maybe after they talked, he'd have a better idea of what was what. In the meantime, he could make a little headway on figuring out the rest of it. The really scary stuff.

He even managed to think this without seeing a picture of Carl, dead in his arms. At least not right away. It was an improvement.

5

By the time she came back, he had the innards of the cook unit spread out on the tabletop next to his makeshift tool kit. "This is junk," he told her as he poked at a corroded bit of electronic flotsam with a bent fork.

"Hey, a fork," she replied. "Pretty sophisticated tools you've got there, Mr. Smith."

"Unfortunately, I left my good repair kit in my other backpack," he told her.

"I kinda guessed," she replied, as she slid into the chair opposite and placed a greasy paper bag down in front of him. He wrinkled his nose. It smelled delicious.

"Fresh doughnuts," she told him. "And some bagels and cream cheese. Don't thank me all at once, now."

She eyed him carefully. He had no idea—or at least she didn't *think* he did—but the time since she'd met him was about the strangest period she'd spent in years. And she still couldn't make up her mind: was he some kind of trap, or not?

Jim pushed the tangle of metal and chips and plastic away with a disgusted wheeze. "Huh, forget it. I can't fix it. Do I still get a doughnut?"

She shoved the paper bag across. He dug around, pulled one out, said, "All right! Crumb cake, my favorite!," and took half the fist-sized pastry in one bite.

"And good manners, too," Cat told him. "Everything I like in a man."

He nodded, cheeks puffed, jaws working. "Mmph, umph?"

"What?"

"I . . . uh . . . waitaminna—there. Okay. So, Cat, where do you go when you won't tell me where you go?"

She tipped her head back. "What makes you think I'll tell you now, when I haven't before?"

He leaned against the back of the chair and crossed his arms over his chest. He was not unaware this made his biceps appear larger than they actually were. "Well, 'cause I thought I'd make a few trades. You probably noticed I haven't had much to say, either?" He thought that came out sounding nicely reserved—strong, silent, even maybe sophisticated.

He watched the pink tip of her tongue dart out, just a flash, and touch the top of her bottom lip. The fleeting glimpse sent another one of those pleasantly annoying tingles rustling up his spine.

She said, "What, Mister Stone? Mister Clam? You, reticent?" She winked. "Not that it matters, though."

"What's that supposed to mean?"

"You may think you're being all discreet and strong and silent, but you're about as easy a read as the funnyvids."

"Huh? Not possible, Cat lady. You're guessing, is all."

"Oh? Then try this for a guess." She touched the side of her nose, then poked one finger up. "First. You're not a Pleb, never have been. Which means you're a runaway, because you are too young to be out on your own—at least in your class of people. Second—" She raised another finger. "Whatever you're running from is pretty nasty, 'cause you wake me up with your nightmares. Third, you don't have any idea what you're gonna do, because it is obvious to me you're clueless."

She smiled, to take a little of the sting away. Still wondering about him, though.

"And, number four: you would like to move from your side of the bed to my side just about more than anything in the world, and I know *that* 'cause you blush whenever you look at me and you think I can't see you. Just like you are now."

"Now I'm embarrassed," he told her.

She grinned complacently. "Go on, am I right, or am I right?"

He shrugged, his cheeks in flames. "Well, maybe about the last part."

"About the rest of it, too, I'll bet." She snatched back the bag of pastries. "Blush all you want, but don't hog my breakfast, buddy." She fished out a bagel, broke off a tiny piece, and nibbled it delicately.

"So," she said. "How about you? What do you think you've figured out about me? And wipe that stupid grin off your face. You look like you're gonna start drooling any minute now."

He grabbed another doughnut to mask his disconcertment. So what exactly had he figured out about her? He bit down and chewed thoughtfully.

"Well, you're mysterious. I think you're about my age, maybe a little older—but you are a Pleb. So I don't know exactly what you being on your own means, except it's probably different than for somebody like me."

She nodded slowly. Encouraged, he continued. "You go places and don't tell me, and you seem to have all the money you need—both kinds, underground cash, and legal chipcredits."

"Well, at least you're reasonably observant."

"Thanks, Mata Hari."

She stared at him blankly. "And that's another thing," he went on. "No offense, but you're not as educated as I am—not formally, at least. I know who Mata Hari is. But I don't think you do."

Her forehead crinkled. "Sure I do. He was . . . uh . . ."

He grinned. "Wrong. *She* was a spy. A real old-timey one, back three centuries or so on old Terra. Prespace, even."

"That what you think I am? A spy?"

He shrugged. "I dunno. You could be, I suppose. An industrial spy, maybe, working for some Terran company. I mean, if you have all this money, why do you live in a dump like this? When you could live anywhere? Unless you're living exactly where you want to—and for the same reasons I am?"

For a moment he hesitated, wanting to say something else, something honest, but afraid to. He was treading too close to too many edges—his own, and perhaps hers as well. But . . . Mentally, he shrugged. *In for a penny, in for a pound.*

"Um, and killing people doesn't seem to bother you too much."

She aimed an opaque glance at him, then twisted off one more minuscule bit of bagel, popped it in her mouth—giving him another delightful flash of pink tongue—and chewed. Her eyes turned somewhat vague. As if she were considering something.

"It's a fair analysis, Jim. Better than I would have given you credit for. You're what—sixteen? You think better than most sixteen-year-old kids. How come is that?"

He felt himself sliding closer to dangerous territory. He couldn't really tell her the truth, could he? Well, why not? It all came down to a matter of trust. Did he trust her?

He tried to weigh it all, but in the end it balanced on his own hunches, feelings, the intuition he'd never known he had, but was beginning to find and trust. She was strange, yeah, but it wasn't bad strange. Not like those murderers who had come to the cabin. Not like whatever awful secret had come snarling out of his hidden past to wreck his present and poison his future.

And God, he so desperately wanted to tell someone.

So he did.

6

"Wow," she said, when he had finished.

Even he had not understood just how much poison had backed up in his system, and how good it felt to spew it out into the bright, cleansing light of day.

But when he finished, a dull fire burned in his cheeks that had nothing to do with Cat, and everything to do with his own shame.

"I'm a murderer," he said, simply. "I didn't want to be, but I am. That's why I couldn't use the molyknife on that Pleb kid who tried to mug me. I didn't want to be a murderer again. Not by my own choosing."

He looked across the table at her, helplessly. Her features were set, almost blank. Her expression frightened him more than anything he'd ever seen on a human face.

"Do . . . do you hate me?" he said.

She made up her mind then.

She stood up, came slowly around the table, and bent down. Her breath was slow and warm in his ear. Gently, she urged him out of the chair, turned him, guided him toward the still-rumpled mattress on the floor.

"You're not a murderer," she said. "And, no, I don't hate you at all."

CHAPTER 6

1

He didn't wake up to a new day. It was more like a new life. Or perhaps his old one, miraculously restored to him, at least as much as it could be.

The morning sun leaked a faded rose glow through the drawn plastic shades, softening the rough edges of the shabby little apartment, draping cool shadows in the corners so that everything looked just the slightest bit unreal. A holovid set, maybe.

Jim pushed himself up on his elbows, the thin sheet across his chest. She was a vague warmth next to him. His slow movement brought her half-awake. She smacked her lips a couple of times, snorted softly, and rolled back over, taking a good bit of the sheet with her.

He smiled down on her—if smile was the correct designation for the expression that stretched his face so wide his jaw muscles ached and his lips felt drawn out of shape. He wondered if it was better than he'd expected, and decided he really had no idea of what he'd expected, not in the face of the reality of it. All his previous notions had been those of a child. Now he'd opened a door and stepped through, and on the other side everything was changed.

Everything . . .

That sadness he would never entirely lose took him then, and under his breath he whispered, "Dad . . ."

But even that shade passed him by, leaving only the coolness of regret, a perfect match for the shadows in the corners of the room, in the corners of his soul.

How could he ever repay her? With her one simple act of giving, of offering the thing every woman possessed, she had rescued him. The act that opened wide space and let in the moon and the stars had worked its eternal and mysterious magic, and somehow she had given him back a future. Not, perhaps, the future he had so innocently imagined even a week ago, but something; the wish to *have* a future, perhaps. So fragile, and yet so incredibly precious. He could still have the stars, if he yet wanted them. That was what she had returned to him: the stars, and the great white ships that sought them.

Today I am a man, he thought to himself, feeling a vague shiver of memory, of a link between those words and a ritual far more ancient than he knew. But this passed as well, as the rose glow of dawn slowly deepened into the red heat of a Wolfbane summer morning, and a cockroach, its ancestors inadvertently imported from distant Earth, ran crazily across the wall.

I have to know, he told himself. *She gave me back my life. But who tried to take it in the first place? And why?*

Mom, hang on. Wherever you are, I'm coming.

2

Later . . .

"So," she said, "now what?"

She was stirring too much sugar into her second cup of coffee, and the longer she was awake, the more distant she seemed to become. He couldn't understand it.

"Is something the matter?" he asked.

"No . . . yes . . . I don't know. Maybe."

"Is it me?"

She stared at him over the rim of the cup, her pale blue eyes wary. Then she nodded. "Probably."

He tried to feel his way into it. But he felt so young, so inexperienced, so clumsy. He didn't want to hurt her. He didn't want to hurt himself, either.

"You, uh, didn't have to . . . you know?"

"Yeah, damn it. I know. That's the problem. Knew it when I did it, and didn't care. I'm not supposed to do stuff like that. But you seemed so . . . I don't know. You needed me, needed somebody, and I guess I just nominated myself."

She paused, sipped coffee, smiled faintly. "Not that it was all that unpleasant or anything. Actually, I enjoyed it. You seemed to be pretty happy with it, yourself." She eyed him demurely.

"Hey," she said. "Did I mention you're cute when you blush?"

He shook his head. She was just too quick for him, especially when he was in this state—whatever this state was he was in. A little voice in the far reaches of his mind whispered that he had just discovered an eternal secret, but that knowing it would do him, a male, absolutely no good at all. No more than if a steer in its slaughterhouse had the wit to understand a hammer. It would make the blow no less strong, nor less ultimately fatal.

"Maybe," he offered, "it would be better if I took off. You know."

But she shook her head. "After I went to all that trouble? Offering you the flower of my . . . uh, flower? Nope, Jim Smith, I now have stuff invested in you. So I think I want you to stick around. Besides, there's somebody I want you to meet."

"Huh? Who's that?" He wasn't sure he wanted to meet anybody. In fact, the thought of stepping out of this tiny cubicle brought an uncomfortable cramping sensation into his belly.

"Just a guy," she said. "Don't worry. I think you'll find you have a lot in common."

3

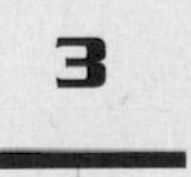

"Lucas Morninglory, son. Betcha never forget a name like that, huh?" He had a jaw like a shovel full of rotten yellow teeth, big teeth, and eyes of the same general color. But jaundice seemed to suit him; aside from the odd golden hue of teeth, skin, and eyes, he seemed healthy enough. Old, though. Very old.

"Please to meet you, Mister Morninglory," Jim said. He stuck out his hand and found it promptly engulfed by fingers like leather-wrapped cable. "Ouch!"

"Lucas," Cat said. "He's mine. Don't break him, okay?"

"Yours?" The irises of Lucas's eyes were small and hard and brown; raisins swimming in buttercream. Sharp. "That true, boy? You belong to Cat?"

Jim shrugged. He had no idea what was happening here, but he assumed if he kept his mouth shut long enough, one of these crazy people would let him in on the secret. Besides, the idea of belonging to Cat wasn't entirely a bad one. If he had to belong to anybody.

The ragged edges of a storm had worked their way over the distant mountains, and now the wind had begun to rise. A set of tarpaulins, tattered and split, suddenly sounded a rippling beat overhead, and a few windblown drops of rain spattered down and marked the aged concrete walkway on which they stood.

"Gonna be a bad one," Lucas observed, smacking his lips. "My elbow joints are acting up already."

Jim nodded. If Cat wanted him to, he was perfectly willing to stand here and listen to this old party babble about the weather for days.

But Lucas squinted brightly at him, then abruptly slapped both seamed palms on the thighs of his filthy jeans. "Enough of the polite chitchat, eh, son? Cat tells me you need to find out some stuff. So, are you ready to take a ride?"

"I guess so . . ." A ride? What the hell had Cat told this ancient, wizened bird?

"We'll see about that," Morninglory said.

Jim glanced at Cat. She nodded. "Lucas is the best hacker in the whole Pleb culture. Here on Wolfbane, at least."

"Anywhere, girlie," he cackled. "Anywhere, and don't you forget it."

She nodded. "Like you said, we'll see about that."

4

"Meet the gang," Morninglory chirped. His voice was high-pitched, cracking, an old man's voice. Yet he moved quickly and surely, youthful as a boy. Jim began to wonder what sort of biological restructuring he'd had done to himself. Fair amount, it looked like.

He had led them into what appeared to be an abandoned factory of some sort; great rusty hulks of shattered machinery loomed upward in the afternoon gloom. Outside, the sudden sizzle of lightning, several long beats, and an answering peal of thunder. A gust of wet wind whipped through murky skylights propped open overhead.

The gang was three other people, two women, both of indeterminate age, and one very young boy whose bony skull was shaved smooth as an egg. He looked up from the huge, cobbled-together pile of electronics boxes that surrounded him and grinned at Morninglory. The two older women both seemed to be busy fetching him plastic bottles of soda, handfuls of computer storage chips, and bags of potato chips.

"The bald one is called Chip, and the two ladies, Frick and Frack." Morninglory bowed toward the trio, and Chip nodded in reply. It was when he moved his head that Jim noticed a cascade of thin wires dropping from jacks behind his ears to the machines around him; six, seven, no ten separate lines. He'd never heard of such a huge number of direct computer–brain connections. The boy looked human enough, but Jim wondered. How could you get that up close and personal with your machines and still remain unaffected? As for the two women, they took no notice of the newcomers whatsoever—in fact, acted far more machinelike than Chip did.

"Chip's my speed demon," Morninglory announced cheerfully. "You need a kid's reflexes for the kind of stuff I do."

Jim looked back and forth between them. Morninglory looked like a derelict. If anybody looked like a hacker, it was Chip. He said so.

"Oh, Chip's a lot faster'n me," Morninglory agreed. "But I know a lot more than he does, y'see. I tell him what to do, and then he does it, faster and better than I could. But he needs me to, kinda like drive him. Think of Chipper as a very fast gravcar. You can do five hundred miles per hour, but without a driver, all you got is a wreck waiting to happen."

Chip grinned. Jim noticed his teeth seemed to be solid gold. "Not true, old man. You may know a little more than I do—you oughta, you're about a hundred years older than me—but it's a partnership, get it? I'm not your car."

Morninglory waved one hand negligently. "Pay no attention to him, folks. His brain's addled from all those wires going into it."

"I'll addle you, you old cranker," Chip muttered.

"But he really is good. Together, we're the best. Trust me."

Jim nodded. "So what do you want me to do?"

"Nothing," Morninglory told him. "Well, I want you to jack into this machine over here—we'll just use your standard virtual-reality jack—so's I can get a picture of what we are looking for. Okay?"

Jim nodded, feeling faintly uneasy. He knew what Morninglory intended. Jim would call up a computer modeling program and then create everything he could remember of that night—through his direct virtual-reality interface. Once created, Morninglory and Chip would feed the results into whatever arcane programs they used and, with luck, perhaps be able to find out who—and what—had attacked Jim and his family.

Maybe even find Mom . . .

He took a deep breath and stepped forward. "You got a jack for me?" He looked at Cat as Morninglory handed him the small connector. Cat nodded, then winked. Jim grinned. "Okay," he said. "Let's do it."

5

No matter how many times Jim "jacked in" to cyberspace and established a direct connection between his own thoughts and the silicon heart of a computer web, the sensation was always strange.

First, a faint, fizzy sensation at the base of his skull, then a momentary flash of darkness while the computer and his brain dickered over who was in charge. Then the moment of blindness passed, leaving him with an odd sense of double vision. He could see the real world just fine, but as if through a pane of glass—clear, but something in between. That was the machine, and the pseudoglass was the screen upon which the computer projected whatever it wished.

He could achieve a link so tenuous that he was barely aware of the computer at all, or so complete that he smelled, tasted, heard, felt, and saw with perfect clarity a virtual world that did not exist except in the agreement between his mind and the computer.

Eerie. But he was well used to it. The jack felt cool between his fingertips as he plugged it into the socket behind his ear. He saw Morninglory plug in three cables. Chip was already festooned with a Christmas tree's worth of high-tech wiring.

"Okay . . ." Morninglory said. "Here we go."

And the real world lurched away into darkness.

Jim floated in the blank and the black, but this time it was not scary. A soft voice whispered in his ear. "Okay, now start remembering. I'll grab it as it comes by and use it to build on. We have an unlimited supply of templates."

Jim nodded to himself, another odd sensation, because he could no longer feel his physical body. How could you nod a head you didn't have?

He began to try to remember everything he could about the night his world fell apart. As the first horrifying images swam into his mind, he cringed. Their emotional heat was still searing, and the effort he had to make in order to hold them was as great as anything he had ever tried to do before. Still, he kept on, until he reached that instant he'd hoped he could wipe away entirely—the moment when his father had died in his arms, that faint, departing smile still on his lips.

"*I love you . . .*"

"Hold it right there," a voice whispered. "You're overamping. Let me take over now . . ."

And somehow Morninglory was there, the blanket of his personality mercifully interposed between Jim and his memories, smoothing them, filtering them.

"See, you saw a lot of stuff you don't remember. Peripheral movement, flashes, memories. Like . . . right there."

Jim saw a face hanging in the darkness. A strange, helmeted

face, helmet mask flipped up to expose pale skin, eyes like ashen pools, blood red lipstick.

"Nasty," Morninglory commented. "Remember her?"

"No," Jim said.

"Well, you do. Okay, I want you to relax, now. I've got everything that's useful, I think. Now comes the hard part."

For a long moment there was nothing but silence. Then, gradually, Jim began to hear the rushing thud of his own blood in his ears.

Click!

"Oh," Morninglory murmured. "Forgot to ask. How do you want me to do this? Filter, or do you want to watch at the machine level?"

Jim considered. If he were to try to watch Chip and Morninglory do their hacking at machine level, all he would see would be the incomprehensible bursts of energy that made up digital thought, the language of computers. A filter would be much better.

"Filter," he said.

"Okay. Any preference?"

Jim shrugged his nonexistent shoulders. Somehow Morninglory picked up the movement. "I've got a nice one. I call it supercity, all right?"

"Sure," Jim said.

And the darkness . . .*twisted.*

6

"Kinda like those dreams of flying, huh?"

Jim nodded. He could see his body again, but he felt like some kind of mythical superhero. He was flying low over a vast plain choked with glowing, multicolored structures. Rapidly moving chunks of light streamed in the interstices between the structures, the filtered representations of data flows. Here and there massive and convoluted shapes thrust high above the general mass. On the flickering sides of these constructions streaks and trails of light blinked and crawled.

"What the hell are those?" Jim asked.

Immediately he felt himself swooping toward the nearest. He glanced to one side and saw two figures flying along with him. One resembled pictures of the ancient Yahweh, the old god, complete with flowing robes, long white hair, and an imposing beard. In his right hand the figure grasped a living thunderbolt, a naked staff of fizzing, spitting electricity. Beyond this amazing figure swooped a younger man—dark-haired, wearing a skintight uniform with a big letter S on the front, and a long crimson cape streaming out behind.

Jim laughed. "Pretty hokey," he said.

Yahweh chuckled. "Keeps our spirits up."

The small party swooshed up close to the towering structure and halted a few yards away. "Don't go any closer," Morninglory said. "This baby is wired about six different ways."

Jim felt his skin crawl. "Where are we, exactly?"

"Main Wolfbane cyberspace. The World Web," Morninglory replied. "We're in a rather heavily restricted area right now. Government databases, military stuff, corporations that would be awfully huffy if they knew we were here."

Jim felt a twinge. "How huffy is that?"

"Killer programs. Brain bombs and neural zappers," Morninglory said. "But not to worry. We've done this before."

"That's nice," Jim said.

"Well, you said you wanted to watch—whoops. Look there."

Something pale, of indeterminate shape, had swum to the surface of the data mass before them. It was vague and ghostly, but it seemed almost aware of their presence.

"Hmm. Seems we've been noticed. Okay, Chipper. Do your stuff."

The boy floated forward until he faced the growing white blob head-on. Pseudopods began to extend from the blob, growing and stretching until they extended out from the larger structure itself.

"Dumb programs, tattletales. But you don't want to let them touch you. They don't let go, and they call for nastier stuff to come help."

"Oh," Jim said. "What is this data mass?"

Soft laughter. "Combined Intelligence Agencies," Morninglory said. "They get a bit touchy about intruders."

Jim swallowed heavily.

Now Chip extended his own hands, palms out. His red cloak billowed out behind him, floating on an unseen wind. Suddenly, from his palms, lances of bright green light sprang forward to meet the oncoming white pseudopods. Where the two met came sharp white flashes, and a sizzling smell like the air after a lightning strike.

Jim knew it was all unreal, a function of the filter Morninglory had applied to what was really happening, but it still seemed as vivid and lifelike as anything he'd ever seen or felt.

"Wow," Jim breathed.

"Chip's using a cracker program. Turns off those alarms, opens the way."

And, indeed, the ghostly white shape was shrinking in on itself, turning dull and dark, and beginning to fade entirely. After several long moments it vanished.

"Good enough," Morninglory said. Where the white shape had been was now a pulsing blue opening in the skin of the data mass. "Door's open, gents. Shall we go see what's in the cupboard?"

Jim felt himself being swept forward, into the most closely guarded—and deadly—dataspace on Wolfbane.

7

In a way it was disappointing. He had jinked around with forbidden bases before, though nothing on this scale. But it had been a whiz breaking into the school's base, scrummaging around in the forbidden grade files, even taking a quick peek at the personnel files for the teachers. Old Doctor Forzwill, for instance—Jim shook his nonexistent head. He was allowing his concentration to wander. Potentially dangerous, not only for him but for Lucas and Chip. He pulled his thoughts together and told himself: *Focus*!

Good thing, too. It looked as if things had sped up. Once they had crashed past the heavily guarded portal, they entered a different sort of space. In fact, space was almost what it looked like, a sea of tiny flickering stars stretching out endlessly before them.

He glanced around and couldn't see Morninglory or Chip, but he knew they were still with him. "What's up?" he asked.

A disembodied voice replied. "Hmm. Very interesting . . . now shut up, boy. We're busy."

This whole false universe began to blink, as they seemed to dart from star to star, but far faster than any human ship could hope to navigate real space-time. For several long moments Jim simply let himself go with this awesome flow, drifting in Morninglory's wake, his virtual mouth and virtual eyes wide with wonder at the monumental vistas of unrestrained dataspace.

"Oh, damn," Morninglory muttered.

A quick chill jittered down Jim's spine, a chill that didn't seem virtual at all. "Damn? What do you mean, damn? Is something wrong?"

Morninglory made no reply, an event in itself upsetting, but very quickly it became obvious why he hadn't—and why no reply was needed.

Off in the vanishing distance a cluster of stars began to throb, and their meticulous constellation to change its pattern. Now, one by one, each pulsating white dot silently exploded, creating an infinity of new stars. Closer stars. Which themselves repeated the process until they now advanced upon a coruscating wall of solid light.

"I think," Morninglory said, "we should probably take our leave."

And, indeed, they began to retreat nicely, the wall before them growing dimmer, until Jim began to relax again. It couldn't be much longer till they were out of the CIA dataspace and relatively safe.

"Morninglory, I need a hand here," came Chip's soft, tense voice. "Zapper's got hold of me, and it's starting to bite."

Just as he was trying to figure out what *that* meant, Jim's vision vanished, and he found himself drifting helpless and cut off, alone again in the blank and the black.

8

The alarms had been sounding for some time now, both on Wolfbane and, via faster-than-light superluminal connectors, on distant Earth itself.

To repel the attack was, in general, work for machines, or at least the software that ran on them. Things moved too quickly for a human response to be of any help—which might have seemed strange, given that the security breach was caused by human effort. The difference was simple—the attackers had the advantage. They *knew* what they were after, but the defenders did not, and so had to make their defense on all fronts. A brute force kind of thing, and far better done by killer software programs like the brain bombs, the neural zappers.

It is in the nature of cybernetic attack and defense that both sides must, to some extent, expose their vulnerable parts: the defenders, of course, reveal that which they defend—their caches of secret data. But the attackers, in order to use cyberspace at all, must mentally enter into it, that is, open their minds to the workings of the computer nets. And it is axiomatic—the way in is also the way out or, more simply, buddy, that's a two-way street.

Neural zappers went the other way.

And one had rolled right down the self-built throughway that Chip and Morninglory had built, crashed through all the traffic barriers, and barreled right into Chip's brain, where it was doing what it had been designed to do: erase data.

The human mind is as much a computer as any manufactured machine and, given that most computers were now grown rather than built, it was not even physically that much different in structure, if a great deal more complex. But the zappers didn't care about complexity—a barbarian may destroy the work of Archimedes as easily as some peasant's kitchen pots. Destruction is always easy.

Chip *screamed.*

The sound was so loud it broke through the barriers Morninglory had built around Jim's perceptions, in order to spare him while he fought for all of their lives.

But Chip's agony, as chunks of his memory literally disintegrated before the zapper's brutal attack, shattered those safety walls and dumped Jim unceremoniously into the chaos of their mutual struggle.

It was an awesome, and awesomely confusing, sight.

The first thing Jim saw when the darkness vanished was what appeared to be an endless stream of multicolored ribbons, twirling and snaking around two figures who already appeared mummified. One was screaming; the other was fighting back, bolts of lightning flickering within the building cloud of the ribbons, blasting great holes in their mindless, choking structure. But even Jim could tell the battle was doomed. No matter how much destruction the bolts accomplished, more twisting ribbons skated in, slick and evil, to bandage the wounds and further smother the thrower of lightning.

And Chip kept on screaming.

The only good thing Jim could imagine was that, for some reason or other, the CIA's killer ribbons weren't attacking him. He presumed that Morninglory's attempt to mask his presence was responsible, but he couldn't depend on the effect lasting, now that he could see the zappers himself. If he could see them, probably they could see him.

For the moment, though, he was free. And he knew exactly what to do.

He closed his eyes, envisioned his own real body, reached up, and jerked the cyberjack from its socket in his skull. A shower of white sparks exploded behind his eyes. For a moment he saw a hazy vision of Cat's face, concerned, floating in front of him, and then the pseudoepileptic seizures that always accompanied an unplanned virtual connection break wrapped him in bands of iron and dragged him down to darkness.

9

"Jim! Jim, wake *up*!"

Something slammed into him hard, and he tried to roll away. No use. It slammed him again, rocked him. Heavy blows. Something flickered, distant, a moment of light.

Wham! Another blow, but somehow refreshing. It knocked away that weird stasis that had gripped him. Now the light began to grow, muzzy gray, fuzzy cotton, brighter—

"*Cat!*"

She'd drawn back her hand to smack him again, and only barely stayed the blow. "What? What's wrong? What's going on?" she demanded.

But he was already scrambling across her, to where both

Morninglory and Chip reclined quietly, their skins pale, their eyelids twitching slightly. As he lunged for them both Frick and Frack moved to stop him.

"Wait!" Frick said.

"You can't do that!" Frack chimed in.

But he burst through them like a linebacker shrugging off downfield blockers and threw himself across Chip's slight body. It was but a moment's work to rip the connections from his skull. Immediately the boy began to convulse. Frack screamed, while Frick unlimbered a small stungun from underneath her shirt, swung it around. Jim got his hands on Morninglory's connections just as the stunbolt buried itself in his skin and turned him off like a cheap lightbulb.

CHAPTER 7

1

"It's got something to do with the Plebs," Morninglory said.

Cat bent over him and touched his forehead. Frack, still holding vigil, stirred at the movement. Cat glanced up. "I won't hurt him," she said.

"Where's the kid, that Jim guy?" Morninglory asked.

"He's resting up. Frack zapped him when he was pulling the jacks out of your skull. He'd already done Chip by then."

Morninglory looked even more haggard than before. Large purple bruises disfigured his forehead and the part of his skull that wasn't covered with bandages. His golden skin had faded, and his eyes now looked like bloody egg yolks. He shivered.

"Kid saved our lives, you know. Neural zapper had both me and Chip for good and square. We couldn't have broken it. He did the right thing, the only thing."

Cat shook her head. "I'll get to him later. How did they get to you? I thought you were the best."

Morninglory grimaced up at her. "I—let's say I'm one of the best, and leave it at that. See, I tried to use Jim's stuff as a key, and it worked. Worked too damned well, because it set off alarms from here all the way to Terra. That wasn't any ordinary piece of killer software came after me and Chip. It was mindslaver stuff, manufactured on Earth, and shipped out here by superluminal interface."

Cat stared at him. "You're kidding, right?"

He shook his head.

She went on. "Morninglory, are you telling me somebody was operating real-time hacker-killer programs on a faster-than-light connection from *Earth*? My God, you could rent a full day on the combined Wolfbane megaprocessor for that kind of money. Hell, you could buy the processor itself, as far as it goes."

"I know," he said.

"What's going on, then?"

"Jim. It's him. He's wired into something big. Bigger than we thought."

"You said it has to do with the Plebs. And mindslaver software. Can we handle it?"

He shrugged. "Maybe . . ."

She looked down on him. "He's a nice kid, you know? I think I'm going to hate myself for this."

Morninglory turned his jaundiced gaze on her. His lips moved, and for a moment she saw his grin peep through. "You're just a kid, too, Cat."

She looked away. "I'm an old kid, Morninglory. Real old."

2

"Uh . . . which one are you? Frick, or Frack?"

Jim's guardian grunted, put aside the skim-mag she'd been viewing, and stood up. Her big thighs jiggled slowly.

"Frick," she said.

"You the one that stunned me?"

She shook her head. "Frack," she said. "Those aren't our names, y'know."

"Where's Cat?"

"She's with Morninglory. You want her?"

"Yes, please . . ."

Frick waddled out of the room.

3

"Everybody made it out?" he asked Cat, after she had shooed Frick out of the room.

"Nice place," she said, glancing around. The room was about the size of a couple of large closets pasted together. Walls of reprocessed fiberboard, scarred and gray. The single window was covered with so much grime, it was hard to tell whether it was daylight outside or not. And the smell of stale curry permeated all visible surfaces.

"Did everybody get out? Yeah, more or less. Morninglory's okay. He's trying to figure out what hit you guys."

"What about Chip?"

Cat shrugged. "He was jacked in the heaviest, so he took the brunt. He's in a coma. Morninglory's got some techs growing a bunch of new brain tissue for him. He says he'll be all right."

Jim felt his stomach turn a slow, queasy flip. In the last few days he'd seen a lot of horror, but the thought of Chip—*brain burned.* Actual brain tissue destroyed by the zappers. How close had he been? He felt an itchy, shrinking sensation at the fork of his legs and involuntarily cupped himself there.

Cat noticed the movement. "Oh? You feeling that much better already?"

He managed a wan grin. "Later, okay? I'm not . . . up for it yet."

For a long moment, silence. He sighed softly. "A waste of time, huh? Almost got us all killed, and nothing to show for it, right? Jeez, I am some kind of a screwup . . ."

"Well, I hesitate to argue that, but as for the rest—no, we got a lot of stuff. Morninglory's running it through analysis now. Listen, Jim, I don't believe much in coincidence, but if there is some *deus* running the big *machina,* She must have had a hand in getting us together. Seems the problem I'm working on just loves everything about you."

He pushed himself up on his elbows, winced, and settled back down. "How's that? Uh, just exactly what is it you're doing, Cat? Somehow we never got around to talking about it."

"Oh, you were close enough. Spy will do for lack of a better job description. Actually, I'm looking for something."

"And now you're going to tell me what it is?"

"Uh-huh. My parents died of the Pleb Psychosis. And according to what Morninglory says, you are cross-referenced a hundred different ways with that subject. Oh, you're the star of another data show as well. Care to make a guess?"

Jim felt his mouth drop open. Almost everything she had just said made his brain feel all dark and fizzy. He wanted to open his mouth and talk in one of those phony robot accents, and say over and over again: Does not compute. Does not compute.

"Couldn't even begin to," he said finally.

"Mindslaver tech. You're all cross-wired into mindslaver stuff, too."

4

Commander Steele took the call from her spot on a treadmill in the ship's rehab center. The little digital monitor said she'd already done twenty-two miles. Only eighteen to go. Overhead, the glowlights spread an antiseptic, even glow. She felt like a bug jogging through an operating theater. Worse than that, she felt stupid. Moving along at top walking speed, while the ship that carried her burned a faster-than-light, superluminal hole through space-time.

"Steele. What?"

"It was almost a good job," the voice said.

"Oh. Hello, there. I don't think so."

"Of course you don't," the voice went on. It was odd, watching Steele striding along, speaking in the general direction of her right shoulder, where there was nothing visible at all. Nor could the disembodied voice be heard by anybody but her, either.

"You killed Carl Saganovich. That's something."

"He was calling himself Carl Endicott."

"I read your report. You've got the woman?"

"Uh-huh. You want her?"

"Enough that I've diverted your ship to the battle satellite instead of direct planetfall on Terra."

"She's that valuable?"

"I don't know. But it's safer, and it's a faster turnaround for you."

Steele slowed a bit. Her heart rate was rising above eighty. Getting old, damn it. "For me? Where am I going?"

"Right back where you came from. We got a line on the boy. Almost nailed him, but missed."

"I've lost my A team," she said.

He chuckled. "Steele, not to worry. This time, I'm sending you back with the whole damned army."

5

It took almost ten days, but now Morninglory was moving around in a motorized chair that responded to commands through the single wire jacked from his skull socket to the chair's brain. The three of them were outside, on the cracked concrete apron around the factory. The concrete smelled of dried oil and sunburned patches of asphalt. Morninglory's chair went *wurzz, wurzz* as they walked along beneath the glazed red light of the sun.

"First thing, what do you know about the Pleb Psychosis?" Cat said.

Morninglory appeared almost recovered, his normal golden glow masking his fading bruises. Cat looked sleek and well fed, and Jim felt as if he would probably survive the bad case of twitches he'd acquired from his first real attempt at serious hacking.

"Pleb Psychosis?" Jim shrugged. "A mob psychology thing. Only happens on Earth. Bunch of Plebs go bad crazy all at once. Usually a lot of violence."

She nodded. "Leaving aside the obvious inconsistencies of that analysis, it has a couple of factual errors as well. First, there have been instances of it here, in the Wolfbane Pleb communities. Second, the violence isn't just usual, as you put it. It is *always* there. Without the violence, you don't have the psychosis. Circular definition, I know, but it's what we work with."

Jim shook his head. "I don't understand, Cat. How could I have anything to do with that stuff? I don't even know enough about it to be accurate when we talk. And you're the first Pleb I've ever known."

Morninglory cackled. "I guess that makes me the second. What do you think, so far, Jimbo?"

"I don't know. Something tells me all the Plebs aren't like you two. Or Chip, either."

Cat stopped and regarded him thoughtfully. "You know, that's an interesting thing to say, because it says more about you than it does about us. Or Plebs."

"Huh? What do you mean?" Jim had the sudden, sinking feeling he had just made an ass of himself. Worse, he had no idea what he had done.

"Well, you think we are not ordinary Plebs. Because, I guess, that we seem as smart as you, or we do complicated high-tech things, like Morninglory there. That we don't just lie around wire-heading, or pick up extra money doing the occasional mugging."

He winced. Although he'd never examined his opinions about Plebs, what she had just described was uncomfortably close to the vaguely formed opinions he did hold. And stated baldly, as she had just done, those hazy opinions sounded woefully immature. Worse, they sounded like bigotry of the most despicable sort.

"I . . . uh, well maybe I might be a little mistaken—"

"Oh, don't be silly. What other ideas could a boy like you have? I mean, raised as a citizen, fully educated, trained to do meaningful work—why would you regard the Plebs as anything but a financial drain on society? And a useless one, at that?"

Her use of the word "boy" hurt. He tried to ignore it—how much pain had his own words just inadvertently caused? Her parents were Plebs, and they had been *killed* in Pleb rioting.

"Listen, Cat."

Morninglory had been listening with half an ear while he monitored something arcane building up in his chair's holoviewer. "Plebs are useless, in general," he said. "That's the problem, actually. I ought to know. I'm one of them."

He glanced over at Cat. "Oh, you hush up now, girl. It's true, and you know it. Simple enough. All through history, the problem for humans was there weren't enough of them. Not enough to plow the fields, hunt the animals, build the cities, run the machines. And then, almost overnight, there were too many of them. Too many hands, and not enough labor. We'd crossed over a line. So what to do?"

He shrugged. "More and more money ended up in fewer and fewer pockets, because only a minority could do work that couldn't be done better by machine. Until finally the people with the money decided to spread it around. There was so much of it, after all."

"Well, of course," Cat said hotly. "You couldn't just let people starve."

"Don't think it wasn't considered. Check your history holos again, and pay attention this time."

They came up to the battered, rusty fence that ringed the whole complex. Strands of corroded barbed wire drooped along the top of the fence. Jim looked up, calculating.

"What would you do if you had to defend this place?" he asked. "This fence doesn't look like it would slow down a mosquito."

Morninglory nodded. "Now, why would we want to defend it in the first place? It doesn't make sense, really. Only people likely to attack it are . . . ah . . . certain sectors of the government. Or some kind of aliens with a death wish. Either way, I doubt even having a Confederation battle cruiser sitting on the cement over there would do much good."

He leaned back in his chair and swept his gaze the length of the fence, back and forth. "Nope, you're right, that old thing *wouldn't* stop a mosquito." Then he cackled again and slapped his knee. "It wouldn't, Jimbo, but I'm not completely crazy. Or a pacifist, either. I do have a few tricks up my sleeve. Since it isn't likely that it's mosquitoes we'll be trying to stop.

"Which reminds me, Chipper's out of the treatment tank, and the readouts say he's good as new. What say we go welcome him back? In a way, he's the best trick I got. My mosquito killer."

6

Steele wasn't entirely satisfied with the shape her knee was in. The limp had almost vanished. But she could only do leg squats with about two hundred pounds. Not much help if she had to drag some shot-to-pieces trooper in full battle armor from here to there.

Well, with a little bit of luck, it wouldn't be necessary. She had a Class Double-A battle team with her this time, the whole damned army she'd been promised.

Now she sat in the shotgun seat of a battlecav sky car, floating over a vague, shadowy area near the outskirts of the city. Overhead, a pair of moons played dice with each other across a Milky Way strangely altered from the one mankind had grown up with.

"There's nothing down there," the tech behind her murmured. "Those few lights we see are automatic, come on at dusk to warn off trespassers. That old factory's been closed for years, owned by some bank."

"Yeah? So why did somebody try an extremely complicated, extremely efficient, and damned near successful hack on the main database of the Combined Intelligence Agency from there?"

The tech shrugged. "You're the boss, so whatever you say. But I don't see any evidence of it."

Steele glanced out the window, her face grim. "You will," she said. And to the pilot: "Take us down."

7

Humans grew up in trees and climbed down from them after enough eons to make it relatively safe, but they never got over their original sleeping habits. So, about six hours after falling asleep, the human body reaches its lowest ebb of the day. Doctors call it lights-out time, because so many heart attacks occur about then, or patients slowly dying of one thing or another pick that moment to just let go.

In an industrial or technological society, possessing clocks, that slice of extreme human vulnerability occurs around four in the morning. Those who fully appreciate this fact, especially certain high-skill civilian police officers, or those of the more esoteric military special operations planners, often make use of it.

At 4:01, the first round of double-AP—all-purpose, antipersonnel—crashed through one of the fogged-over glass panels in the roof of the old factory, fell to the floor, and exploded a blue-green cloud of gas into the interior of the shadowy building.

After that, all hell broke loose.

8

In physics, a fully ionized gas containing approximately equal numbers of positive and negative ions. This is the definition of plasma. Plasma occurs in nature in several forms, including ball lightning, the stuff in the centers of stars, and at the edges of nuclear explosions. Shortly after the dawn of the third millennium, some bright weapons researchers figured out how to generate and project beams of plasma.

Over the years, they refined this concept until they were able to build small, floating generators suitable for use as mobile artillery on the battlefield. These two-man weapons platforms, which resembled slightly chubby snowmobiles, became known fondly as buzz saws. The amount of simple, mindless destruction they were able to generate was enormous. Picture cramming a portion of the original atomic weapon detonated over Hiroshima, in old Nippon, into a beam approximately one inch wide. Now picture the tip of that beam touching any readily flammable material—say, plate glass. Or granite. Or case-hardened molysteel. Or diamonds . . .

At the kiss of plasma, all these substances are only slightly less flammable than tissue paper or high-octane hydrocarbon fuel. By 4:02 A.M., there were two buzz saws floating at either end of the factory, wreaking a rather amazing amount of havoc.

"Jim! Where the hell are you, boy? Down that hatch, that one, right there with the steel doorway."

Morninglory whirled his chair in a tight circle, trying to shout loud enough to be heard over the monstrously deafening sounds of battle. The air here near the center of the factory was full of smoke and chemicals, and sudden blasts of superheated air. Jim's eyes burned as he waited for Cat to catch up. He stood next to the open hatch at his feet and ignored Morninglory's frantic commands.

"Not till she gets here, Morninglory."

"You young idiot, she might be *dead* for all we know. God damn those bastards! Where the hell did they come from?" He glared at Jim. "Forget I said that. I didn't really mean it."

Oh, yes you did, Jim thought. *They wouldn't be here at all if you hadn't set off a bunch of alarms and nearly got yourself killed. And that wouldn't have happened if I hadn't come along. And you are exactly right, Morninglory. I am a damned Jonah. Everything I touch dies!*

When the first blasts had shaken the old buildings and rolled Jim right out of his bed, the first thing he'd grabbed for was the S&R .75 pistol that now was never more than arm's length from his body. In this case it had been under his pillow, making for a somewhat lumpy, but secure, sleeping situation.

Morninglory, his hair flying, the lower half of his face covered by a respirator that doubled as a microphone, rode his chair like a small bronco, urging his people down into the deeper safety—at least he hoped it was—of the underground shelters beneath the lowest factory floors.

"Chipper," he roared. "Chip, are you there!"

Jim heard the disembodied voice reply, "Here, boss. I'm already below, and working on it. Just about got it, in fact. You want to come help?"

"In a minute," Morninglory grated. "Jim, I told you to get your young ass down below."

"No, Morninglory, not till Cat gets here. I told you."

Morninglory stared at the weapon in Jim's right hand. "You know how to use that thing?"

Jim nodded slowly. "Uh-huh."

"Good. Then if you insist on standing here doing nothing, would you mind killing those two troopers running down the hall toward us with their big ugly rifles?"

"Oh—*Jeez.*" Jim ducked and whirled, and the blinding blue laser beam that would have taken his head neatly off at the neck sizzled harmlessly overhead. Ten years of habit swung into play; Jim brought the forward sight of his weapon into line with the first trooper's armored chest.

His inner voice was babbling: *Hold steady, focus on the front sight, not the rear, keep the front sight on the target, that's good, now squeeeeeze slowly . . .*

He didn't realize he had pulled the trigger until he saw the awesome result of an S&R .75 slug strike its target head-on. The armor the first trooper wore was quite good. It slowed the entry of the slug down for an appreciable fraction of a second. The reason for this was that the armor itself was flexible, at least if you hit it hard enough. Thus a fist-sized portion of the armor, pushed by the slug, punched out a larger-than-fist-sized hole in the chest and rib cage beneath it.

But this situation only lasted for an instant. Then the depleted uranium slug, handily exchanging velocity for heat, became a minibeam of plasma on its own, and vaporized everything in front of it for a half dozen feet—including the second trooper. What Jim saw was a blinding flash of light, and two indistinct figures in the center of it exploding backward as if jerked by rubber bands powerful enough to bungee-jump main battle tanks. The effect was so spectacular that it didn't hit him immediately that he'd just killed two men.

"Good shot," Morninglory hollered. "See if you can do it again over here. Quick, now, here comes your girlfriend, too."

Jim spun toward the sound of his voice and saw Cat about ten yards away. As he watched she wheeled, knelt, and snapped off a couple of shots from the tiny slug thrower she always carried. Jim could see one shot graze off the side of the battle helmet the trooper wore, but the hit had no other effect. The trooper was swinging his own rifle up when Jim introduced him to the laws of physics, as interpreted by the S&R .75, and blew his head, and most everything else above his belt, into the far wall of the factory.

"Over here," Jim screeched. His voice was raspy in his throat, and he realized he must have been shouting at the top of his lungs for quite some time. Odd. He hadn't noticed a thing.

Cat came loping up, somehow managing to seem poised even in the heart of chaos.

"Down there?"

"Yeah. Go on. I'll get Morninglory."

"Won't do any damn such thing," Morninglory wheezed. "Now listen, you two children. We ain't got any time. The both of you just pick me up and toss me down that hole. And then you come on down and pull the damn thing in after you. Okay, now, do it!"

"But what if—" Jim's protest went nowhere, because Cat had

already jumped over and grabbed one of Morninglory's bony shoulder blades.

"Give me a hand, here!"

He took the other side and they heaved the old man straight through the hatch. The throbbing sound of one of the buzz saws suddenly crescendoed, and a blinding burst of light blew through the ceiling far overhead. Steel girders simply dissolved, and the entire roof began to come down.

"After you," Cat said sweetly.

"Hell," Jim said. He looked down and saw blood on his hands. But he dived through anyway.

The shelters were little more than a labyrinth of crude tunnels hacked out of the swampy earth beneath the factory's foundations, reinforced with crumbling slabs of sweating concrete.

They found Morninglory at the bottom of the shaft, in the middle of a tunnel, trying to right his chair. Cat tipped him up. It was very hard to see anything; the light, supplied only by a few widely spaced glowstrips, could barely penetrate the dust-filled murk; and every explosion up above sent shudders through the walls down below, squeezing more clouds of pulverized cement into the air.

"This way—" Morninglory tossed over his shoulder as he charged off down the tunnel.

They followed at a dead run, until, like Alice disappearing down the rabbit hole, Morninglory turned hard right and vanished.

9

The figures looked eerie as they picked their insectile way through the dust and rubble. Most of the roof overhead was gone, and only one wall still remained at its full height, though most of its windows were now gaping, empty holes. The first pink light of dawn tinted the entire surreal scene with the colors of a garden party. Steele, garbed in a force-multiplier cyborg suit, moved through the destruction, stepping carefully.

Her cyborg suit wasn't battle armor, not precisely. It did have some defensive capability, but essentially it was a molysteel alloy skeleton which wrapped around Steele like the shell of a crab. Once she had a direct neural connection to the many small armored brains that controlled the suit, it functioned as an extension of her own nerves, bones, and muscles. Except it was about 150 times as strong as she was, and carried weapons similar to those of a small military gravcar. Her right forefinger, for instance, was a full-power battle laser. All she had to do was point at something to destroy it.

"Not many bodies," she remarked.

Her executive officer, a black woman called Margot, but known more familiarly among the enlisted personnel as Iron Maggie, gazed off into the distance for a moment as the latest casualty reports were interfaced directly into her skull.

"So far, we have . . . two of them. And seven of us."

Steele winced. She hated losing her people. She took it personally, with usually fatal results for whoever had caused the loss. She didn't intend for this operation to be any different. Still, it was puzzling.

"I told that idiot pilot there was something down here. And I was right. And it was good enough to take a full frontal attack from a Double-A tac team at four in the morning, survive, and inflict more than three casualties for every one of theirs. What does your analysis say about that, Captain?"

One of the two troopers escorting them whirled with the preternatural speed of jumped-up cyborg reflexes, and cranked off a couple of antipersonnel grenades from the launcher built into his left elbow. A spot about forty yards away suddenly erupted in flames. The shock wave sent their gyros humming to keep them stable in the blast.

"What the hell?" Steele said.

"I thought I saw something," the trooper replied sheepishly.

She stared at him until his cheeks began to flame bright red, then turned away. "Captain, what do the battle computers say? We've got two bodies that aren't our own. Where's the rest?"

Iron Maggie had her head cocked to the side, listening. Her gaze was distant, until, with an abrupt shake of her head, she snapped back.

"The orbiting fleet carrier just finished a long-wave radar survey of this area. There's a network of tunnels below the factory level. It's quite extensive. I'm transferring maps to your battle axe now."

Steele nodded, waiting, until her personal battle access box beeped. She told it to generate a holomap immediately, which it did. The map hung in the dusty air, wavering eerily.

"Okay, it looks like we're close to one of the entrances." She paused, swung to her right, then nodded. "That pile right over there. We need to get that moved. Okay, Captain?"

Iron Margot tossed off a sloppy salute. "Heads up," she called. Steele and her two troopers both turned away and crouched. A moment later one of the buzz saws plummeted down from above, hovered, and let loose with a plasma beam. The mound of shattered concrete, twisted steel, and melted glass vanished in a huge clap of light and thunder, leaving a twenty-foot-deep pit with smooth, glassy sides. The heat of the plasma had fused rock, sand, and metal into a thick coating of glass. At three points around the pit, holes yawned darkly: the tunnels, now exposed to the open air.

"Okay, gang," Steele said. "Let's get to it."

10

"Where'd he go?"

Clots of people rushed frantically by, paying them no attention. "Hey!"

"Forget it, Jim. They're not worrying about us. Hmm. He must be around here somewhere." She turned and began to check the walls.

Jim looked, too, but saw nothing out of the ordinary. Only the concrete slabs, and here and there a patchwork of rusting rebar. No clues at all, until a scrawny arm stretched *out* of one wall and grabbed Cat by the wrist.

"What the—" Jim had his pistol out, but Cat was already waving him off.

"No, come on," she said, half-laughing. The disembodied hand jerked at her, pulled her forward, and she vanished. Jim shrugged, marked the spot, took a deep breath, and—stepped forward into a small, brightly lighted room crowded with way too many busy people.

"Welcome to battle central," Morninglory said, as he settled into a tank while a busy tech hooked up what appeared to be *hundreds* of input jacks. Next to him, Chip's pale features, framed by a similar tank, were almost hidden behind his own festoon of wires. It was the first time Jim had seen Chip since the hacking incident. If the boy was fully recovered, it was the unhealthiest recovery Jim had ever seen.

"Here's the deal," Morninglory was saying. "You two are getting one-way tickets out of here. Cherry, over there"—he nodded at a small, monkeylike figure who turned out to be a young woman with a cheerful, nut brown face, a thousand-watt smile, and reflexes like a cobra—"Cherry will get you out. A lot of these tunnels are shielded. They'll find them eventually, but not right away—and they connect into the Wolfbane tube system. Once you're out of the main battle area you should be fine."

A shower of sparks erupted from Chip's tank. His thin body arched, then subsided. His eyes were closed, and his lips drawn back against his teeth in a white snarl.

"Hey, I'm not going anywhere," Jim said. It was slowly coming to him that he had killed at least three men back up above—and he had done it, in part at least, to defend this irascible old man now being strapped down into a tank that looked too uncomfortably like a coffin. As the techs worked on Morninglory, Jim saw the spreading red splotch on the upper left part of his chest.

"You're hurt!"

"Uh-huh. Don't have time to bother with it now. And I want you to stop this foolishness. I don't need your help. What I need is for you to get yourself and Cat out of here—before those bastards bring down the whole thing on us."

Cat moved closer to him. "He's right, Jim. Morninglory will be okay. He and Chip can take care of themselves. They've been doing it for a long time."

Cherry came up and rapped him sharply on the shoulder. "Listen to her, bub. She knows, and you don't. Now, are you gonna go, or not?"

Jim glanced back and forth between the two now-silent figures resting in their tanks. He had an idea of what was going on. Morninglory and Chip were about to throw everything they had into a cyberwar version of Custer's Last Stand—and while doing battle in the virtual worlds, they didn't want to be bothered with their bodies. So the tanks would take care of that, and let them worry about the real stuff.

Yes, they look like they know what they're doing, Jim thought. *I know, too. They're committing suicide, because somewhere up above, orbiting directly overhead, is a full-scale Confederation battle cruiser, and if they become too much of an annoyance, this whole area will simply cease to exist.*

He could even visualize it: the long, probing finger of a spaced-based phased laser array, almost invisible as it lanced down to stir the earth like a spoon made of lightning.

"I don't want to go—" he said.

"And I don't care what you want," Cat said abruptly. "What I want to know is what you're going to do? Now, are you coming, or not? Me, I'm out of here." And she strode on past him without a second look.

He stood there, utterly torn. Everything he had done, every person he had touched in the last few weeks, had turned to bitter dust. One missing, some dead, and now more to come. Nor was it a consolation that most of the damage had come to those who were defending him, or trying to help him, even after he'd brought down danger on them all.

I can't run away again, he thought desperately. *I just can't!*

Morninglory lifted his head slightly. His cracked, crazed eyes focused on Jim's face. "Go on, boy," he said. "I know what you're thinking, but go on anyway. You have some things to do, and you won't get them done here."

Jim raised one hand in denial, but the old man continued, his voice stony as a grave. "Listen to me! All you can do here is die, and not even take your revenge for it. So go on, get out of here, and do what you have to do. Leave the rest to me. I'll hurt them."

He paused, licked his lips, and nodded. "Jim," he said gently. "This isn't really about you. My war goes back before you were born. I always knew it would end like this. Why do you think I have this setup? I fight for the Plebs, and I do it any way I can. Even if that way is what the Japanese call *kamikaze.* So don't take whatever happens to me on your own shoulders; it isn't your burden to bear. We always have the right to choose, Jim. That's what free will really means. Remember, you *cannot* make a slave of a free man . . . you can only kill him."

His gaze pierced Jim. "And I *will* hurt them, son. You can make book on it. That's a promise."

"But . . ."

"No buts, boy. You want to do something for me? Carry on the fight. Cat will show you how. You make me *that* promise, Jim, and whatever happens, I'll rest easy."

A deathbed promise, Jim thought, as the old man sank back down and his eyes fluttered closed. But he nodded anyway. "I promise, Morninglory."

He thought he saw a faint twitch of assent, of acceptance, and knew he had taken on a great commitment, one he could not break. A *deathbed* promise . . .

It frightened him.

Now the techs gathered around and slowly closed the armored lids of the tanks—whatever happened here, Morninglory and Chip would be the last to feel it. Their shields wouldn't last forever, but maybe long enough.

The techs had no such final protection, and they knew it. Nevertheless, no one made any move to leave. A few exchanged hugs, others clasped hands or even kissed, but that was all. Then they were back at work, hunched over their consoles and axes and holovids, getting ready to lead the hopeless charge.

Jim felt his eyes go hot and wet. "Are you coming, or not?" Cat asked again, but softly.

"Yes," Jim said. "I'm coming."

He turned and followed, but as he did so, he made himself a silent promise: *Never again!*

And another brick in the great structure of himself slammed into place, cemented into the very foundation of what he would become. Never again would he abandon friends to danger. It was the promise of youth, and it would not always be kept. But Jim would never forget it, as long as he lived.

"Let's go," he said, and they did.

11

The ConFleet starship CSS *Henry Templeton*, a line cruiser fully staffed with a complement of 1,680 sailors, floated white and silent 420 miles out, precisely over the abandoned factory where the lids were just then closing on Morninglory and Chip.

Captain Jock Sturbridge sat in the chair on the upper level of the bridge, where he could see everything below simply by shifting his eyes. In the old days of saltwater navies, the bridge had been the eyes of the ship, even open to the ocean air. Now, of course, things were different; the bridge, which fronted the Battle Command and Control (BCC) room, was, like its neighbor, buried deep in the guts of the ship, protected by layer after layer of the heaviest armor. Nevertheless, the huge screens which lined every wall of the bridge were so perfectly clear, down to the smallest of details, that sometimes Captain Sturbridge had to remind himself he wasn't gazing at wide-open windows.

Now, one screen showed the view forward along the vast, dish-shaped top hull of the *Hank Tee*, as she was fondly known among the crew. Another portrayed a computer-enhanced real-time screen that showed a picture of the factory area, as if seen from a height of three or four miles. Sturbridge could touch any part of the smaller control screen on his own console and blow up that same part of the larger screen for better viewing.

Spread out before and below him, as if in a theater, were several levels of consoles, each manned by the officer of the day for one particular part of the ship's operations: exec officer, engineering, command and control, weapons, navigation, and all the other departments necessary to keep a star cruiser humming with efficiency.

And all of this, though filtered by the department heads or their deputies, banks of computers, and finally the executive office, eventually funneled into Sturbridge's console, where he made the decisions that only he could make.

He now examined the data flowing across his various screens and murmuring in his ears and into the cyberjack he wore when he sat in this chair, and made one of those decisions.

"Commander Steele requests standby backup. A little problem with some shielded and armored tunnels, it appears. Gunnery Officer?"

A smart, golden-skinned woman at a console two tiers below him nodded. Her face appeared on his own console. "Prepare a fire pattern to accomplish the objectives as stated by Commander Steele."

Gunnery Lieutenant Sylvia Chen said, "Aye, aye, sir," and forwarded the command to a series of dedicated computers and their spaceman technicians in the command and control room behind the bridge. After a moment, new targeting instructions for the *Hank Tee*'s gigantic phased array lasers began to rush across her screen.

In her mind's eye she could see the huge guns move microfractions of an inch as they adjusted their fire patterns. Phased array lasers were the latest wrinkle in big-ship armament; a single laser, no matter how large, could only hold peak power for a fraction of a second. If run full blast any longer, delicate parts of the big gun simply melted. But if you hooked up ten or twenty of these lasers in a repeating series, something like the old-fashioned Gatling or chain guns, you could create a more or less continuous beam that operated at a power level impossible for single guns to reach.

The *Hank Tee* had two phased array lasers; each consisted of *thirty-five* linked battle lasers. If necessary, she could turn entire cities into boiling sludge in a few microseconds. Or the beams could be fined down by electronic microdirection to punch holes no more than a few feet wide from a distance of several hundred miles.

"All batteries ready, Captain," Gunner Chen reported.

"Stand by," Sturbridge replied.

On a third screen he was watching a thrashing, jumbled picture of armored, skeletal figures stumbling through murk and dust and darkness. The sound was good, though jumbled; Steele rapping out orders and warnings, two scouts up ahead carrying on their own chatter, all punctuated by the occasional flash or thrumming ripper-zipper of squad weapons.

"We're beginning to uncover more of the tunnel network," the intelligence officer reported. Sturbridge acknowledged the IO curtly: "Keep it coming, and keep handing it over to Commander Steele." Perhaps the most important thing the *Hank Tee* was doing at the moment was the real-time deep radar mapping of the enemy site. Every second broke down more shielding and revealed more of the warren, both to the cruiser and to Steele as she rushed along the tunnels themselves.

"Yes, sir," the IO replied. "And we're getting just a bit of—"

His voice broke off suddenly. Sturbridge raised his head and peered across his own console. "Intelligence Officer," he said. "What's the problem? Report—"

The IO, a grizzled vet of twenty years of service, suddenly stood up from his console and began to wrench desperately at his full-helmet virtual-reality link. His screams almost drowned out the abrupt honking of Class One Emergency warning sirens.

Red lights began to flash everywhere. Sturbridge glanced down at his own console screens, and for one instant saw something that made absolutely no sense at all: each of his miniature screens, representing the output of one entire and separate part of the ship, all showed the same thing.

The face of a young man, surely no older than twelve. Grinning like a demon.

Then the face was inside his *skull*, and Captain Sturbridge also tried to scream. But he couldn't.

He wasn't in control any longer—of anything at all.

12

Cherry led them at a full-tilt run through the chaos of the tunnels. After what seemed like hours, but was only ten minutes or so, the small woman brought them up to what appeared to be an ancient, rusted-shut sewer lock of some kind. There was a big, corroded crank on the front of the circular plate. The whole thing looked as if it had not been touched for generations, but when Cherry stepped up, took the crank in both hands, and twisted, it began to spin around as if greased.

After a moment, she had the hatchway open. Light, clean and pure, gushed out.

"It goes into a service well for the public tube system. Go ahead, get your butts on through there."

She held the hatch open while first Cat, then Jim, scrambled through. As soon as Jim hit the other side he stopped and reached back to hold the hatch for Cherry, but it was already swinging shut in his face.

"Hey!"

"I'm not coming," Cherry said. "What'd you think? Watch your fingers, now."

And with a dull, metallic thud, the hatch slammed shut. Jim heard the faint cry of metal on metal as Cherry redogged the hatch, then nothing. Slowly, he turned and saw Cat staring at him.

"I know," she said softly.

His face felt stiff and hot. He wanted to feel something, to let something show, but he couldn't. His shame and misery were just too great.

"Let's go," he said at last. She nodded. They moved off into the bright, glow-panel glare of the service tunnels, and were gone.

13

Steele saw it, too, that face. In her own heads-up helmet screen, it blinked for just a fraction; the boy, grinning, his eyes like embers buried in ashes. This grisly vision superimposed itself on the real-time maps that the *Hank Tee* had been sending down, and she knew something had gone wrong.

"Landing team leader to mother ship, come in. LTL to Mother, do you read?"

No reply.

She froze, her head slowly swiveling. Then she flipped over to local command and control and latched on to one of the mobile buzz saws.

"I need a hole, right now," she said, and gave the coordinates. Then she waited, jiggling her right foot, whispering, "Come on . . . *come on*!"

The plasma beam sliced through about ten feet in front of her. When the blinding dust had settled, she saw the opening to the sky and took it.

"Liftpacks—fire!" she ordered.

They popped out of the hole in the ground like corks from a bottle, a handful of tiny figures arcing straight up, then out and away from the site.

Out of the corner of her eye, Steele saw a black dot in the sky, growing.

And in her screen, an old man suddenly appeared, cackling. Her earphones crackled. She couldn't be sure, through all the static, but it sounded like he was saying, "Gotcha!"

The earth moved.

14

The lights in the tube train flickered, then went out. Slowly, the chain of cars settled from their invisible antigrav rails until they rested on the track bed itself.

A great hand silently lifted the car, gently shook it back and forth, then set it down again. After a few moments a dull roar filled the air.

"What was that?" Cat whispered.

"Morninglory. Taking his revenge," Jim told her.

CHAPTER 8

1

They took half an hour, cutting crosstown on foot from where they'd climbed up from the stalled tube system. Like some monstrous, bent-backed old man, a pillar of flame-shredded smoke stooped over the horizon and touched the spot where the factory had been.

Cat shivered as they walked. Jim only felt numb.

"What do you think he did?" Cat asked.

"I think he dropped that space cruiser right on his own head," Jim replied. "It felt more like an earthquake, not just a big explosion. A cruiser crash would feel like that."

He tried to picture it. He knew all the public statistics about ConFleet ships. There had been over a thousand sailors on that vessel. And how many more in the warrens hidden beneath the factory? Even Cherry had gone back . . .

He saw that Morninglory's wrath had been terrible. And in that moment Jim understood what a blessing the old man had given to him with his final words: he had taken the guilt—the literally unbearable guilt—of those deaths from Jim and placed it firmly on his own shoulders.

Free will, Morninglory had said. *My fight is older than your entire life . . .*

And I, Jim thought, *have taken up his battle. I promised.* But what did that mean? It meant, he realized, that he might be called upon make the kind of decision that Morninglory did. To choose to reap human lives—even his own—with both hands.

Can I do that? Can I bear such choices?

He shuddered. A tight ball of nausea curdled in his gut as he realized, for the first time in his life, the kind of decisions a starship captain might be called upon to make. Life-and-death decisions, with real lives—and real deaths.

What had the captain of that cruiser been thinking as his ship plummeted like a stone while he wrenched futilely at controls that no longer responded? Had he seen his death approaching, his and his crew's?

Yes, of course he had. Jim felt an icy lump slowly fill his chest. No games. Not anymore. It was all too horrible and bloody and real. "Cat?" he said.

"What?" She seemed preoccupied. They had passed through the center of town, and were walking briskly toward the spaceport out beyond the edge of the city. The landing-field control tower had begun to loom over them, a twenty-story needle that handled all interstellar passage to and from Wolfbane.

The sounds of a massive emergency filled the air: sirens, distant cries, alarms that sounded like the raucous clamor of electronic birds. Vultures, perhaps. Awkward vehicles with flashing red lights choked the gravlanes and, overhead, massive flying platforms floated ponderously toward the pillar of smoke.

Here, on the pedestrian paths, all was green and cool and peaceful. Yet even on these lanes they walked apart, though he could feel the physical nearness of her, and was soothed by it. But some wall now existed between them, and he didn't understand what had built it so quickly. Sadness? Regret? The simple memory of things too awful for humans to share?

"Do you want to talk?" he asked her.

She shook her head. Up ahead, a pretty stone bench, set in a bed of dark purple flowers, appeared. "Let's sit," he said, pointing.

"We don't have time . . ."

"Cat, we have to make time. I don't know what we are supposed to do next. Do you?"

She paused, turning. Her face seemed empty of emotion, her eyes dull. There was a lifelessness about her, and he wondered if he presented a similar impression. Emotional overload.

"They're dead, Cat. All of them. Morninglory, Chip, Cherry, all the rest. And the ones in the cruiser, too." He stopped, searching for the words. "It's called survivor guilt, I think . . ."

"Don't lecture me, Jim!"

He recoiled. "I didn't mean—"

She sighed heavily. "Look. Forget it. Just forget it. You don't really understand, do you?"

He didn't want to hurt her—not her!—but now he was floundering. And his own anger was churning inside him, seeking an outlet. He felt the incoherent words bubbling in his throat, and forced them down. He no longer had the luxury of childish tantrums. She was his only connection to—

And he stopped. Connection to what? He had no idea. His father dead, his mother gone, the deaths of hundreds still fresh in the eye of his mind, and . . . he didn't *know*!

"Cat, please . . . let's sit. Even if you don't, I have to talk. I need to talk."

She nodded stiffly. "All right . . ."

2

Steele had heard them on the ship, screaming, all the way down. The blast had caught her team still in the air, and tumbled them like feathers, like dry leaves before a storm.

She had come to a rough landing perhaps two miles from the center of the explosion, crashing through the leafy canopy of a small park. For a moment she'd blacked out, and come awake shaking her head, a slab of pain radiating dully from the base of her spine.

"Report," she whispered, her throat suddenly dry and constricted. The extent of the horror had not yet penetrated to her conscious thoughts, but she could sense it down below somewhere, waiting to belch up like hidden swamp gas.

For a long moment there was no response, and fear closed her voice box. She licked her lips. "Report . . . ?"

The main com channel, only moments before so busy with professional, businesslike voices, now echoed with a distant electronic hollowness, meaningless clicks and scratches of static. Then Iron Maggie's voice: ". . . down in a suburb somewhere. My satellite locator isn't working. I don't know where I am. Or you, either . . ." She paused; Steele listened to the ragged sound of her breathing. "Commander, what the hell happened?"

"They took out the cruiser somehow. Crashed it right on top of the factory." Steele still hadn't got her mind around the implications of that. Was this all that was left? Her and Margot? But how could that be?

She shook her head. That damned kid. This whole thing was jinxed. A curse on Carl Endicott and all that touched him!

But underneath the bright flame of her rage, a question: was his curse on her, now? Once she had loved him, and then, because of the bitch, she had hated him, but it didn't seem like enough. Not for this vendetta stretching down through the years. But he was dead. Surely that ended it?

She thought of the boy. His son? *Her* son? Delta would know. Perhaps. Or Carl Endicott, but he was gone.

Yet she knew: the link remained. The net in which she was caught, she and all the rest of them, had snared the boy as well.

It wasn't over yet.

3

She sat at one end of the white stone bench, facing away from him. He sat at the other, hands folded in his lap, and stared at his feet. He had been jittering with a sick, fevered energy, but now that toxic intensity drained away as he sat, leaving him cold and empty. He waited for her to speak, but she was better at waiting than he was, and so, finally, he broke the cheerless silence. "What do we do now, Cat? You'll have to tell me. I don't know."

He watched her lips move, but nothing came out. She wouldn't look at him. She tried again. "I . . . maybe you don't do anything, Jim. Maybe for you it's over."

He touched her shoulder. "Cat? How can it be over for me? Look at me. Please."

Slowly, she turned. Her skin was pale as fine marble, and as cold.

He groped for the right words. "I don't have anything left, Cat. I'm . . . only sixteen. I thought I knew a lot. But I don't know anything. What am I supposed to do?"

"Nothing is . . ." She shook her head. "Jim, you saw what just happened. You probably can't imagine anything more horrible. But I can. I've seen that many people die in half an hour, and it was only a beginning. Morninglory was . . . important to me. But there are other people also important, not just to me, but to millions of others. The Plebs, Jim. That's the important thing to me, all of them. It's what Morninglory called his cause. But it's mine, too. Don't you see?"

He tried, but he couldn't see. He didn't know enough. And she wouldn't tell him. He shook his head slowly. "Can you help me to see? That's all, just a little help?"

Some hints of animation had come back into her expression. Her eyes didn't look so blank and unfocused anymore. She looked down at his hand on her shoulder and put her fingers gently on his. Her fingertips felt cool and dry.

"It's not your fight, Jim. How can it be? It's not a fight you take up. It's a war you are born to, and you weren't born to it. That's all. I have no right to—"

He lifted his fingers and touched her lips to silence her. "You have no right? Don't you remember what Morninglory said back there? That we all can choose? That we have free will?"

She stared at him, waiting.

He nodded. It suddenly felt right to him. "I can choose, Cat. I may not be Morninglory, as old and wise and as brave as he was, but that doesn't mean I can't choose. So I do. You remember what he found? What we found, when we hacked those databases? Cat, there's a *connection*. He thought so, and so do I. Somehow, what has happened to me is connected to whatever it is you are doing."

"Jim . . ."

"No, *listen*. I know the evidence, whatever it was, is gone now, but—why are you shaking your head?"

She shifted her backpack off her shoulders. "Oh, it's not gone. We never got a chance to really analyze everything, but I have it. All of it, chips full of it. That was my next mission. To carry it to Earth. They'll know what to do with it there."

He felt a rush of relief. "You saved it?"

"Sure."

"Then that's where we're going," he whispered, his thoughts surging with certainty. "We're going to Earth!"

For the first time, she smiled. Faintly. "You may be right."

She hoisted the pack back to her shoulder. "But not together," she told him.

"Huh? What are you talking about?"

Something had changed her mind, had decided her. Now her features warmed, and a shade of their old familiar glow returned. "You want to choose, is it? Well, if you choose to do what I do, it won't be easy. You understand?"

"I . . . think so."

"I have a way to get back. I won't tell you what it is, for obvious reasons."

Hurt, he murmured, "Because you don't trust me. Well, I guess I understand . . ."

"No. I don't trust anybody. You think you could keep a secret, but you can't. Jim, I couldn't. No human can resist the drugs and techniques, not if they want to use them." She paused, thoughtful. "I'm going to Earth, and if you want to go, then do it. Go. But don't tell me how, because I don't want to know, either. All right?"

Overhead, the soft breeze carried the breath of distant fires. It seemed peaceful here, but it wasn't. He could picture the entire city convulsed like a kicked-over anthill. And in that swarm, searchers. People looking. For them? The *two* of them?

"I understand," he said.

She stared at him for the length of several heartbeats, then leaned forward and brushed his cheek lightly with her lips.

"Good. I hope you make it." She stood. "I wish I could offer you more, Jim. You're a nice boy. If things had been different . . ."

"But they aren't," he said. "So we'll work with what we have. Okay?"

"On Terra," she said, "there is a place, a bar. Outside the TerraPort main gate, in the Plebtown there. It's called Shawn Fan. Go to the bartender. Use my name. Somebody will come for you."

He nodded. "Well, then . . ."

"Jim? Be careful."

"Yes. I will."

And then he took her into his arms and squeezed. He didn't realize until after she had vanished down the winding path that the moisture on her cheek was tears.

4

Wolf Port, the Wolfbane spaceport, was less than a piddle compared to the awesome spread of TerraPort, but taken by itself, it was still a huge and awe-inspiring construction. Jim was reminded of this all over again as he stood in the shadows of the inevitable commercial communities that always grew up around great transportation hubs. In this case, Spacetown, as it was called, extended right up to the tall fences that marked the limits of Wolf Port.

He leaned against the front wall of a dive whose windows were so filthy they might have been solid concrete. Across the front, holographic images of unclad women cavorted. Jim watched them from the corner of one eye, amusing himself by trying to figure out how any creatures so top-heavy as these would be able to walk at all, let alone dance as these pictures did.

He'd thought about going inside, but decided against it. It looked invitingly dim in there, but he'd never been in such a place before. Why take chances?

The men and women who passed by here paid him no attention: they were bound on other errands, some inside the bar—FLASH-DANCE FLASHDANCE FLASHDANCE—some in the dilapidated building next door that advertised ROOMS TEN CREDS HOUR.

Why would anybody want to stay in a hotel room only an hour? Jim was sure he was missing something, but unsure precisely what. And he had no intention of asking. He'd caught a glimpse of himself as a smudgy reflection off the barroom windows, and was relieved. He looked ragged enough that he doubted anybody would think him out of place. There was a certain safety in appearing to be a Pleb. Plebs were sort of everywhere, just like signs or ornamental bushes, and no one paid them any attention. Which was fine: the last thing he needed or wanted was attention.

He edged toward the corner of the building, keeping in the shadow beneath the broad eaves that extended out over the window. On his left, half a block away, the object of his study erupted into a sudden flurry of activity. He shaded his eyes with his hand

and watched intently as a pair of large, steel gray trucks glided up and came to a halt before the tall gates set into the fence.

On the outside of the fence, at the edge of the gravlane, was a pillboxlike guard kiosk. After the trucks had stopped, a guard wearing half-body armor with a heavy slug pistol at his belt stepped out and walked slowly toward the lead vehicle. A window slid open in the truck's cab to reveal a face, hands, a plastic card handed over. The guard ran the card through a reader slot and checked the result. He handed the card back and tossed off a derisive salute. As he did so, the massive gates began to swing wide. In a moment the two trucks glided on through and vanished beyond, as the gates swung shut.

Neat, simple, efficient. It looked to Jim as if this entry point was not operating at any special level of alertness. The guard had made no effort to search the truck. Perhaps the emergency had not reached down to this level yet. But he thought it probably would, and soon. As soon as the shock of what had happened at the factory had lessened a bit. At some point the authorities would begin to consider the possibility of escapees from that holocaust, and things would tighten up.

Even so, this cargo gate was a better bet than a public entrance. Travelers had to show identification to enter in those places—and he couldn't do that.

I don't have much time, he thought to himself, *but maybe enough.* He began walking—not toward the gate, but in the general direction of the crowded warren of gravlanes leading up to the entrance. Those trucks would have to slow down here and there, maybe even stop, as the automatic lane controllers juggled traffic through the choke points before the gates. And with a little luck, he just might be able to . . .

5

It turned out to be even easier than he'd hoped. A huge, lumbering van slowed, then pulled onto the edge of the lane and settled ponderously to the ground in an emergency parking slot. The driver climbed out, looked around nervously, then ran across the lane and disappeared into a small corner grocery. That was good, but when Jim darted up to the rear of the van, he saw something even better: the door handle was turned down, in the unlocked position, a small green bulb winking in welcome above it. He took a deep breath, tugged on the handle, and jumped inside.

It was dark, and smelled of old leather, stale cigarette smoke, greasy fried chicken, and—something weird . . .

Frantic, he wormed his way forward. There were no windows, and once he'd pulled the door shut, he was plunged into darkness. He worked by feel—and finally made himself a little nest beneath what felt like stiff, furry blankets. He hoped there were no infrared cameras trained on the interior of the cargo hold—and no sensor alarms either.

But what was the point of worrying? This would either work, or it wouldn't. And so he curled up into as tight a ball as he could manage and waited. After a few moments he felt the van rock slightly, then heard the door to the cab slam. The van lifted off.

Next stop: the gate.

In the darkness, something snorted softly.

His heartbeat did a nasty little double clutch. *Something was in here with him . . . .*

6

He remained frozen in terror the rest of the trip, not even noticing when the van bumped to a halt at the gate. Dimly, he heard muffled voices and a sudden bark of harsh laughter. But what he really listened to was a chorus of soft rustlings, what sounded like multiple stomachs rumbling, several more sharp, snorting sounds, and once, a low, mewling whine.

This went on for what seemed like hours, as he realized that what he'd thought was the smell of leather was something warmer and more lively: it was the stink of whatever was in here with him.

The sudden burst of light from the rear of the cargo hold shocked him and he gasped. Noise flooded in: the roar of engines, rough shouts, barked commands.

Got me! he thought.

But they hadn't. The back door was open wide. From his place of concealment, he could just see the face of the driver as he bent down and yanked out a ramp from the floor of the van.

"Come on, you ugly pussers! Get your shaggy butts out of there!"

Sheep. He'd stowed away in a van full of sheep! And yes, these were sheep hides covering him, and, boy, did they ever stink.

He timed his moment perfectly, and was out of the van while the driver was dealing with a dozen or so blinking, complaining animals. He moved away from the van briskly, noticing for the first time the legend on the side: KELVEY'S INTERSTELLAR ANIMAL SHOW AND CIRCUS.

Sheep? In a circus?

His pulse rate began to slow as he realized he had made it. He was inside the port. But where? He stopped and slowly turned a full circle, trying to take in everything.

The ceiling was at least a hundred feet overhead, vanishing in a bright haze from the hundreds of skylights that flooded the vast structure with filmy light. The space echoed with random noise—human, mechanical, and electronic. He stood at the intersection of a pair of corridors that stretched out in every direction, so extensive he couldn't make out where they ended. The walls of each corridor consisted of rack upon rack of crates, boxes, and reinforced shipping containers. Long cranes dipped down with insectile grace from the upper reaches, plucking, searching, replacing. Automated flatbeds raced up and down the centers of the aisles, loaded with cargo.

Very well, then: the cargo docks. He rubbed the side of his nose. Was this the place? At the moment, he felt fresh out of ideas. But was this the way out?

He considered. Stowing away in a spaceship's passenger compartments was, for all intents and purposes, impossible. The public areas would not hide him for long, even if he were somehow able to make it past ticket agents and shipboard personnel and automated sensors. And if he were found aboard, there was no place to run. Whoever was searching for him would have him, neat as a bug in a bottle.

Something unpleasant wafted into his nostrils. He raised one hand and sniffed. Ugh. The stink was his own—well, not exactly.

He'd never thought of sheep as being quite so rank. After all, they were white and fluffy.

He thought about sheep for a moment. An interstellar circus. Sheep. Now, how would you transport sheep between the stars? And a sheep, full-grown, weighed just about as much as he did . . .

He began to grin.

Baa.

7

Cat took the tube directly into the heart of Wolf Port, got off, and walked through the passenger-scanning station. She waved her ID chip vaguely in the direction of the reader, her face empty of expression, bored . . .

The chip, with its embedded fake identity, should work. Morninglory had provided it, and he was the best. Then she remembered that *was* happened to be the operative word, and once again felt an overwhelming wave of sadness. Would it ever end? Or would the mysterious enemies of the Pleb class continue their mindless slaughter?

Morninglory had been her father's half brother, her uncle. She had not let Jim know. Her grief, she felt, was too sharp to share; that it would somehow be a disservice to Morninglory's memory to parade her own bereavement like some cheap emotional toy.

Besides, Morninglory wouldn't have approved. What he would have wanted was what she was doing now: carrying on the battle. He had cracked the hidden databases, and she had the fruit of his theft in a handful of chips no larger than seeds. And that was exactly what they were, or so she hoped: seeds which, properly planted and nurtured, might grow into a weapon with which to bring down his, and her, enemies.

She passed on through the passenger gate without challenge. A few minutes later, whisked along by high-speed escalators, she boarded the *Terra Boy* through the economy-class entrance. It took her a while to locate her own tiny cubicle, and not until she was behind its safely bolted door did she, finally, allow herself to mourn.

After a time she took out the handful of chips and stared at them. So tiny, so harmless-seeming. But she knew more about their contents than she had let on.

It was a gamble, turning Jim loose on his own as she'd done. But there was no choice. Together, they would not have stood a chance. Still, he was resourceful. She hoped he would find a way. Not for his sake, but for her own people's hopes.

He was, it seemed, a key of some sort. The chips were the thing, she told herself, the most important thing. But he was important, too. She was not quite able yet to admit that he was important to her, though.

Nor did she—or anybody else, at that point—understand that while Jim was indeed a key, he held within himself the lock, too; a lock that guarded things of greater importance than anybody had imagined. Had she known that, things might have turned out very differently.

8

It was a problem he'd never thought he'd have to deal with: how do you murder a sheep? And though the thought revolted him, he couldn't see any other choice.

The problem was simple enough. He'd come to realize that nobody paid any attention to people working here in the cargo docks. They were here, weren't they? Security worked at keeping the unauthorized out, not checking on those already in.

So he felt relatively safe as he stood a few feet from the temporary holding pen that contained eleven disgruntled, shaggy beasts. Out beyond the pen, neatly arrayed alongside a loading conveyer, were eleven self-maintaining animal containers. Eleven sheep, eleven containers. But if one of those containers was to be his ticket to Terra, one of those sheep had to vanish. And quickly.

He stared at the sheep and mulled over the quandary. As he did so, two dockworkers ambled up; one muttered something under his breath and pointed at the sheep pen. The other laughed out loud. Then they got to work.

Jim felt his stomach sink as he watched them expertly snare each twitching, irritable hunk of four-legged stubbornness and wrestle it into a container. It went quickly, though they had to attach some obvious plumbing to each animal after it was in its container. The sheep weren't pleased with the operation, and made their displeasure obvious.

Now what? Jim wondered. There was a sheep occupying his stateroom. He stared at the enigmatic containers as if hoping a solution was written on their shiny sides, and when the answer did come to him at last, it was so simple he wondered why he hadn't seen it at once.

He checked out the area and saw nobody nearby. Then he walked over to the nearest container, unlocked the catches, and began to wrestle the protesting fur ball out onto the floor.

"Go on, boy. Shoo," he said.

The sheep eyed him warily. Finally, Jim stepped around and booted the animal as hard as he could, right in the hindquarters. The sheep let out one sharp bleat, and took off at full speed down an aisle. Jim watched until it vanished in the distance. Then he climbed in, settled his backpack, and began to fit himself into the cramped confines of the container.

After a few moments of thought, he realized what those connections the dockworkers had hooked up were for. Sheep generated waste. So did humans.

Groaning softly, he dropped his pants and began to hook up the plumbing.

This was going to be one hell of a trip.

9

The human mind is a funny thing. It doesn't take well to isolation. Magpielike, it craves constant stimulation. It demands things to see, to smell, to hear, to taste, to feel. When it is deprived of these things, it begins to manufacture its own substitutions.

Psychologists call these ersatz stimuli sensory-deprivation hallucinations. Jim waited in the warm darkness for what seemed like hours—though it was only a few minutes—until suddenly he felt himself lifted, then dropped hard onto the moving conveyor belt. More movement, a sharp jerk, a harsh, clanging sound, and then—

Silence. Darkness. Emptiness.

It went on and on. Finally, he began to dream . . .

10

. . . a baby, crying.

He floated. The sound was insistent, irritating. He tried to make it go away, but it wouldn't. Slowly, light bloomed. Yellow light, dim. The baby was unhappy. Cold, tired, sore.

The baby's eyes weren't developed. Its world was small, tight, closed in. It didn't understand what was happening to it. Uncomfortable things—things that hurt—touched it, penetrated it. The baby felt a sudden rush inside itself. It didn't understand . . .

A face. A woman's face. It didn't know the difference between men and women, and it didn't care. But this was a special woman, a special face. It had a name.

Mama . . .

Mama was *doing* something to him. The baby didn't understand this, either, but it didn't like it. The sensation was sort of like feeding, because gradually the baby began to feel full. Then more than full. Then almost bursting.

The baby wailed louder, and *Mama's* face came back. Soothing, meaningless sounds. Words without shape. Slowly, the glutted sensation began to subside. The baby's throat felt raw.

Something inside, something in the deep and the dark. The baby closed its eyes and swam, down and down, into the darkness. Into itself.

Later . . .

"Kootchie, hoo baby, hoo, boy. Cutie Jimmy, cutie baby."

The words meant nothing. The face a blurry fuzz, familiar. Daddy . . .

And more faces. One like an egg, hairless, with tall, arching eyebrows. Familiar. The shape familiar. More words. *Mama's* face, Daddy's face, the other.

Faces, shapes, sounds.

Down again, into the secrets. Into the *inside.*

PAIN!

11

. . . Pain.

The noise shook him from the deep hallucinations, the deep dreams, and he exploded to the surface of his mind as a diver climbing to the surface of a pool, into the light and noise.

"What the hell . . . ?"

Rough hands grabbed him, shook him. He fought back blindly, fists swinging. Somebody grunted.

". . . *out* of there!"

Pain in his lower regions as the waste connections were ripped away. He felt himself lifted up, the light, the painful light burning through his closed eyelids. A wedge of pure agony transfixed him as he landed hard on hipbone and elbow.

"It's a kid! It's a damned kid!"

He tried to curl up into a ball, into the soft warm ball of dreams, but the noise, the smells, the light, the whole panoply of *sensation* roared over him in unceasing waves.

"Let me *go* . . ." He knew that voice. It took him a moment to realize how he knew it. It was his own, trying to make its way through his clogged throat. He shook his head. His hands and feet began to tingle. After a time, it felt as if his extremities were being dipped in boiling water, and he screamed.

"Kid. Open your eyes."

He shook his head.

Fingers clamped on his jaw. He tried to bite. No good. "Hey, damn it!"

The fingers went away, leaving an ache. Then something crashed into the side of his head. Stars exploded in his skull, and his eyes popped open against his will.

The light poured in, searing as the sun.

Vaguely, he realized that something was wrong. He needed to do something, to . . .

Run.

"He's coming around," another voice, low and angry, muttered. "Jeez, look at him."

A part of him was still in the long, deep, dream, but the rest began to piece it together. My God, he'd made it! This must be Earth! And with a sinking sensation, he suddenly understood the rest of it.

Caught!

"Leave me alone . . ." He blinked. Slowly, like a computer graphic painting itself across his vision, he saw their forms and figures coalesce out of the blinding light.

Two men, one tall, one short, both burly. Wrinkled green jumpsuits, deep stains in the armpits and on their bellies. They stared at him.

"Kid?" the short one said. "What the hell you think you're doing?"

He turned his face away from them. Then he bit down hard on his tongue and felt his mouth fill with hot, coppery tasting warmth. He turned back and looked up at them.

"Kid . . . ?"

He belched a mouthful of red blood down his front.

"Lordy!" the tall one said. "We need a doctor here!"

He turned and ran. And when the shorter man turned to follow, Jim groped for his pack, staggered to his feet, and lurched off as quickly as he could in the opposite direction.

"Hey, you, wait a minute . . ."

He shambled around a corner into the chaos of the TerraPort cargo docks, and was gone.

CHAPTER 9

1

Lonely, hungry, constantly terrified, Jim walked for what seemed like hours. It was eerie. He had thought the cargo docks on Wolfbane were huge: now he realized you could take their entire vastness and lose them in one small corner of these docks. But what was even more unsettling was how empty of life this fantastic place was.

Here, too, were the endless aisles, the scuttling machines. But, unlike the docks on Wolfbane, there were almost no people. Sometimes, off in the hazy distance, he would see a single figure, perhaps holding a small computer, or maybe just strolling along. But the work was done by machines, cool, silent, efficient.

There would have been thousands of workers on Wolfbane. Here, there were only a handful. Abruptly, with a twinge of fear, he realized how lucky he had been to pick a sheep carrier: no doubt it was the living cargo that had brought human stevedores to unlock those containers. Otherwise, he might have remained inside, locked in dreams, until he died of thirst.

He shivered at the thought, then pushed it away. He had other problems to worry about now—and the first was the simplest. How to get out of here without getting caught?

He wondered if his two rescuers would spread an alarm. He thought they might not—they had looked like workers at the lowest level, not inclined to rock any boats they didn't have to—but there was no sense in taking chances. The quicker he got out of the confines of TerraPort itself, the better. But how? He rounded one more nameless corner and found himself at the edge of a broad, open space. The ceiling was so far overhead it was hard to make out. Complicated metal girders, robot cranes reaching down like ducks bobbing for food, lights like miniature suns. The whole space illuminated in harsh blue-white light, shadows like razors.

Beyond the open space, which was dotted with piles of loose cargo, was a broad metal wall, perhaps twenty stories tall. Hundreds of dark, cavelike openings punctuated the immense face of the wall. As he watched, a small train of tanklike containers rode a steel track into one of the openings and vanished. Closer examination revealed a great deal of movement: many such trains, and here and there, large, snakelike tubes whose sides vibrated faintly.

From his vantage point it looked like a kid's train set, until he noticed what he was leaning against: a tank, similar to those that made up the distant trains. But the tank was thirty feet tall and a hundred feet long.

Everything here was *huge*. Suddenly he felt like the hero of one of those fairy tales, dumped into a world of giants. He smiled at the thought, but it wasn't getting him any closer to his goal.

An ugly, familiar stench wafted over him. He wrinkled his nose, trying to remember. Oh, yes. That plumbing he had hooked up to himself in the sheep carrier. It had been designed to fit sheep, and had not made as tight a seal on him as it should have. The stink of his own waste had permeated his unconscious dreams, and now he smelled something very similar.

It was not a pleasant smell, nor even a pleasant thought, but it seemed to tug at him, as if the idea was trying to reveal something to him. Something necessary . . . human waste.

Turds.

The ships would generate tons of waste as they traveled the stars, and like all things organic, even turds and pee were far too valuable simply to throw away. No, they would be shipped downplanet for recycling.

He glanced around, then turned to the tank that towered next to him. There was a metal ladder, a series of rungs, set into its side. He hitched his pack onto his shoulders, took a deep breath, and began to climb.

At the top, ranged along the flat center of the tank, he found a series of round metal hatches. The stench up here was very strong. He began to breathe through his nose. When he undogged one of the hatches, the stink just about blew him over. He peered inside.

There was about four feet of space between the top of the tank and the dark, sludgy liquid below. He grimaced, then bent down and stuck his head into the tank. Deliberately opened his nostrils and sucked in a breath.

The odor was nearly unbearable, but there was oxygen. Enough to support him? He didn't know.

He pulled his head out and mulled it over. There was another ladder extending from the inside of the hatch, down into the sludge. He could cling to it and keep himself out of the worst of the muck—if the tank didn't get shaken around too much. The major advantage he could see was simple: nobody would be inspecting the interiors of these tanks very closely. Not without a gas mask. After all, who would be crazy enough to hide in a tank full of shit?

A sharp, metallic crash broke his reverie. He peered over the row of tanks. Three tanks down, one of the overhead cranes inserted its steel pincers into fitted sockets, and lifted. The tank swung away into the air.

He stood up and took one long, deep breath of relatively clean air. Then he climbed down into the tank and pulled the cover shut behind him.

No sensory deprivation here. His nose had just about all the sensation it could handle.

2

"Kid, I hate to be the one to tell you, but you smell like crap. And I don't mean that as a figure of speech. You really stink."

Jim looked down at his jeans. They were coated from the thighs on down with a brown, flaky crust. The sun had dried the pants, but couldn't remove the evidence. That tank *had* jiggled. Quite a bit, in fact.

He was seated next to a stunted palm tree, in the center of a tiny park. Most of the grass here had been worn away, leaving a thin veneer of dusty earth, and patches of greenish gray weeds otherwise.

It was a thoroughly repulsive place, even frightening, but to Jim it felt like a small slice of heaven. He had found it after climbing out of the tank, finding himself in an incomprehensible warehouse full of liquid, chugging sounds, and getting out of that place as quickly as possible. Into a brand-new world.

The sun was high overhead, hotter, brighter, whiter than the light of Wolfbane. It worried him for a moment, as he wondered about solar burns. Then he remembered that he was human. His body had been designed for this planet, not for Wolfbane. This sun wouldn't kill him.

The thought was so stupid that he started to laugh. After everything that had happened, to worry about terminal sunburn. The more he thought about it, the harder he laughed. And, evidently, the lanky number who came over and settled himself next to Jim didn't find anything too odd about a kid covered in dried crap, sitting next to a palm tree, laughing his head off at nothing discernible, for, after making his observation about Jim's body odor, he went on calmly: "You new here?"

It took Jim a moment to realize somebody was talking to him. He turned. His fellow sun worshiper was completely bald, had an evil scar that extended down the right side of his face, and wore an illegal wirehead rig strapped openly on his upper arm. A month earlier Jim would have simply run as fast as he could from such a character, but now, all he could feel was gratitude at the sound of another human voice.

"Uh-huh. New," he agreed.

The man had strange eyes—now green, now brown, now blue, depending on the way he cocked his head against the light.

Hazel, Jim thought. *That color is called hazel.*

"Yah, you're new all right. Wolfbane, right? You got the accent . . ." He paused. "Didn't know they had very many Plebs on Wolfbane."

Jim eyed him warily. Well, at least one good thing. This man, obviously a Terran Pleb, thought he was one of the fraternity. Which was probably a good thing. Plebs on Wolfbane were a relatively new phenomenon, and there weren't many of them. Here, according to legend, the Plebs were an endless swarm. All the better to hide in.

Jim nodded. "Got one less, now."

The man chuckled, then stuck out one grimy hand. "Put her there, kid. Though I can't imagine why you'd leave a nice, clean place like Wolf's supposed to be, and come all the way to hell on Earth. Uh, my name's Jackie."

Jim took his hand. "Jim," he replied.

"Nice socket you got there," Jackie remarked. "Doesn't look gov ish."

"Huh?"

"Gov ish. Government issue. Looks custom. Rich-folks stuff. You sure you a Pleb?"

Jim shrugged. "I wasn't always. You know. Things . . . change."

Somehow, it was the right answer. At least it seemed to please Jackie a great deal, because he reached over and slapped Jim on the back. "Yeah, that's how it *is*, isn't it? One day you're just fine, or your family is, and then some damned robot or computer comes along and makes you obsolete. Boom! And then you're one of us."

Jim nodded. Suddenly he thought of the vast and echoing emptiness of the TerraPort cargo docks. No doubt they had once swarmed with workers, just like those on Wolfbane. But now the workers were gone. Maybe they were sitting out under stunted palm trees now, all over Terra.

"Sorry about the stink," Jim said.

"I smelled worse. But there's public baths, you know. Or maybe you don't. You just get in?"

Jim nodded. "Well. I don't know what you got yourself into"—Jackie chuckled sharply—"but I sure ain't one to judge. A dime-cred will get you fixed up."

Instinctively, Jim's hand went to his pack, where his small cache of cash was hidden. Jackie's gaze followed the movement brightly. Suddenly Jim knew it would be a good idea to put some distance between himself and the other man.

"Jackie?"

"What's that?"

"You ever hear of a place called Shawn Fan? A bar?"

Jackie stared at him oddly. "Now why would you want to go there?"

"I'm meeting somebody," Jim said.

Jackie drew back from him, as if he had somehow suddenly become more formidable. "Well, you want to go there, I'll show you. You just be sure to mention it was me that took you, okay?"

Jim had no idea what Jackie was talking about, but he nodded. Jackie brightened. "You want to go to a bathhouse first? Kinda get cleaned up?"

For the first time since he'd parted from Cat, Jim felt a surge of hope. Somehow, maybe things would work out after all.

"Yeah," Jim said. "That would be great."

3

The man with the bullet-shaped head sat behind his broad desk, his features lost in the bright glare of light from the window behind him. He wore a dark suit and a white shirt with a ring collar. His thick-fingered hands rested on the polished surface of the desk without movement. Like fat, perfectly manicured sausages. His voice was deep, a resonant baritone, filled with color and warmth.

"Steele, I really wish you had managed to put your hands on that wretched little SOB. I'm afraid you are beginning to disappoint me."

Commander Steele had been sitting in a capacious black leather armchair in front of the desk. Now, with some painful effort, she hoisted herself up, grunting.

"Your back?" the man inquired politely.

"Will be fine," she grated. "I'm a disappointment? Listen, this was your mission. You set it up. Did you plan on losing a ConFleet cruiser? I mean, my God . . ."

"Yes," the man agreed. "That was a tragedy." The way he said it gave Steele the idea he didn't think the demise of the *Hank Tee* was much of a tragedy at all. "But, you know how it is. You can't predict everything."

Steele shook her head. "If anybody can predict everything, it ought to be you. Damn it, I lost almost my whole team. Again!"

"Steele, Steele. So fierce. These things happen."

"Not to me," Steele grated. "Anyway, I'm done, right? I'm out of it. That kid is toast. Burned toast. So I can go back to doing the everyday dirty work, just your basic murder and rape and pillage, right?"

"Well . . ." the man said. "Not exactly." He flapped one hand at a large holoscreen. The form of a teenage girl began to appear. She was sitting disconsolately in an otherwise empty cell, staring at her feet.

"Look what I found," the bullet-headed man said. "Her name is Cat."

4

Shawn Fan. Jim stared up at the weathered wooden sign, incredibly old, that creaked softly on its hinges over the door of the bar. Next to him, Jackie wrinkled his nose. "Did a good job, Jimmy, my boy. Can't hardly smell you at all no more."

Jim grinned. "Yeah. Thanks, Jackie."

"You remember. You tell 'em I brought you, okay? You promised . . ."

"I will, Jackie. I'll remember. Aren't you coming inside, though?"

Jackie recoiled. "Me? In *there*? He chuckled uneasily. "Oh, no, I don't think so. You go on. You'll be fine."

And with a final, nervous smile, Jackie bobbed his head once, turned, and scuttled away. Jim turned back around and stared at the sign again. Jackie was weird, true, but something about this place frightened him.

He thought about that, and then squared his shoulders. Shawn Fan, outside the main gate of TerraPort. Go there and mention my name to the bartender. Someone will come . . .

Jim squared his shoulders, tried to ignore his doubts, and stepped through the door into the dim coolness beyond.

"You want what?" the bartender said.

"Soda. Cherry soda . . . please?" Jim told him. Uneasily, he thought that the manners his parents had taught him as a child might not be the proper code of conduct here. This was shortly confirmed as the bartender, a man of average size, middle-aged, with greasy black hair topping a face almost obliterated by colorful tattoos, said, "Kid, get out of here before I have to throw you out." He paused, glared, and said, "Go on, beat it. You smell bad, by the way."

Hmm. Evidently the bathhouse hadn't been as effective as he'd hoped. He slid off the barstool, unmindful of how that piece of recreational furniture had remained basically unchanged over four centuries. Nor did he give much thought to the idea of a human bartender in what was nothing more than a low-level dive. An equivalent restaurant would have no human servers, only robot systems. Of course, he couldn't begin to imagine the chaos possible in a place that served intoxicating drinks and drugs to a clientele already predisposed to violence. And if he couldn't imagine it, neither could any robot system. In some niches, human resilience still reigned supreme.

"I'm . . . uh . . . sorry. Somebody told me to come here. Maybe you know her? Name of Cat . . ."

The bartender, who had been applying a greasy paper rag to the greasy bar top, paused. "What's that?" he murmured, leaning closer. "No, don't say it again. I heard the first time. How do you come by that name, kid?"

Jim shrugged. He seemed to be getting someplace, though he wasn't sure exactly where. At least Cat's name was familiar here.

"I knew her. Someplace else. Wolfbane."

"You don't say? Wolfbane . . . ?" The bartender eyed him sideways. "Tell you what. You go over into that corner over there and sit down and pretend you're invisible. Okay? I gotta make a call . . ."

Jim nodded. "Can I—"

"We don't serve no sodas here, kid. Not unless you want to mix them with rotgut whisky. Get me?"

"Uh-huh."

"Good. Go sit."

Jim went to the table and sat. The corner was dark. He scrunched down in the booth until only his head was visible above the table. It seemed stupid and melodramatic. He'd never been in a place like this, but it didn't look as if the police monitored it very closely. Still, the atmosphere was tense and wary, from the bartender's attitude on down to the furtive watchfulness that cloaked the few other patrons who sat, hunched and silent, over glass tumblers they guarded with the air of feral dogs protecting chunks of meat.

Hurry up and wait, Jim thought. *I seem to spend most of my time waiting for things I have no idea about. Whether they are good or bad. Whether someone will come to help me, or kill me.*

He felt helpless. Again, damn it . . .

He was still thinking about this when they did come for him. Two men, one thick, one thin, otherwise indistinguishable from each other. Both had the hard, competent air of men used to enforcing their requests with their fists. Or worse.

They came through the front door and walked directly to Jim's table. "You. Up," Thick said.

Thin glanced at the bar. "Thanks, Max. We got it now."

The bartender nodded, then looked down at his endless polishing. Jim got the idea that Max wouldn't look up again, not even if Thick and Thin decided to dismember him on the top of the table.

"Where are we going?" Jim asked, as they frog-marched him out the door between them.

"Shut up," Thin said.

"Yeah," added Thick.

5

"So you claim you were with Cat on Wolfbane . . ." the stone killer named Jonathan said.

They sat across from each other at a simple wooden table, in a small, nondescript room. The same description—small, nondescript—would have applied equally to Jonathan, Jim thought. He looked like some kind of low-level clerk, with his short, sandy blond hair, his unathletic body, his pale, long fingers unmarked by any evidence of hard physical labor.

His eyes were watery and blue, and he was reluctant to focus them on anything. Whenever Jim tried to catch his gaze, those eyes would dart away, as if fearful of direct contact with another human. Even his voice was anemic, soft and almost lisping; his speech was so hard to make out, Jim had to lean forward to make sure he understood what Jonathan was saying to him.

Small, frail, silent, evasive: what was it, then, Jim wondered, about Jonathan that was so completely terrifying? As he strained to hear what Jonathan was saying, he thought it probably had something to do with what he'd felt when Jonathan had listlessly offered his soft handshake. Jim had taken those limp fingers and dropped them immediately, the skin on the back of his neck quite literally crawling. He had resisted touching his own neck, because he knew he would feel gooseflesh there.

It had been the psychic equivalent of taking up a handful of blind worms, warm and slimy and writhing with fevered life—and Jim didn't believe in anything psychic at all. But he believed in his own instincts. . . . In the case of Jonathan, every instinct he had was screaming at him: *run . . . hide . . . run away now*!

Jonathan even acknowledged this in some manner; when Jim gasped and dropped his hand, Jonathan smiled faintly, as if to say, "Oh, yeah, I understand. People tell me it's awful. Happens all the time."

There was something monstrous about this harmless little clerk-man. And the monstrosity was so plain, so obvious, that Jim wondered how people could stand to be around him at all. Maybe that was why this room was so faceless, so utilitarian. Only the table and the two chairs, and a rack of digital screens on one wall, six screens running silently, pictures of places Jim didn't recognize, faces that were alien as eggs.

"Tell me about Cat . . ." Jonathan went on, gentle, insistent.

Jim was grateful for the enigmatic screens. Their colors and quick-change movements gave him something to look at besides Jonathan's watery, evasive gaze.

Jim shrugged. "I met her on Wolfbane. She—helped me a lot."

"Did she now? How, exactly, did she do a thing like that?"

Jim watched the screens as he told his story, and finished with the unlikely tale of his transit from Wolfbane to this little room. Just as he completed the story, something moved on one of the screens and snagged his attention.

Jonathan's pinkish lips moved; he hawed in soundless laughter. "In the turd tank. Excellent. So you stink, it washes off. But nobody looks in a bowl full of turds for the missing diamond."

Jim looked away from the screen, and the tiny spark that had caught him disappeared from his mental radar. "Is that what I am?" Jim asked. "A diamond?"

Jonathan fixed him with one sharp glance, before his attention dissolved and he looked away again. "Maybe. I'll find out. You can be sure I'll find out."

Jim's bowels suddenly turned cold and runny. "What's wrong?"

"Cat seems to be among the missing . . ."

"Missing?" Jim knew his lips were hanging open, but he couldn't help himself.

"Yes. So the logical thing, I suppose, is to find out exactly who you really are. Or, more to the point, *what* you are. James. Endicott . . . is it?"

6

"This won't hurt," the woman said. She was short, with iron gray hair done in a neat bun, a shapeless flowered dress, and a motherly expression on her sagging features. But her puffy hands were encased in rubber gloves, and over her dress she wore a white medical apron, as if she feared something might splash on her.

Jim felt even sicker, imagining the sort of things that might splash. He chuckled weakly. "My doctor program used to say that."

"Mm hmm . . . ?"

"It always hurt," he told her.

"Deep breath, now," she said, and just as he hitched up his shoulders, she hit him on the arm with a hypospray. For a moment he stared at her expressionless features in surprise, the sharp hiss of the spray echoing in his ears. Everything began to waver and blur, and then he was gone.

CHAPTER 10

1

"Well, you're who you say you are. At least, *you* think you are," Jonathan said.

Jim stood next to a large window and looked out. He guessed he was at least forty stories up, and even so, the tops of nearby buildings vanished far above, into what seemed to be a permanent mist.

Off to his left, the antique structure of the Golden Gate Bridge, now a ramshackle collection of condominiums, glowed in the dim light. So he was in San Francisco. The idea that at least he knew where he was, if not much else, gave him some comfort.

"Huh . . . ? What does that mean? Of course I'm who I am. Who else would I be?"

Jonathan came up behind him. He moved as quietly as a ghost. When he spoke again, his nearness startled Jim, made him jump. Of course, everything about Jonathan made him jumpy.

"Oh, Jimmy, how naive you are. You could be anybody. You could believe you're anybody. The human mind is a malleable thing . . . just like the human DNA."

This made so little sense that Jim turned and stared at him. "What are you talking about?"

Jonathan shrugged. "Your DNA, for instance, is very . . . interesting."

"I don't give a damn about that. What happened to Cat? What's going *on*, Jonathan?"

"Well, now, that's a trick question, isn't it? We had you under for three days, my boy. You're a regular treasure trove."

"Jonathan . . ."

"Oh, all right. Miss Cat is . . . missing, as I said. But no longer presumed dead, if that sets your mind at rest."

Jim let out a long, relieved sigh. It had been in the back of his mind, that somehow she was gone, and worse, that it was his fault. Everything seemed to be his fault, why not this, too?

"Tell me . . ." he said, excited. "Where is she?"

"Well now, that we don't know. Exactly. But first, young James, I think we need to have a long talk. I mean, aren't you curious? You should be, you know."

Jonathan wandered away. The room was furnished with a couple of sofas, a table, chairs, some cheap holoprints. It might have been an inexpensive hotel room. It had that faceless, anonymous feeling to it. Finally, Jonathan perched on one of the sofa arms. "Doesn't it strike you odd, Jim, that so many people should be so concerned about you? So . . . *interested* in you?"

Jim turned back to the window. Jonathan's quiet, insistent lisping made him even more uneasy. "Of course," he said finally. "I'm not an idiot. My dad told me . . ."

"Not enough, it appears. You dad was an interesting man, Jim. He had a history. What's even more interesting is that, despite the fact we turned your deep memory over like an unmade bed, and we know everything about Carl Endicott that you do, we still can't trace that history. Old Carl, he was a real mystery man."

The thought seemed to make Jonathan happy.

"You could have just asked me."

"Oh, we did, Jimbo. Jimmy, we did. Doesn't your head ache?"

"As a matter of fact, it does."

"It'll pass. Ignore it. Anyway, time for a history lesson. Maybe a mystery lesson, big Jim." Jonathan slid off his perch. He couldn't stay in one place very long.

"You know this guy, Jimmy?"

A standard issue holoscreen hanging on one wall burped into life, revealing some kind of press conference. Important-looking officials gabbled silently. The camera panned the group, then settled in tight on one man who stood behind the others, and made no effort to speak.

Jim felt a jerk of recognition. "Yes . . . uh, no."

"Well, I doubt you've met him recently, but you do remember him, right?"

"I . . . saw him when we talked the last time. He was on one of the screens in your room. I just noticed. That must be why I remember."

"Well, not quite. One of the things a full mind scan does is comparison studies. We flashed a lot of pictures at you, and you reacted to some things you shouldn't have twitched on at all. Like . . . this."

A second picture of the man suddenly appeared. It was plainly the same man, but much younger. There was a fringe of black hair on his bulletlike skull, and he was thinner, his features sharper.

Jim stared, wondering. "It seems like I ought to know him . . ." he said. "But I don't, not really. It's like . . . déjà vu. But I've never met him in my life."

"His name's Delta. Well, that's what he calls himself nowadays. He has, for all intents and purposes, obliterated any records of his past. A man and a woman died to obtain this one picture. Does it . . . ring any bells?"

Jim shook his head. But he *did* know him, didn't he? The younger version, at least. How, though? His head began to throb again.

"Delta? No. What's his real name?"

Jonathan sighed. "We don't know. It is one of the best kept secrets in the whole Confederacy. We know who he is, though."

Jim stared at him, waiting.

"Delta runs the Combined Intelligence Agencies. The CIA. He's the biggest spook there is." Jonathan paused, then added, offhandedly: "He is my enemy, if that matters."

Jim felt his thoughts creak dangerously. It all made a horrible kind of sense. Ever since his world had fallen apart, he'd felt himself at the mercy of vast forces. Things had happened so quickly, he hadn't really thought about it, but surely it would have taken somebody very powerful to orchestrate all the disasters that had occurred?

"Delta . . ." he said slowly. He shook his head. "Jonathan, I don't know him. Really, I don't."

"Well," Jonathan replied. "Maybe that will change. As it turns out, he says he wants to meet you."

2

The interrogator was a young woman. Cat thought she wasn't much older than she was, and supposed it was standard operating procedure. Try to create a bond between the subject and the questioner.

"Catherine," the woman said, "we know you passed the chips on, and we know to whom. You can be certain we will locate that person, so we really don't need you, do we? But there are a few things you could help us with."

Cat shook her head, determined to remain stubbornly mute. She had no doubt they'd mind-reamed her for hours—there were suspicious blank spots in her memory—but she had been trained to withstand certain things. There were fail-safes and cutouts burned into the physical structure of her brain, so that before she would give up some things, her entire mind would collapse.

The techniques for imposing these kinds of blocks were intensely painful, and she'd always wondered if the results were worth the agony. Now, facing her kind, soft-spoken tormentor, she decided they were. The blocks had held, even under mind-reaming. So she still had cards to play.

But what was the game? For what stakes? And, most important, who were the players?

"Oh, come on, Catherine. Give me just a little. Something . . . maybe I can help you. Why don't we start with your young man? With Jim Endicott? What do you know about Jim Endicott?"

3

"Jim, what are the Plebs?"

The question took him by surprise, and he stammered. "Uh . . . well, I guess you could call them an . . . underclass?"

Jonathan shook his head. "That's what you would call us, I suppose. We don't get the best publicity . . . not, mind you, that there isn't some truth to what we do get. We're all violent, lazy thugs, addicted to wireheading. Lie around all day on the Confederacy dole, wires stuck into sockets behind our ears pumping the old joy juice right into our pleasure centers. Something like that, right?"

Jim remembered, with some shame, his conversation with Morninglory. Shame, because that was exactly what he'd thought—until Morninglory, a Pleb, performed one of the bravest acts of self-sacrifice he'd ever imagined.

"Yes. I guess that's what I used to think."

"You mean you don't think so now?" There was a mocking tone in Jonathan's soft lisp, and when Jim turned to look at him, he saw that same mockery in his expression.

It ticked him off. "Listen, I thought you just read me like some comic vid. That's what you said. So you know how I feel. Right?"

"Ooh. Baby's all upset. Calm down, Jimmy. No harm intended." Jonathan's nasty grin said otherwise.

"Stop calling me Jimmy! My name's Jim!"

"Whoa. All right . . . Jim. So then we agree that the Plebs aren't the scum you were brought up to believe?"

"Morninglory . . ."

Jonathan nodded, suddenly serious. "Yeah, the old Glory man. I have to give him credit, from what you remember. He popped them a good one. I have to confess, I didn't think he still had it in him. Took down a whole damned cruiser. All right to that." And for the first time, Jim thought he saw a glint of honest emotion in Jonathan's gaze: fierce, triumphant . . . bitter.

Those hundreds of deaths would not weigh on Jonathan in quite the manner they did on Jim. Jim felt grief and horror and regret. But Jonathan *exulted* in the immolation of over a thousand ConFleet sailors.

"The Plebs are the inevitable products of technology," Jonathan said finally. "There is no shame in our existence. Humanity gave itself to the machines. Nobody seemed to understand, or care, that in the process, most of humanity became surplus. I suppose we're lucky they didn't just murder us all." He paused, and once again Jim saw that impossible well of bitterness flicker out of his eyes. "And maybe that would have been for the best, after all."

"Jonathan . . ."

"Spare me your sympathy, Jimbo."

Jim slid his gaze at Jonathan, then away. It was like watching somebody peel off a section of his own skin with a sharp knife.

Jonathan hated. If you knew that, you knew everything you needed to know about Jonathan. But this was going nowhere, Jim thought. All these wordy little games. Plebs. *Where was Cat?*

"Jonathan. You said that Cat . . ."

"Forget Cat a second, Jim. Listen to me instead, okay? That's a good boy. We'll get back to Cat when I say so."

Then, just like that, Jonathan went blank. Jim could feel it, as if Jonathan had turned himself off. He . . . went *away*, and he stayed *away* for almost a minute. It was the eeriest thing Jim had ever seen. He thought that if he closed his eyes, all his senses would tell him the room was empty, lifeless.

Jonathan grunted, and came back. "What . . . oh. Jim, Plebs are everywhere. Even on Wolfbane now. They weren't there, not at first, because it was a frontier planet. Our next frontier, they said at the time. But now the machines are there, too, more and more of them, and so are the Plebs. More and more of *them*. And you want to know what I think, Jim?"

Here he paused. But Jim was lulled by his lisping voice, just drifting along, and didn't answer.

"Jim, are you still there? Hello, Jimbo?"

" . . . sorry. I was thinking."

"Well, stop. Pay attention, because what I'm going to say is a matter of life and death." He flipped out that switchblade grin again. "Your life and death, probably."

Jim stared at him.

"Something is using us, Jim. Using the Plebs. I've known it—sensed it—all my life. I don't know how, but that much human meat, it's got to be a resource. And in our world, resources never go to waste. Not for long."

He sighed, and Jim got the feeling that he went *away* again, but this time only for a second.

"So a long time ago I decided to find out. See if I could get a handle on what was utilizing this particular resource. Cat helped me look, and Morninglory, too. And a lot of others. And you know what? A funny thing . . . everybody who helped me look ended up on Delta's shit list. Don't you think that's funny, Jim?"

"I don't have any idea what you are talking about, Jonathan," Jim said simply. And he didn't. He felt as if he were at the end of his rope, trapped in an unbreakable web of horrible circumstance, locked in this transient room with a man who scared the hell out of him, and bored him to death at the same time. What was Jonathan, anyway? Good or evil? Or did such things even apply to him?

"Jonathan, I don't want to talk anymore, unless it's about Cat. Just tell me what happened, okay? I don't give a damn about Plebs, or you, or anything. Just Cat."

Jonathan pulled gently at his lower lip, staring at him. "Well, you're honest. Even if you don't care much for the big picture. . . ."

He smiled suddenly. "So, okay, Jim. Here's the deal. Delta says he has Cat, and he wants to trade her. Guess who he wants instead?"

It made no sense, of course. None of it had, so far. But he had promised never to abandon one of his friends again. And Cat was more than a friend. Much more.

"Rhetorical question, I guess?"

Now Jonathan's smile became a lamp, fearsomely bright, beaming out of his pudding face. "Good answer, Jim. That's right! He wants you!"

Then, more softly, "And isn't that just the most *interesting* thing?"

4

They bound her wrists with plastic handcuffs before they took her into the huge, dim room. He waited at the far end, a black shadow-cutout against the light blazing from the window behind him. She felt the ceaseless tick and hum of hidden machines, and smelled his odor: thick, muskily perfumed, somehow frightening. The room was designed to set him off, a frame to better illustrate his power. The room of a festering egomaniac.

Her guards were faceless and interchangeable. They marched her halfway across the room and then stopped, not from any signal she could see, but from what she sensed was long practice. The guards had brought many helpless victims to this spot. They stopped and waited, fingers clamped tight around her biceps.

Her lower arms began to tingle and go numb from the pressure of their grip, but she ignored it and waited, silent.

"Hello, Cat," he said.

Deep, warm, almost fruity. A politician's voice. Soothing, fatherly. Utterly untrustworthy.

"You've kidnapped me," she said. "It's against the law."

"Oh, Cat. So harsh. So *fierce*." He twisted the tail of the word so that it became a private joke, shared between the two of them.

"But not to worry, my dear," he continued. "Your . . . captivity won't last much longer. There. Doesn't that make you feel better?"

Not particularly, she thought. *There's more than one way of ending a captivity. And at least one of them is fatal. . . .*

"You're letting me go, then? Isn't that dangerous?"

He laughed out loud. Once again it was an attractive sound, rich and booming, full of real humor. Meant to disarm. She resisted. "Dangerous? To whom, my dear girl? Me?"

"I've seen you . . ."

"Well, no, you haven't. Not really. And even if you thought you had, what would it matter? Consider. If you think you *do* know me, then you must understand how little it *would* matter. Correct?"

Delta. She knew him, how could she not? And he was right. Delta could make things disappear. Her, her memory of him, anybody else's recollection of this meeting. Like all spymasters, his greatest strength was just that: making things vanish.

It could all be wiped away. As far as she was concerned, his power was effectively unlimited. He ought to have terrified her. She wondered why he didn't.

"So?" she said at last. "Why are we having this little chat, then?"

The shadow moved. She felt the pressure of his examination, his watchfulness. Maybe that was it. He wanted to see her in the flesh. Some men were like that, not trusting their machines, only the evidence of their senses. Who needed sensation to make things real. She knew the word for people like that. Psychopath. She felt a heaviness in her chest, her belly.

He reminded her of Jonathan.

"I'm not afraid of you," she said at last. Even to her own ears it sounded stupid, juvenile. But it was all she could think to say.

He laughed again. "But why should you be, my dear? You haven't been harmed. The effects of our . . . questioning will wear off in a few hours. And we will be releasing you shortly, to continue on your journey. You should be safely at your destination only a day or so late. Hardly worth the upset, I would think."

"It's that simple, is it?"

"Just that simple, Cat. Let me be honest. You are of some marginal interest to me, if only because of the effort somebody expended on you to make it difficult to, ah, examine you. A very thorough job, that, let me add. Given time, of course we could break you, but—my congratulations to whoever did it."

She watched beefy shadow arms rise, and imagined blunt fingers coming together beneath a broad, heavy chin.

A crazy bravado seized her. "I'll be sure to tell them."

"Oh, Cat. I plucked you up once. I can do it again. Do remember that."

The dull, heavy feeling in her belly, her chest, intensified. What had they done to her? She thought of the possibilities: tiny sensors, buried deep inside her flesh. Chemical bomblets, alarms woven from her nervous system. No doubt she now glowed in their sensors like a bonfire.

She was still alive, but they'd killed her, at least as to any further usefulness to her own cause. How he must be laughing at her.

"I hate you . . ." she said.

He must have been waiting for that, because now his voice sounded softer, as if he were turning away from her, losing interest—though he didn't move at all.

"It's been interesting knowing you, Cat. But I think we're done here now, don't you?"

She had to know. "Why are you letting me go?"

"Why, I traded you, dear. For that pesky boyfriend of yours. Jim . . . you remember him, don't you?"

"You . . . bastard."

"Well, of course, Cat. What did you expect?"

They turned her around and marched her out, back to her cell, and locked her in. She sat in the pitiless light and tried to think what it all meant, but she couldn't.

Jim. What was so important about Jim?

Why *him*?

5

"Jonathan, what's so important about me?" Jim asked.

Jonathan shrugged. "A better question would be why Delta thinks you're so important. *If* he does—we really have no idea why he wants you. Maybe he thinks he can get more from you than from Cat . . ."

Something about the way he said this last sent warning tremors up Jim's spine. "Has Cat been hurt?"

"Probably not. At least not physically. But you can be sure she's been questioned."

"Her mind . . . ?" Jim knew something about modern interrogation techniques. Anybody could be broken, if enough time, technology, and determination were invested. But if time was short, the most effective methods tended to be the most brutal.

"Who knows?" And in Jonathan's reply, Jim heard the unvoiced thought: *Who cares*?

He made up his mind in that moment. Every second Cat stayed wherever she was, she remained in danger. But Jim could get her away from that danger, if he was willing. He'd had no choice with Morninglory. The old man hadn't given him any. But this was different.

"Trade me, then," he said. "Set it up. Let's get it done."

Jonathan quirked that odd, soft, almost pitying smile at him. "My, what an eager little beaver you are . . ." But some respect, too. "I give you credit for bravery, though."

Then he nodded, turned, and walked out of the room.

6

Commander Steele stood at parade rest in the exact spot where Cat had been only a few minutes before. She held her position, though her back was giving her all kinds of grief.

"I have alerted all the special tactics units," Delta said, in that syrupy, booming voice. "I don't think your people will be needed, but just in case, you might step up their ready status a notch or two."

Steele nodded. "What there are left of them . . . May I ask what is about to happen?"

"Steele, you sound bitter. No doubt your back is hurting. Why don't you relax, unbend a little? All the years I've known you, you've always had that military poker up your rear."

"Yes, sir. And every time I've relaxed, things have gone straight to hell. The most recent occurrences are an excellent example."

"Well, you may be right," Delta murmured blandly. "I'm not sure I could get used to you if you suddenly became . . . loose."

"Indeed. Is this why you called me? To practice your dry wit?"

Delta laughed out loud, and this time there was genuine mirth in his voice. But it only lasted a moment, and then he became coldly serious.

"What is about to happen is a sad outbreak of Pleb Psychosis. This will be a particularly virulent seizure, affecting a sizable percentage of the Terran Pleb population, and a smaller, though significant, portion of the Pleb community on Wolfbane."

Steele stared at him for several seconds, then shook her head. "What does sizable mean, exactly?"

"Hmm. What percentage of the Plebs do you suppose indulge in wireheading?"

Steele thought about it. The best guess she could come up with was approximately 32 percent. About a third. Wireheading, the practice of directly stimulating the brain's pleasure centers with a trickle of current delivered via a wire plugged into a skull socket, was very prevalent among the Plebs, less so in the higher classes—the so-called working classes. Installing the socket was cheap, simple, and, although illegal, not really proscribed—especially since a normal cybersocket could be easily modified to do the trick.

She offered her estimate, and Delta nodded. "I'd say you're close enough. So prepare for—let's see, there are three billion or so Plebs—that would make it about a billion screaming, violent psychotics." He paused. "You think anybody will notice?"

"You enjoy this, don't you?" Steele said.

"No, I don't. But I do it anyway."

"Why is that, sir?"

"Because," Delta said, "the alternatives are even worse. Oh—I want you to supervise the transfer of the girl."

"Yes, sir."

"One less thing for me to worry about. And, Steele?"

"Sir?"

"Are you excited about getting your hands on the Endicott boy?"

Steele thought about all the deaths that had sprung from her efforts regarding that one young man.

"Only in that I would like to kill him, if I may, sir," she said carefully.

"Not right away, Steele. You take very good care of him at first." The big shadow moved against the lighted window. It might have been a shrug. "As for later, well. Who knows? Go make ready, Steele. Go make ready."

She nodded, and did.

7

Delta watched Steele's ramrod back as she marched from the room. Odd woman, that. They went back almost to the beginning, to the time of the great and secret discoveries which had launched him on the road to power.

Had he—had she—made mistakes back then? At the time he'd thought not. He was not particularly an introspective man. It had never been in his brutally forceful nature to second-guess his own actions and decisions. But time itself had a way of demanding new evaluations, and what time had now coughed up—Jim Endicott—forced him to examine things and incidents he'd thought locked irrevocably in the past.

It was not a pleasant sensation, and Delta did not intend for it to continue much longer. Cat had been moderately instructive, although much of her thought had been too well shielded for the time limits involved in her questioning. He'd gotten a few things, though.

So the Plebs had begun to connect him with their travails? Their machines had sifted and analyzed and decided that his name came up too often in correlation with the Pleb Psychosis?

Perhaps that was inevitable. But such things were not threats, at least not yet. And since he'd considered the possibility of discovery right from the start, he had contingencies long in place to handle such threats.

Jim Endicott, however, was something else. He ran the tape in his mind once again: the minicams every one of his special forces people wore on their uniforms had filmed and recorded that touching final scene between Carl Endicott and his son. What had it meant?

Carl Endicott obviously thought it meant something. He had spoken with his final breaths in this life—and God, how Delta had hungered to hear those breaths, preferably gasped in painful extremity—but what he'd said remained a mystery.

Slowly, he stood behind his desk, a broad, heavy man who seemed to carry his own shadows with him. He moved slowly, with the automatic prudence of a big man who must be careful, lest he crush what he walked on. . . .

In his time he had crushed them all, all his enemies, all the ones who'd been unwilling, or unable, to comprehend the great web of danger only he saw, and only he had the strength and will to oppose.

Now, a sixteen-year-old boy might be the greatest threat he'd faced since Carl Endicott, who had not called himself Endicott then, and a beautiful woman named Kate had conspired to deprive him of the only things he'd ever loved.

He moved to a door hidden in the side of the room, behind a tall swath of black draperies. As he lumbered along, he mumbled, almost an aside, to his ever-present machines: "Bring me the boy's mother. I'll speak to this Tabitha Endicott."

And then we'll see, he thought.

CHAPTER 11

1

"Tell me what you've done," Jonathan said to an entity he knew only as The Fountain.

They were gathered together in noplace: that is to say, the place where they chose to meet, in fact the *only* place they deemed safe enough for all of them to join together—did not exist in the physical world, but only in the nebulous regions of cyberspace. Which did not mean their meeting was not real. It was. Deadly real, and vast amounts of thought, wealth, and force had been spent to make sure this insubstantial meeting ground was secure. Here they existed only as clouds of electrons, but they could be damaged nonetheless.

They were eight. Eight apparitions in cyberspace, where appearance was a matter of choice—and some of the choices these eight had made were outlandish. Picture The Fountain, for example: it—Jonathan had no idea if The Fountain was male or female—hung in the shadows and poured out of them, now a spew of bloodred fire, now a boil of steaming liquid, now a creeping flow of tiny, clicking insects. All this always in motion, always welling up from some hidden source.

There were times Jonathan wondered about his fellow conspirators, as he tried to imagine the kind of mind that would choose to present itself so. But he could never know, nor did he want to: none of those gathered here had ever met, in the flesh. The computer world was sufficient to their needs, and far safer. What could he tell an inquisitive interrogator? That his chief scientist's most preferred self-image was some sort of endless technological vomit?

"Picture a great and ancient city," The Fountain intoned. "Picture Jerusalem."

In their varying ways, all of the eight signaled assent.

"Jerusalem, within its high walls, is incredibly busy. Merchants, builders, buyers and sellers, priests and wives and hordes of screaming children. In the center of Jerusalem is the Temple, and in the Temple is the Book. From the Book, the smallest part of this great city, come all the rules by which it governs itself.

"The Book tells the people of the city how and what to eat, how to make love, how to buy and sell, how to build and fight. It orders their lives down to the smallest degree, this book at the heart of Jerusalem."

The Fountain paused, and Aker Bilk, charged with the military affairs of the conspiracy, who chose to manifest as a gigantic, neon-crusted praying mantis, muttered, "Yes, yes. Go on."

"Picture Jerusalem as a human cell," The Fountain continued. "The analogy is exact. Within the walls of the cell countless smaller things hurry and bustle, grow and build, die and change. In the center of the cell is its own temple, called the nucleus, and in the center of the nucleus is a book. The book is extremely tiny compared to the rest of the cell, yet in it are all the rules and blueprints that govern everything that goes on inside the cell. The book of the cell is like the Book of Jerusalem. We call the book of the cell its DNA."

Rose Lovely, who ordered all of the human spycraft the conspiracy undertook, and who manifested as a huge white blossom of her name, whispered softly. "We know this is true, Fountain. But what have you done?"

"DNA," The Fountain mused. "In one cell a pair of entwined molecules that if unwound would be a meter long, and so thin you could pack ten billion of them inside a human hair. This strand of DNA—that we also call the genome—is itself divided into smaller books, as an encyclopedia might be. The DNA contains twenty-three smaller books, called chromosomes. And the sentences that make up the articles in each of these smaller books we call genes. Finally, the tiniest of the divisions, the letters, if you will, are the base pairs of the spiral helix. Like the twenty-six letters of the alphabet, these genetic letters can be combined to form an infinity of meaning and information. Thus is the book of human life written, in the heart of the city of the cell. Do you understand?"

Cracker, who manifested as a very young man, though he had

recruited Morninglory to the cause many, many years before, said in his clear and trilling voice, "I could run a hundred thousand hacker programs before you come to the point, you old fool. Of course we understand. This is childish gibberish. What did you do?"

If anything, Cracker's insults caused The Fountain to slow down a bit. The Fountain, as the most brilliant scientist of the Pleb conspiracy, knew its own value. Perhaps too well sometimes, Jonathan mused.

"As in the Book of Jerusalem, there is space in the book of the genome that goes unused, or has things written that no one reads or understands. Yet if properly coded, the words of the genome will go out and work their will as inexorably as the codes that create blue eyes—or loudmouths, Cracker."

"Humph."

"What did I do? I put in a few new articles in young Endicott's genomic encyclopedia. Instructions of my own devising. It was very difficult."

"And why was that?" Jonathan asked.

"Because somebody had been there before me. Much of the space that should have been empty was filled, with genetic words and sentences—almost a whole sub-book's worth—so I had to work with what was left."

Rose Lovely spoke, her tone startled. "Are you saying that somebody has already encoded something in young Endicott's genome? What is it?"

The Fountain began to belch bluish phosphorescent slime that smoked thickly as it dropped to vanish in the nether regions below. "I have no idea," The Fountain said. "The code was of a level so complicated I doubt the legendary Mindslaver Arrays—even if they did exist—could unravel it."

There was a moment of deceptive silence: deceptive, for in their various ways, each of them conferred with others at extremely high speeds.

Cracker spoke. "You tried digital decryption, with no luck? Pity."

Aker Bilk said, "Are we giving away a great playing piece to our enemy, Fountain? Doubtless this code is what Delta seeks."

"To no avail, I assure you," The Fountain replied. "He can no more read Endicott's secrets than I can. At least, not in the time I will give him. Let me tell you what I have done."

"About time . . ." Cracker murmured.

"We know Delta has science equal to ours. Perhaps greater. We know he is suspicious and paranoid to his very bones. We know he will take young Endicott apart almost molecule by molecule before he allows him into his presence. So I have put there nothing for Delta to find. No secret chemicals, no hidden physical bombs, no complete bioviruses or dataviruses.

"I mixed my codes in with the others. Certain molecules within those codes are timed. They will only begin to carry out their instructions *after* Delta has finished with his examinations. The examinations themselves will be their triggers.

"As a further safeguard, the boy has been psychologically programmed without his knowledge. His body will release certain hormones only in the event he approaches Delta physically. The hormones will further trigger the process already begun by Delta's probes."

"And that process is what, you dithering ninny?" grated Cracker.

"Two-pronged. The Endicott boy's breath will become laden with chemical codes programmed to cause death in any male other than himself. Second, he will begin to manufacture free-floating codes programmed to attack electronic systems of all kinds. An interesting—and difficult—melding of biological and computer viruses. A cybernetic virus, if you will. It lives in air for half an hour. Should be long enough to find a host."

"And the boy. . . ?" Rose Lovely wondered aloud.

"Oh, the process will kill him. Eventually it will eat him alive. I rather imagine, though, that Delta will kill him before it ever comes to that. The results of the codes I've implanted are rather . . . spectacular. Delta will certainly understand what has happened in time to take some destructive action, before he himself succumbs."

Aker Bilk broke in. "Are you sure about all this?"

"As sure as we are likely to be, all things considered," Jonathan said. "We have all seen the correlation. Delta did not manage to stop Cat's chips from Morninglory getting through to us. They make our long-held suspicions nearly certain. Delta has some intimate connection with the Pleb Psychosis. So, it seems, does this Endicott brat, but no matter. Jim Endicott's true value to us is simple: he may be the first weapon we've ever had that can strike at Delta in the heart of his power. Win or lose, we can't afford to pass that up."

"Agreed," said Aker Bilk. "Yes," said Rose Lovely. "Okay," said Cracker. "Yes, yes, yes," said all the rest.

Now Jonathan smiled. "I will lead an attack on Delta myself, timed to synchronize with the triggering of Endicott's booby trap. If everything goes as we hope, Delta's impregnable fortress should be coming apart at the seams just about the time we hit it with everything we've got."

Rose Lovely breathed softly. "And if you're wrong?"

"Then I die," Jonathan said simply. "And so does Jimbo Endicott. The microscopic molecular machines inside him will have pretty much used him up by then to make our killer viruses, anyway—and so what? Eternal life isn't in anybody's contract. Not yet, at least."

And so in a myriad of electronic scratches and scrawls they agreed to the project and broke apart. Jonathan found himself sitting in a chair in an empty room, blinking at the fading memories of his conspirators made as real as he was ever likely to see them, these ghosts in their machines.

Now the ghosts would strike for flesh and blood. He raised his slender right hand and stared at it, shuddering at the desire in his own sere and damaged soul.

Lusting for the kill.

2

They stood on an open observation deck squinting at the sun that burned off the water into their eyes, with the salt wind whipping at their hair. Jim, his mouth hanging open, stared at the terrific apparition before him.

The North American Skysnake rose up from the Pacific Ocean forty miles west of San Francisco TerraPort. It and its four sisters were the largest constructions ever built by man. The idea was a simple one: place a satellite in stationary orbit above the earth and drop an elevator cable from it to the ground. Simple in concept, but huge and difficult in execution. This one, the first, had taken twenty years to build. But the Skysnakes were Terra's lifeline to space. Up and down their sinuous lengths traveled all of earth's cargo, in huge, gondola-like elevator barges the size of football fields that climbed and fell around cables 150 miles long.

Jim stared up in awe at the gigantic column that rose before him. "I came down that?" he whispered to Jonathan.

"Of course. Everything does. Most efficient cargo mover ever built," Jonathan said. He seemed distracted.

Jim nodded. "How much longer?" he asked.

"We're on the next barge," Jonathan said.

"And then . . . ?"

"When we get to the distribution satellite at the top, we'll meet a scooter ship from Delta's headquarters; his place, the CIA Command Satellite, Comsat One, is farther out. A three-hundred-mile orbit."

"That's where I'm going."

Jonathan shrugged. "I presume. All I want is to make the trade. What Delta does with you after that is up to him."

"What do you think he'll do?"

"I can't imagine. Up to now, it seems he's been trying to kill you." He shrugged again.

Jim nodded. He glanced around the wide platform. Here and there, trying to look unobtrusive, several guards of both sexes provided an ever-shifting protective screen for them.

"You're going up with me?" he asked.

Jonathan nodded. "Some things," he said, "if you want them done right, you have to do them yourself."

Jim shifted the weight of his backpack. It reminded him. He'd carried it all the way from Wolfbane. In it were the things he'd packed back when his life had been something entirely different. He felt a stab of loneliness, and a more sickening pang of hopelessness.

"I've still got my gun."

"Hmm?" Jonathan's eyes turned on him, glittering.

"My S&R .75. My dad gave it to me, back . . ." He trailed off, remembering the pain of that memory. "Will the detectors catch it?"

Jonathan grinned. "We're not going up like tourists, Jimbo. Plebs have resources. Don't worry, we'll get you and your antique hand cannon to the transfer in one piece." He paused. "Delta's people will pick it up, though."

Jim knew that, but the idea of the gun was comforting. Maybe somebody would make a mistake. Maybe, somehow, he would get to Delta and still have the .75 with him. And if so—?

He didn't know. Could he kill a man in cold blood? Perhaps. If it was the man who'd killed his father. The wind bit at him through his thin, ragged jacket, and he shivered suddenly.

"How much longer?" he asked.

"Soon, Jimmykins. Soon enough."

3

"Your name is Tabitha Endicott," Delta said.

She blinked, her mind still numb from days of questioning, from terror, from the tiny cell in which she'd been confined. Now she stood in a tall, shadowy room, and tried to think, tried to pull herself together.

Come on, Tabby . . . She nodded. "Who are you?"

"Mmm . . . call me Delta." The voice was booming, full of reassuring cheer. She watched as the shadowy figure behind the desk stood and, moving carefully, came around, away from the concealing glare, into the light. She stared into his face, not knowing it was her death sentence to see it plain.

Big man, with a big, bullet-shaped head. The skin of his face seemed curiously stretched; his lips were thick and wide, above a shovel-like chin. He was bald as an egg. His eyes were like half-buried black marbles, their fearsome attention fixed on her. He wore a beautifully tailored blue suit that did not quite disguise his heavy belly, but did accentuate his large, muscled shoulders. His hands were broad and thick-fingered. He looked like a wrestler, and moved like an overweight ballet dancer. He flapped his right hand at her.

"Sit down over there, on that sofa, Tabitha," he urged softly. "We need to talk about your son."

She had not expected so simple a sentence to cause her the agony it did, but the thought of Jimmy was like a blow. She had no idea what had happened. Carl had been a secretive man, and had carried his secrets into death, leaving her behind. She knew Carl was dead. She didn't know how she knew: her last memories were of throwing herself at a huge, armored figure, and then sudden, blinding pain. She'd awakened in her tiny cell, feeling in her core only the hollow sense of loss where her love for Carl Endicott had once been.

But . . . Jimmy! She felt the two guards turn her, gently, as if she were an invalid, and guide her to the sofa. She sat, her heart racing. She looked up at the big man treading toward her, his balloon face wreathed in an impossibly oily smile.

"Jimmy . . . ? What about my boy? Is he all right?"

Delta seated himself with great care in a large chair across from her. He folded his thick fingers across his broad belly and sighed. "I'm afraid there are some . . . problems."

Panic stabbed through her foggy thoughts. "What do you—talk to me, damn it! Tell me the truth! *Is Jimmy okay*?"

She half rose from the sofa, but, from behind, heavy hands pressed her back down. She squirmed against the pressure a moment, then subsided, breathing hard.

"Now, calm down, Tabitha. The boy is all right, at least he was the last I heard. And guess what? He's coming here. Quite soon, in fact." Delta nodded to himself. "Yes, I'd say the two of you will be together quite shortly. There. Is that good enough for you?"

Wildly, she searched his features. He was smiling, everything about him signaled solace and encouragement, and yet she couldn't shake the feeling that she was in immediate danger, that there was something deeply evil about the man sitting before her.

She knew she shouldn't let any of this show. Somehow, she had to think her way out of this, as best she could. "Can you . . . tell me what happened? Why I'm here? Did you have something to do with why those people attacked my family?" She stopped, struggled with the question, then went on: "Is Carl . . . my husband . . . dead?"

He listened attentively, nodding as she spoke, then steepled his fingers beneath his chin. The way he did it, she got the idea it was a habitual gesture, one he didn't notice even as he did it.

His expression turned serious, even grave. "Your husband is dead, Tabitha. I am so sorry."

Even though she knew it, to have the news delivered so baldly was a naked thrust to her heart, and she gasped. She managed to choke back any sound, but tears began to roll silently down her cheeks.

"It was a mistake," he went on, as he watched her. Something in him stirred. "Your husband had . . . reflexes that, in the end, served him badly. He resisted the team I sent to pick you up—resisted violently, I'm afraid, with predictable results. I didn't intend for him to die, Tabitha. I didn't intend for anybody to die. You must believe that."

But she didn't. He sounded plausible, but even in her shattered state, she heard the fraudulent undercurrents beneath his words. And following that idea, she suddenly understood how deadly a situation she was in.

Keep him talking, she told herself. *Anything, any one little thing, might be valuable. He hasn't killed me yet. There must be a reason.*

Yet she felt so *helpless*, and if she blamed Carl Endicott for anything, it was that. He had not told her the things she'd needed to know. He was a secretive man, but some secrets he should have shared. He hadn't, and look at her now. She had no idea why this nightmare had happened, no idea how—or if—there was any way out for her. *Or for Jimmy*, she thought suddenly, remembering he was supposedly on his way here—and when Delta had told her that, she had felt the ring of truth in his words.

"I don't understand . . ." she whispered finally. "*Why* did you send people to get us? Why like that? You could have sent . . . oh, I don't know, a letter. Or regular policemen. You're a powerful man, aren't you? Somebody high up? How could we have resisted?"

He said dryly, "Tabitha, you may or may not know it, but your husband was a dangerous man. A trained killer. If you recall, he resisted quite effectively."

She knew that even this, so brutal and straightforward, was a lie. May or may not know? She thought this man knew everything she had ever known, knew it as intimately at the tips of those blunt fingers he seemed so intent on examining now.

"Be that as it may," Delta continued, "it doesn't solve the current problem. I can't tell you why my . . . agency needed to speak with you, but I can say that you, Tabitha, are not involved. I've verified that to my satisfaction. On the other hand, all the indications I have now say that your son, Jimmy, is of crucial importance to me. So why don't we talk about him?"

"Jimmy is just a boy, Mister—Delta. Sixteen years old. How can he be important to you, to anybody?" And she wanted to scream at the top of her lungs—*Are you crazy?*—but she didn't. She had a feeling they both understood the answer all too well.

Delta moved his big shoulders quickly, a surprisingly delicate shrugging motion.

Behind his outward concern, he had been watching her.

Beautiful woman, really, with her fluffy blond hair shot with streaks of silver, her clear skin, her frank, unassuming, ocean-colored gaze. And there was a strength to her as well; small and thin-framed, but tough. A fighter. He could see it in her, in the way she tensed, in the way she seemed almost coiled. Perhaps even a dangerous strength?

It excited him, and he was puzzled at that. Very little excited him these days. Then he understood; though they were different, there was a sameness between her and another woman, long dead. A woman he had loved, a woman he still, in some twisted way, loved even now.

Carl Endicott had possessed both these women. Had stolen—*stolen!*—the first, and found the second. This was Carl's woman, and in many ways she reminded him of Carl's first woman. No doubt Carl had seen the similarity, too. Had he been introspective enough for that?

Possibly. But Carl was dead now, and his woman sat before him, helpless. And once again he felt that curious, powerful attraction—an *urge*. Could Tabitha Endicott see or understand the long skein of the past, which had led her unwittingly but inexorably to this moment?

The temptation to unburden himself was suddenly overpowering. After all, what harm? She would never leave this place alive. She belonged to him utterly, whether she knew it or not. But nobody knew the whole story but himself, and the dead. The dead could no longer speak . . . but he could.

Finally, he wanted to talk to her, just as one person to another. Modern interrogation was thorough, but it was still, in some ways, a blunt instrument. Chemicals and dreams dulled the mind. Opening the secret doors revealed the truth, but only if you knew what to ask for. He had asked everything he could think of, and come up empty. Yet there might still be hidden pockets of truth. And perhaps, in something so basic as simple conversation, he could find one or two . . .

I'm a fool, he told himself, but he went on anyway. There was time yet, even time for foolishness. He leaned forward.

"Sixteen . . ." he mused softly. "Let me tell you what happened, Tabitha, more than sixteen years ago."

4

Steele led the small group of special tactics forces out into the open space of the broad reaches of the distribution satellite that anchored the orbiting end of the Skysnake. It had been an uneventful trip over from Comsat One, but in the back of her mind she remembered Delta's prediction of the upheavals to come.

She wasn't privy to his plans, but she believed in taking as few chances as possible. Plebs were not generally employed in the satellites—the satellites were too important as Terra's lifelines to allow any possibility of disruption—but there had been instances of Pleb Psychosis even here. Her team, though in civvies and innocuous-seeming, was armed heavily enough to handle anything she could foresee.

She hadn't foreseen this.

It was plain to her trained military senses the moment she stepped into the vast concourse, with its bustling crowds transferring from one ship to another, chattering and buzzing, a thunder of noise in the enclosed space.

There was a good-sized battalion of armed people here—she'd walked into a trap!

She couldn't tell anybody precisely how she knew it. She spotted Jim Endicott right away, standing near the center of the swirling crowds next to an older man who looked like a psychotic accountant. And that man was familiar, too, wasn't he?

She pushed that thought aside, concentrating on the ominous signs she understood better. There was a random, almost Brownian motion to moving crowds, like stray molecules ceaselessly bumping against each other. But she saw the others—many others—who seemed to move, but didn't. They drifted back and forth, but always in a circle of a few feet, and held their positions against the flow of bodies. And all of their eyes were watching her.

She'd brought six of her best people. But there were at least fifty of these watchers scattered about, fifty that she could see, and God only knew how many more concealed away from her line of vision.

She tapped the side of her throat and spoke subvocally into the microphone embedded there.

"Heads up, people. This isn't what we expected."

Quickly, she told them what she saw, and gave a rapid series of orders. Her team closed in around her, taking up their own unobtrusive positions.

Steele swept the area again and saw that her team's movements had been echoed by the others. What the hell was going on here? Hell of a place for a firefight . . .

She took a deep breath and marched up to Jim Endicott and his lethal-looking friend.

"You're James Endicott?" she said abruptly.

It startled him, she could tell. He whirled, his mouth falling open. "Uh. Yes, I'm him."

He was so puppy-dog jumpy that she almost laughed in his face, but then she remembered that this puppy had already demonstrated teeth. And the one next to him was no laughing matter at all. Steele, who'd dealt with her share of bad people, knew a monster when she saw one.

She nodded at this one. "I'm Steele," she said. "You ready to do the trade?"

Jonathan eyed her with his vague, watery gaze. "I know who you are," he murmured. Steele felt the flesh on her arms begin to crawl.

"What is this?" she said suddenly. "You've got too many people here . . ."

Jonathan inclined his head slightly. "Would your own master travel with any less?" He looked around, taking his count of her escort. "Where's the girl?" he asked abruptly.

"She's here," Steele replied.

"Bring her out, then."

"Not so fast. You have too many people."

Jonathan stared at her. "It's a trade, Steele. That's all it is. You can have the kid." He jabbed Jim in the shoulder, pushed him forward. "Go on, take him. He's yours."

Steele nodded, started to turn.

"Wait. The girl." Jonathan paused. "This is why so many, Steele. You can have the boy, but *I want the girl.* And you won't get ten steps unless I have her. Do you see it?"

Steele stopped, waited, then moved her head in assent. "Yes. Hold your britches, then." Her lips moved. Everybody waited.

Two more special forces people appeared at the far edge of the concourse, supporting a dazed-looking Cat between them.

"It's a harmless sedative," Steele said quickly. "To keep her from getting in any trouble. Wears off in an hour or so."

Jonathan nodded. "Okay, then. Off you go."

Several people who otherwise looked like simple travelers gathered around Cat. Her two escorts peeled away and moved toward Steele, who led Jim back the way she had come. She watched the boy as he passed the girl at some distance. His hand moved as if to wave, then dropped aimlessly to his side.

She recognized the expression on his face. *Poor bastard, he's in love,* she thought, pitying him. Then she remembered all her dead, and the moment passed.

"Let's go, you," she said.

Jim had been moving as if dazed, but the sound of her voice stopped him. He turned and stared at her.

"I know you," he said.

"I know you, too," she replied.

No two wolves, legs stiff, backs rigid, and fur bristling, had ever done it better.

CHAPTER 12

1

"More than sixteen years ago, Tabitha . . ." Delta mused. "Two very gifted scientists, a man and a woman, made an amazing discovery. It took them years, but, in the end, they were successful beyond their wildest dreams. They learned how to join human minds into a linked computer array. Picture it!"

Tabitha squirmed on the sofa. Delta's face had grown hot, swollen; emotions that frightened her boiled beneath his stretched, reddened skin. His eyes were fiery black dots. She stared at him.

His words began to tumble over themselves. A thin line of saliva leaked from the corner of his mouth.

"The human mind is the most complicated computer we know of, Tabitha. And those two scientists had figured out how to link thousands—no, millions!—of them into one huge thinking machine. It was the single greatest discovery humankind had ever achieved."

Suddenly he subsided. He lifted his big hands, then dropped them into his lap. "But one of the scientists—the woman—could only see the drawbacks. You see, there were problems. The other—the man—saw the potential, saw what the discovery of the mind arrays could mean for humanity's future, but she couldn't see it."

He sighed heavily. "It seems," he went on, "that when the linkages were made and the array created, the individual minds, though properly functioning, underwent a kind of psychosis. Unconsciously, those minds contributed their individual powers to the array, but some part of them couldn't take the pressure, and became violently disoriented. A linkage-induced psychosis. You see?"

She shook her head. What she saw was a kind of madness. Linked minds? Mind arrays? What did such things have to do with her?

He saw the puzzlement in her features and smiled faintly. "The two scientists argued. The man said that it didn't matter, that this psychosis was a small price to pay for the great gift of the arrays themselves." He stopped, glanced at her. "You have to understand the situation, Tabitha.

"Humanity had been in space for generations—and we were failing. All around us were the others, the aliens, races older and more established than we were. Our science was puny compared to theirs. Their machines were greater than ours. We were second-class citizens in the galaxy—no, make that third-class." He grinned. "Trash is what we were. Dependent on their kindness. I could see—the man could see—where that road was leading us. But no more! The mind arrays finally gave humanity the hole card it needed. We could use them to advance our science in unimaginable leaps and bounds!"

She blinked. The concept—human minds enslaved in some awful cybernetic link—horrified her. "Did those poor—did the people who went crazy know what was happening to them?"

His lips narrowed. "What does it matter? The fact is that it worked, Tabitha. If there was some pain, it was better than not having the mind arrays at all. Tabitha, we are talking about the survival of the human race! The ends justify the means, Tabitha. They always have, and they always will."

She looked down at her hands, so she wouldn't have to look at him. She thought she had never heard a better definition of pure evil: that the ends justified the means. Behind those few words were every monstrous thing that humankind had ever done to itself. He sickened her. But she couldn't let him see it.

And she wanted to keep him talking, had to keep him talking. "These . . . mind arrays. Did you keep those people locked up?"

He responded with a huge smile. "Oh, Tabitha. It's much better than that. The links, the connectors, were childishly simple. I . . . retired . . . the original subjects. I didn't want just a few links. I wanted millions! And it was so easy to find them. Can you guess where?"

She shook her head.

"All over the earth were useless humans. Surplus of the technological age. The Plebs, doing themselves and humanity no good at all. Parasites. Many of them addicts of the worst sort. Wireheaders. Content to—how do they say it?—plug in, turn off." He smiled bitterly. "So it was self-selecting. I arranged it so that 90 percent of the wirehead sockets implanted in those useless people were links to the arrays. They picked themselves, Tabitha! They chose to drop out of the human race, and by their choice, they gave me the way to save it, instead. Imagine that . . ."

And he smiled again, so obviously pleased with the elegance of his solution that it was all she could do—imagining the vast damage the Pleb Psychosis had wreaked on those helpless victims—to keep from spitting in his obscene face. Everybody knew about the psychosis. Now she knew what caused it—and understood that he could not let her live.

But her own plight paled before what this man had done. Had she thought of Stalin, Hitler, Vos Valt? Compared to this monster before her, they were children, harmless infants.

"Yes . . ." she mumbled. "I suppose so." And bit down hard on her urge to vomit. "So what happened to the woman?"

"What happened? Oh, many things happened. Did I tell you that the two scientists loved each other? The man would have brought the woman around, given time. After all, he was right, and eventually she would have seen it. But there was a third person, another man."

He stopped, and now that dull brick glow began to rise from his neck again, as he thought about it. "Yes, another man. A soldier, a killer, brought in to supervise security for the project. He worked closely with the two scientists, perhaps too closely. As it happened, the woman began to confide her silly fears to him. And—this from a man who should have understood, who should have put the safety of humanity above such petty things—this soldier, this cheap killer *agreed* with her."

Good for him, Tabitha thought. *Whoever he was.*

He chuckled. She'd never heard such a mirthless sound. Delta made that odd shrugging motion again. "Well, you can guess what happened. She turned to this soldier, and the two of them conspired against the other scientist. The soldier twisted her against the man she truly loved, and eventually, he stole her away entirely."

"That's . . . terrible," Tabitha said. And it was a terrible story, though not in the way Delta evidently thought she meant it.

He closed his eyes. He hadn't been wrong. Carl Endicott had stayed true to form. This was a woman like his long-dead Kate. Maybe there was room for some kinship, some feeling, even here. Maybe he wouldn't have to kill her . . .

"Yes," he continued, that hot eagerness seizing him again. "She ran away with him. She betrayed everything she knew—her true love, her science, the human race itself. She let him fill her with a child, and she tried to destroy the project itself. She let loose a virus that should have destroyed everything in the project computers—but she'd underestimated the man she dishonored with her squalid lust.

He—I—caught it in time, though undoing what she'd done took so much of my concentration, of my energies, that she was able to make good her escape, she and her killer man and their child." An expression of disgust filtered across his heavy, swollen features. "She even tried to pretend the brat was mine . . ."

He looked up at her then, his eyes bright as those of a hungry bird. "Your adopted son, Tabitha, and your husband. That cheap killer, Carl Endicott, and little Jimmy Endicott. I found them once, but Carl and the boy escaped."

He stopped, suddenly empty. "Now do you understand?"

Her heart leaped. She'd never been prouder of Carl Endicott, nor loved him more, in her whole life.

"Yes," she said softly. "I understand."

Perhaps Delta heard something in her tone, because his expression tightened. He stared at her a moment, almost as if disappointed in something, though she couldn't imagine what. He waited a beat, then shook his head.

"Well, now you know what my interest is. I've searched for them, the boy and the man, even while I used the mind arrays to rise to my present . . . position. I knew that if I waited long enough, the man would make a mistake. As it turned out, I was wrong. It was the boy that gave them away. It was Jimmy."

"That application to the Space Academy . . ." Tabitha said, suddenly understanding it all. And wishing once again that Carl had confided in her, though now knowing why he hadn't. His intentions had been good, but the road to hell was paved with good intentions. Poor, desperate Carl!

"Yes, that application. Of course all government data systems are open to me. Jimmy's and Carl's genotypes stood out like a pig's in a bowl of soup. And when I examined them, I realized that the dead woman I loved had not been content to try to destroy me. She'd left something else behind—and do you know where she hid it?"

Slowly, Tabitha shook her head.

Delta clapped his hands, a sharp, popping sound of triumph. "In Jimmy Endicott's DNA. She had the knowledge, she had the tools. She had the boy, and she hid her filthy secrets in him, and now, Tabitha, I *will* know what they are!"

He stopped for a breath, an expression on his features of surprise, almost astonishment, at his own passion. "I have used that discovery to nurture, to protect humanity in a hostile universe for almost sixteen years. These fools and their wish to align with the aliens who will destroy them, this federation they want to create . . ." He shook his head sadly. "Well, they are fools, but I am not. And I will not let the hand of that dead woman jeopardize all my work, jeopardize even humanity itself . . ." Suddenly he realized to whom he was speaking, and his voice softened. "Even if it means Jimmy's—"

"Yes," she said dully. "I know. The ends justify the means . . ."

He smiled. "Exactly."

2

Steele slipped a pair of plastic cuffs on Jim as she backed him away from Jonathan. "I'll take that," she told him, and lifted his backpack from his shoulders. "Hmm? Don't like that? Something you want inside? Ah."

She fished out the S&R .75 and grinned at him. "Pretty big gun for such a little guy."

Jim stared at her face, now clear, but dimly remembered from the fire and flash of that awful night on the mountainside. The circle had come fully around: this was what his father had died to prevent.

He felt a flash of regret, and quickly rejected it. He was here by his own choice. Well, maybe. He sort of suspected Jonathan might have made the decision for him, had he decided other than he had. But no matter. Cat was safe. That was what mattered.

"Where are we going?" he asked.

"To see a man about a dog," Steele told him, and flipped him a nasty grin. "And after that, maybe you're going to see me."

All this time their little group had been working its way out of the humming concourse. Jim didn't have Steele's experience, but even he sensed that they were the focus of many watchful eyes.

"What's happening?" he asked, as they reached the edge, then turned and began to march briskly down a long, gray tunnel. As soon as they were within its protective confines, Steele seemed to relax a bit.

She glanced at him. "Despite my initial misgivings," she told him, "it looks like what's happening is that we're gonna get our butts out of here. And that suits me just fine."

Jim nodded as their pace quickened. He straightened himself and squared his shoulders. Whatever was coming, he planned to face it head-on.

He was sure his father would have done the same thing.

3

Jonathan watched the little group vanish into the eddying crowds at the edge of the concourse, a vague smile twitching his lips. When they were gone, he touched his throat mike and got busy.

"Status on the barge, please," he murmured.

A burst of voices, quickly overridden by his command frequency. "All stations secured. Ready on your mark."

Jonathan glanced at his thumbnail watch and counted seconds. He took a deep breath, wondering if this would be his last mission. He didn't really care, as long as it was a successful one. The analysis had not been one hundred percent certain, no analysis could be. But within absolute limits, everything pointed to Delta. And Delta, even if he wasn't the prime mover behind the Pleb Psychosis, had done enough harm to his people over the years that, if ever a man needed killing, Delta was that man.

All in all, even if he didn't survive, it would be a most satisfactory way to exit, stage left.

"Okay, people, let's do it. On my mark . . . mark!"

The distribution satellite shuddered. Then the lights went out. In the dark, the crowds began to scream, a primal, shrieking sound that raised the hairs on Jonathan's neck.

He flipped on a pair of glasses that spread a map of the satellite across his vision, and began to make his way through the crowds.

The Skysnake raised and lowered vast cargo barges. At the top, here, the football-field-sized containers detached, became huge, lumbering cargo ships, and made their way to waiting star cruisers.

In a few seconds they would own one such barge. It would make a dandy landing craft for the small army he'd brought with him.

His thoughts turned incandescent as he thought of Delta. The killing rage took him then, which was as it should be: all the others of the Pleb leadership had specific talents. He did, too.

He was their killer.

4

Steele felt the jolt as Jonathan's attack shut down much of the power on the distribution satellite. She began to run.

"Come on, out of here!"

They dived through an entry hatch at the end of the tunnel, then into a long, flexible boarding tube. The lights were out here, too, but a faint, phosphorescent glow from the emergency glowstrips lighted their way.

They dived pell-mell through the open spacelock at the end of the tube, Steele sputtering orders as she moved. Jim felt himself lifted, tossed like a sack of flour, and then he slammed into a steel wall. He was suddenly weightless: the abrupt transition brought a belch of bile into his throat.

Alarms rang. He lay stunned a moment, watching the spacelock cycle shut. Then somebody grabbed him, dragged him up a ladder, and thrust him into a small chamber. He looked around: a head, cramped toilet facilities. But there was a lock on the door. He heard it snick shut.

A moment later, the ghostly hand of acceleration pressed him against the deck. It wasn't very strong, nor did it last more than a few seconds, or he might have been badly hurt. As it was, he tried to stand up, but his shackled hands betrayed him, and he slipped, banging his head. So it was with ringing in his ears and stars whirling in his eyes that he started the last leg of his long, strange trip.

The circle finally complete, the snake eating its tail.

Back to the beginning.

5

Cat shook her head, trying to jar the cobwebs out. She had passed from Steele's care into Jonathan's hands in one smooth transfer, and had barely noticed Jim heading the other way. Something must have sparked, though, because now she remembered how his hand has risen in greeting, then fallen again. Waving. Waving at her.

"Jonathan!" she screamed suddenly, caught in the grip of a pair of Plebs. "What have you done!"

But Jonathan wasn't there, and if he was listening somehow, he didn't make any reply.

Now, an hour later, she stood in the vast, echoing emptiness of a cargo barge and watched an army of Plebs make ready to go to war.

Everybody seemed to have forgotten her. Her two rescuers had brought her here and left her sitting on a low pile of soft tarps, and here she had stayed while her senses gradually began to clear, to sharpen again.

For the past several minutes she'd felt almost normal, though there was an undercurrent of fear in her mind: what had Delta done to her? Had the interrogators damaged her permanently?

And Jonathan. What the hell was he doing? God only knew what kind of sensors Delta had hidden inside her. It wasn't inconceivable that everything she saw with her own eyes, heard with her own ears, was somehow being directly relayed to Delta himself.

"Jonathan!" she shouted, and this time she saw him turn, in the center of his small group, and glance over at her.

Grunting, she pushed herself up. Her legs weren't quite right yet, it felt as if she was walking through sludgy water, but she kept on. He watched her as she came, that infuriating smile on his oatmeal face, and made no move to help. He just waited.

So like him, she thought suddenly, and realized that she'd never really liked him at all. She wondered why this would come to her now, as she stumbled toward him, and then she knew: comparison.

Jim Endicott wasn't like that. Jim wouldn't watch her with that clinical scorn, as if she were little more than some interesting bug. Jim would have come to her, helped her, done anything he could. And he would have never looked at her with that expression on his face.

"Jonathan . . ." she said, as she finally reached the group, and it parted, letting her in.

"What, Cat? I'm busy . . . got a little assault here to run."

"Is that what this is? An assault? Jonathan, have you lost your mind?"

He stared at her, waiting.

She licked her lips, trying to pull herself together. "Jonathan, I'm probably bugged six ways to hell. Delta wouldn't let a chance like that go to waste."

He grinned. "Is that it? Listen, little sister, don't worry about it. Of course he bugged you. Didn't you notice those two dudes with the hand scanners? You lighted them up like Christmas at the Confederation Center."

She still didn't get it. "Then he knows? Delta knows what you're doing?"

He glanced at the others, then back. "Maybe . . ."

"What do you mean, maybe?"

"Listen, Cat, why don't go back over there, sit down, rest up a bit. Things'll start to get hot soon enough."

"Jonathan . . . what's going on here? What did you do?"

He gave her one final hard glare and turned away. But she wasn't having that. She grabbed his shoulder, jerked him around. "Jonathan, *talk* to me, damn it!"

He whirled, some of the milkiness gone from his eyes. "What the hell, Cat? You think two can't play at Delta's game? We made a trade, understand? You for your boyfriend. You for Jim Endicott!"

And then she got it. Something hard and cold fell into the bottom of her belly. "What did you do to him? What did you do to Jim?"

He raised his hands, flapped them as if to shoo her off. "Go sit down, Cat. Nothing you can do about it anyway . . ."

"*What did you do, you frigid bastard?*"

He sighed. "I did what I had to. A couple of microvirus assemblers, a little of this, a little of that. Put it this way. Delta's about to get one hell of a surprise when he unwraps our little package."

She froze. "Microviruses? But . . . there's only one way to get something like that past Delta's scanners. . . ."

"What's your problem, Cat? You'll find another guy to play snuggle with. Hell, there's a million of us out there. Now go on, get the hell away from me, leave me alone. I've got work to do!"

She slugged him in the mouth with every ounce of weight she could put behind it, but all that bought her was a quick trip back to her tarps.

"Look, Cat, I understand where you're coming from, okay?" said the tall blond man, one of Jonathan's bodyguards, who'd wrestled her away from Jonathan. "But don't pull a stunt like that again, or I really will put you down the next time. I mean it, all right?"

Sullenly, she nodded, as she pulled her knees up against her chest. "Bastard . . ." she mumbled.

"What's that?"

"Nothing. Go away. Leave me alone."

He eyed her, then stepped back, but not too far. Jonathan came over and spoke quietly to him. They both looked at her.

Obviously, she was now a prisoner. Jonathan didn't trust her. And he was right, she thought. She would betray him in an instant if she could save Jim. She put her head down on top of her knees and closed her eyes. Poor Jim. Delta would . . .

She shivered. The ghost of an idea began to form, and she raised her head slightly. Her guard was back, looking slightly sheepish.

"Jonathan," he said. "He told me to stick with you. He's worried you might try something . . . stupid."

Blinking back tears, she forced herself to smile up at him. "Well, sit down, then. It's Joey, right? So, Joey, I guess if you gotta keep me prisoner, you might as well get comfortable."

They were still sitting there, half an hour later, Joey glancing at her uncomfortably every once in a while, when the lights of the vast barge flickered and she felt the whispery lash of acceleration.

Whatever was going to happen, it had begun.

6

One hundred fifty miles farther out, Delta smiled, his eyes coals in the furnace of his face.

"Jim Endicott!" he boomed. "You have no idea how pleased I am to finally *meet* you."

CHAPTER 13

1

Jim stared up at Delta, at that horror of a face, stretched tight and gleaming with good cheer. To Jim, Delta looked insanely happy, but the insanity definitely had the upper hand. And, yes, he remembered him. Not the face that loomed over him where he lay, strapped to an examination table while machines chattered and hummed as they combed every inch of his body for hidden surprises, but a younger, rougher, more human version. Somehow, somewhere, this man had sung lullabies to him.

The memory was not now a comforting one. Yet, oddly, with the memory came another, almost as an overlay on that grinning hobgoblin: once, beneath the bloated flesh he saw had been another man. A man of high and serious purpose, whose purpose had been reflected even in his bones and skin. He could see it now, though of course he'd been too young then. But still he knew it: once there had been beauty in those features, perhaps heroic beauty, and still the ghost remained. That was the most horrifying thing of all, the terrible ruin of what had once been lofty and pure, the thing maybe only he could see.

Delta paused, hovering, and leaned that face down until Jim could see the lines hidden underneath those balloon-skin features, could smell the sweet, chemical odor of his damp breath.

"Well . . . hmm. It looks like they didn't put anything too nasty in you, Jim. A couple of amateurish monitor things." He withdrew, sighing, and added, "I suppose I shouldn't have worried. They are Plebs, after all."

"Let me up," Jim said. The examination hadn't been painful, nor had he lost consciousness during it, or at least if he had, he hadn't noticed. He had, however, remained transfixed by the sight of Delta, the man gliding about like some huge, demented ballerina, humming to himself, muttering occasionally, but always coming back, always bending low to examine Jim as if he were some exotic specimen of insect or animal, stretched upon the table for his own private amusement. And he did seem amused, Delta did. His smile remained almost constant, high, wide, and radiant, and that was the scariest thing of all. The triumph in it.

But Jim couldn't read it, couldn't figure out why Delta seemed so *happy* with everything. And then, abruptly, he couldn't look at him anymore, and turned his face away, to the side. Tried not to think about Delta for a moment, since there wasn't anything he could do about him anyway. Better to try to learn what he could, see if there was anything that might offer some hope of escape.

The room was lighted like an operating theater. The entire ceiling spilled down a diffuse waterfall of white light, banishing shadows, making the brushed steel and aluminum of computer housings, data screens, holographic generators, and all the rest of the equipment glow as if lighted from the inside.

It had the feel of a laboratory, a place where science of some kind was done. The only jarring note was the slick stainless table on which he lay, shackled with leather cuffs at ankle and wrist, with a pair of wider straps across his chest and pelvis. He'd already tried: there was no give in his bindings at all.

"Comfortable, Jim?" Delta murmured. "Don't worry, we're almost finished here, just have to make sure, is all. Then we can sit down and have a nice talk. You'd like that, wouldn't you? A nice talk?"

Jim had the feeling that even if he replied to this, Delta wouldn't hear him. The man seemed lost in some inner world of his own, seeing things far away, or long, long ago.

A large, black metal device slid on ceiling railings from one side and halted directly above him. It made a whirring sound, and extruded a long probe that had a glass tip on the end. He flinched, but the probe stopped about an inch from his skin and, with a sharp, ratcheting sound, began to trace the contours of his body.

"Last thing, Jim. We're almost done," Delta caroled.

Jim imagined he could *feel* whatever bizarre rays or frequencies the probe thrust into him, tickling his cells, massaging his molecules. Or was it his imagination? There really was no sensation, but still . . . somehow, on some deep level, he knew that strange, arcane processes had begun to take place inside him. Almost as if the probe had triggered something . . .

He drew in a quick breath and tried not to think about such things. No doubt his mind, already keyed to a fever pitch, had begun to play tricks on him. His throat began to itch. Nervously, he coughed.

And a cloud of tiny engines, so small that millions could fit inside a single human cell, burst out of his mouth and throat, riding on minuscule aerosolized bubbles of moisture, floating away from his lips in invisible clouds, spreading out, some searching for other male human hosts, others for ways into the vast network of computers that maintained Comsat One.

And some equally small part of himself vanished, taken and remade into those molecules, and now the process began to accelerate. He didn't know it, but the tiny machines that The Fountain had encoded into his DNA had begun to eat him alive. . . .

Delta drifted back, still grinning like a Halloween pumpkin, and Jim looked up, looked into that broad, sweating face, and said, "I know you."

2

"We got lift-off," Jonathan announced to the small circle of lieutenants surrounding him, as they all felt the ghostly hand of slow acceleration. Jonathan seemed calm, almost amused, though his doughy features were serious. "We should make Comsat One in exactly . . ." He checked his thumbnail watch. "Forty-three minutes."

"Jesus," a tall man with a bright purple wen on his left cheek, under his eye, said. "Is that enough time? We get it wrong, they'll blow this washtub out of space so quick . . ."

Jonathan eyed him. "Our techs already got the go. The kid made it in, and evidently Delta triggered the nanotech stuff inside him. Some of it's already out, into Comsat's computer systems. Delta's own systems sent the message."

"Nanotech?" the tall man said, doubtfully.

Jonathan eyed him sideways. "Subcellular machines. Computers a few molecules in diameter, cellular machines a billionth the size of a human hair. Don't worry about it, Haller. They work okay."

Haller nodded. "Just so they do. This ain't gonna be easy, even so."

"Why, hell, Haller." Jonathan slapped him on the back. "I don't remember telling you it was gonna be *easy*."

The huge barge plodded on, inexorable as an avalanche.

3

"You know me, hmm?" Delta said, as he unstrapped Jim from the table, then reached out one beefy arm and helped him to sit up. "Wait a minute, let the circulation come back into your hands and feet. Pins and needles, right?"

Jim nodded, rubbing his hands together.

"So where do you think you know me from? Seen my picture someplace, is that it?"

Jim shook his head. "No. I . . . remember you."

Delta's eyebrows rose and wiggled slightly above his beak of a nose.

"Remember me? How can that be?"

"I don't know," Jim said. "But I do. You're younger, somehow. Your face is thinner. But I remember you. You used to sing to me."

Delta turned away quickly. He didn't want Jim to see his face, see the shock he felt blooming there. Because the memory suddenly filled his mind, dragging him back willy-nilly to a time and place and even a person far different than the man he now was.

Yes, he had sung to the baby Jim . . . and it was not a place to which he was willing to return. But he couldn't help himself, and back he went, astonished at his own helplessness in the face of the boy's simple words.

You used to sing to me . . .

Delta closed his eyes and was there, *living it again*, when his body was slimmer and his name was more real than a word that meant only a symbol. When he'd thought the boy was his, and not knowing the truth, he'd cradled the tiny, delicate form in his big hands and felt the life, imagined he felt his own blood, throbbing in the flesh he'd believed was his own.

My son . . .

And Kate was there as well, sweet, burning Kate, and he saw her as she had been, before she disfigured her own image in his mind forever:

Thin, muscular, aflame with intensity, her great intelligence lighting her sharp features from within like an ocean of candles, her lion-colored hair unkempt from where she ran her fingers distractedly through it. Her expression concentrated, focused, watching him, watching the baby . . .

"What's that?" she asked.

He looked up, across the room in the dim light, picking her watchfulness from the shadows. "Scottish folk song. My grandmama used to sing it to me . . ."

"Sweet," she said. "A pretty song."

Jimmy stirred in his hands, his rosebud lips twisting, his eyes squeezed fiercely shut in his pink face, wanting more, more song, more proof of love. Delta smiled down on him, joggled him a bit, and began to sing again, knowing how much he loved them both, his woman, his boy-child, his perfect life . . .

"Tcha!" He shook his head as he came back, sliding down the chute of the years, landing finally in this hard room sixteen years later, standing in the bright lights and the hard glare of Jim's accusing gaze.

"That was . . . a long time ago, Jim," he said. "It doesn't make any difference now. I knew you. I knew your mother. Of course I did—and you remember me? The human mind is amazing, isn't it?"

And he chuckled, because it was better than weeping, or putting his big hands around this boy's neck and squeezing until he'd utterly destroyed the final evidence of that woman's treachery.

The betrayal of love. He stared at the boy, wondering what was going on behind that green gaze, so angry and opaque. Did the boy hate him? Of course he did. He must. He'd killed the boy's father, and Jim knew it. He had won, in the end, and Jim's presence in this room was tangible proof of that triumph. So why didn't he feel triumph? Instead of what he did feel: sadness, betrayal, disgust—and an endless *wistfulness* for what might have been, for the lost years that could have put an entirely different expression on the face of this boy he'd once loved with all his heart.

But he'd sacrificed them, hadn't he? Sacrificed the woman, sacrificed the boy on the altar of the greater good, on the altar of duty to his species, on the altar of the ends that must, that *had to* justify the means. Had to justify the *sacrifice* . . .

The aliens had been pressing in, with their terrible science, so far advanced. He'd had no choice, really . . .

Who could blame him? He had no illusions. Still, he'd expected anything but this. This terrible emptiness.

"You knew my real mother?" Jim whispered.

Delta stared at him. "Yes," he said finally. "I did."

Jim nodded. "Can you tell me about her?"

4

Jim had no idea why he'd suddenly asked that question: from the expression on Delta's face, it wasn't anything he'd expected to answer. Well, that was fine: it wasn't any question Jim had expected to ask. And then, as he stared into Delta's moonfaced features, he realized that it was *exactly* the question he'd expected to ask, had been hoping and *praying* to ask ever since Tabitha had let slip the truths that had turned his life upside down.

I'm not your mother, and perhaps your father isn't your father, and maybe . . . you aren't even you.

Childish nonsense, Jim thought. *I am me, who else could I be?* But the certainty wasn't reassuring, not as he stared at Delta and realized that yes, this man could, if he chose to, answer those questions. For without a doubt, Delta, whoever else he might be, had been a man who'd known them both, his real mother, and Carl Endicott, who might or might not be his father. Jim had known Carl, too—but only for sixteen years. All his life he'd believed that was enough, that he knew all he needed to know—only to learn, in the final moments of Carl Endicott's life, that he knew almost nothing. Nothing, at least, of the most important part of Carl's life: the time before, the time that answered all the unanswered questions Carl had left behind.

He sat on the edge of the table, hunched slightly forward, his elbows resting flat on his thighs, hands dangling awkwardly between his knees, waiting.

Delta started to speak, stopped himself, pursed his lips. Unconsciously, he raised his hands in a warding motion, then let them fall. He exhaled.

"Do you know? I just had a surprising experience. I was going to tell you about your mother, about what a treacherous, evil woman she was, about how she risked the future of humanity for her own selfish sentimentality, and—"

He shook his head. "Well, perhaps it's true. But I can't look at you, look you in the eyes, and say that. Your mother was a wonderful woman, Jim. A beautiful woman—there is a lot of her in your face, your eyes are green, but they have a bit of her blue—and a strong, intelligent woman. I see some of that in you, don't I? You must be strong, to have come this far after all that's happened?" He stopped, and his gaze wandered off, as if he was surprised to find himself standing here.

"What did Carl—what did your father tell you, Jim?"

"He told me that somebody wanted to kill him—kill us, all of us. Me, too. I guess that's you, right?"

Delta shrugged uncomfortably. What Jim said was true, but put so baldly, it sounded wrong. It made him see it from the boy's point of view, just a kid, and somebody trying to murder him. Somebody who'd already murdered his father.

"Jim, don't—I mean, now that I've met you, perhaps . . ."

But Jim shook his head. "Then let me go. If you're not going to kill me, what do you want me for? What kind of crazy thing are you doing?"

The word lashed at Delta's sensibilities, and he flushed. "I'm not—don't say that. Crazy. I'm not crazy, boy. You—you just don't understand."

Jim stared at him. "Then tell me. I don't understand anything, you're right. So why don't you explain it to me?"

Now Delta paused, his thoughts slipping through his mental fingers like tiny, shining fish. Jim. This kid he'd held in his two hands and sung lullabies to. The only living connection, aside from Steele, that remained from the days when he'd made huge and terrible decisions. And suddenly he realized it was more important to him than he'd ever imagined that this boy know what he'd done, why he'd done it. He'd felt a glimmer of that obsession when he'd talked to Tabitha, and it had unlocked things he'd not spoken of for years. But with Jim Endicott the urge was even stronger. Surely he didn't think he needed to *justify* himself . . . ?

He coughed suddenly and, like an echo, Jim also coughed. They stared at each other. Jim shrugged. "Dry throat, I guess . . ."

Delta said, "Come with me," then turned and led Jim from the lab. After they were gone, the lights remained on, bright, hard, unyielding. And in the air of the room, moved by tiny currents, the submolecular machines drifted, seeking entry points into Delta's infinitely larger machines. Seeking, and finding. After a time, warning lights began to blink, like the eyes of foxes peeping from the forest.

5

The command bridge of the cargo barge was little more than a small room with a few screens and a couple of control stations. Jonathan stood behind one of these, watching over the shoulder of the woman who murmured into a throat mike as she kept track of things on a small display. Her pitted features, reflected in the high-impact plastic, were concentrated and intense. "There," she said. "We're past the inner screens."

Jonathan exhaled softly. For all his icy confidence, he hadn't really believed it would work. Too much chance involved, getting the boy, the Trojan horse, inside Delta's stronghold, then hoping Delta's electronic search instruments would trigger the nanotech hidden inside Jim—and that Delta wouldn't spot the trap until it was too late.

A lot of things had to go exactly right for this to work, and in Jonathan's experience, operations like this one never went the way they were supposed to. But they'd made it past the screen of ships, made it past the inner electronic wardens and their ceaseless sweeping guard. Now they approached the heart of Delta's empire,

Comsat One. Jonathan stared fixedly at the monitor. He'd seen pictures, but this was different. This was real.

Spread out in front of him, vast, growing . . .

Comsat One, the headquarters of the Combined Intelligence Agencies, was an elongated collection of spheres and cubes bound together by thick girders: there was a haphazard feel to it, as if it had begun as something much smaller and grown huge over the years. Scattered about the surface were antenna farms, dishes and spikes tipped with brilliant white strobe lights. Long stretches of armored plastic windows glowed like arcane hieroglyphs, and here and there maintenance cranes crawled across the surface like insects, bending, testing, probing.

It was at least ten miles long. Jonathan knew it was the largest human construction in known space, larger even than the distribution center atop the North American Skysnake.

It was supposed to be impregnable, but he was past its defenses, watching it spread itself naked before him, open and vulnerable. A fierce dark joy filled him, tingled his fingertips, jazzed his heartbeat. For a moment a red fog drifted across his vision.

"How much longer?" he whispered.

The tech glanced up. "Twelve point two minutes," she told him.

"Turn on the intercom speakers."

She nodded, flipped switches. "Ready," she said.

"All boarding parties to main landing gates," Jonathan said. Throughout the huge barge, his voice echoed off high steel ceilings, and down into the listening ears of nervous Pleb soldiers. They shifted uneasily as their leaders issued quiet orders into throat mikes, and grasped their weapons in sweaty hands. Some of them would die before this day was over. But all were volunteers, and finally their day had come.

The tech looked up again. "There it went," she said.

"What?"

She smiled. "The nanotech. It just took out the Comsat's operating computers. Look—down there. All the landing doors are sliding open."

Jonathan stared, his breath shallow with anticipation. "Yes, come on. Open wide for daddy . . ." he whispered.

He turned. "Let's go," he told the others. "Carpe the frigging day."

The barge drifted down and down, crammed with death. Inside Comsat, the wounded computers began, at last, to scream for help.

6

Jim sat quietly, listening to the drone of Delta's voice. Such soft words, but they were tearing him up inside. He listened as Delta told him about his real mother, and about what Carl had done. He didn't know this woman, the Kate that Delta kept circling back to, like a dog who couldn't resist ripping at the same bone, over and over again.

Once, he interrupted: "You and my mother made the Slaver Arrays? You're responsible for *that*?"

Delta bridled, then went on. "Don't you see it, Jim? We—humanity—had to have them. Without some advantage, we were—we are—helpless. The aliens had all the advantages."

He paused, remembering. "Jim, you should have seen them, their great ships, their science so unimaginably far ahead of us. It didn't take any kind of genius to understand what would happen. It was no different than if we found an island of savages, somewhere on Terra today. Their society, their culture could not stand against ours. They would fade away, would simply wither in the face of our technologies."

He sighed. "And the same things were already happening. Things were changing too quickly, had been for years. Why do you think we did what we did? We were looking for a key, a weapon, a defense. Something to save us from the irresistible tide of alien power. They weren't evil, those aliens. They aren't today. But they would have destroyed us as surely as we would destroy that island full of savages. Because that's what we were to them. Savages."

He fixed his eyes on Jim. "The mind arrays saved us from that, gave us a breathing spell. We were able to hold our own, at least for a while. At least so far. Your mother had reservations, deep reservations. But what could I do? Let humankind vanish, simply because of her squeamishness? You think the choice was easy? It wasn't. But it had to be made, and I made it."

He paused, licked his lips, and fixed Jim with a searching stare.

"Tell me," he said quietly. "Before you judge me. What would you have done? Would you have done any better?"

And Jim couldn't answer. His mind was overwhelmed. Too much history, too much unwanted knowledge. The tale of Carl and Kate—of the discovery of the mind arrays—of the terrible choices they all faced back then—it was too much. He didn't know what he would have done, or if he could have done anything better.

He thought of Cat, of the anguish on her face as she'd told him of her parents' deaths. The human fallout of Delta's decision. But what about the rest of it? What if Delta was right?

"It's . . . it was wrong," he mumbled, but his reply was weak. He knew it, and so did Delta. The older man showed his teeth and leaned forward.

"Wrong? I repeat, Jim. What *would* you have done, that was right? Can you separate your personal feelings from the larger reality, from the risks humanity itself faced then, and still faces today? I wasn't thinking just of myself. I had to consider all of us."

Jim shook his head. Delta sounded so calm, so reasonable. His words fell like soft raindrops on Jim, wearing away his certainty, until all that was left was a jumbled mishmash.

"Wrong . . ." he said again.

They were in Delta's tall, bright room, but Jim sat at the side of the huge desk, out of the glare of the window behind, with a clear view. His nemesis was seated in a chair so large it was almost a throne, and on his head was a round, silvery helmet, from which extended a spray of glittering cables.

"It hurts, doesn't it, boy?" Delta asked softly.

Jim nodded, reluctantly.

"I know. It hurt then. Can you believe that? They weren't easy decisions. I did the best I could."

"The ends don't justify the means!" Jim burst out. How many times had Carl told him that?

"They don't? Never? Sometimes? Always?" Delta asked gently.

Jim shook his head again. He wanted to hate this man, but he couldn't. He didn't know what he felt anymore.

He coughed, then coughed again, surprised at how weak he felt suddenly.

"Nasty cough, boy," Delta said. "Maybe we ought—" Delta stopped, a surprised look crossing his broad features. Then he began to cough, too, a long, moist, racking explosion. A rope of saliva dangled from his chin. He wiped it off, surprised.

"Now, what . . . ?"

"I feel funny," Jim said.

Delta sat up straight in his seat. Suddenly the room was full of the sound of sirens. Delta reached up, adjusted the position of the helmet on his head. His lips moved silently. He closed his eyes, then opened them and stared straight at Jim.

"God damn it," he said finally.

Jim shivered. There was a kind of madness in Delta's new examination of him. Madness, and fear. Then a whirring sound, and the seat on which Delta sat rose up, as the desk fell away. Delta glared down like some vengeful, angry god.

"What?" Jim said.

"It's you," Delta said. "I should have known . . ."

7

Jonathan stepped out into Comsat One's central receiving bay. Ragged wisps of smoke hung like half-burned curtains in the dry, hot air. Most of the overhead lights were out: flames crackled redly in a distant corner.

He cradled a military maser rifle in his arms. His eyes were hooded as he scanned the shadows, moving forward. A bell rang sharply and he turned.

"What's that?"

One of his techs said, "Alarm systems still going off."

"I thought we took out the central computers," Jonathan said. Something clutched at his ankle. He looked down, saw a young marine clad in olive drab, a spreading red splotch on his chest.

"Help me . . ." the kid whispered.

"Right," Jonathan said. He let the bulbous snout of the maser drop, center. He pulled the trigger.

The tech recoiled in horror. Jonathan only smiled. "You were saying?" he said.

"Uh . . . I don't know." The tech's face had gone the color of candle wax. "Probably some low-level automatic response."

Jonathan kept on moving. Most of his people were in. The defenses were collapsing before them. Astonishing, how soft the core of this armored fruit was. If he'd known before . . .

He shook his head. "Let's go . . ." he muttered, as much to himself as anybody.

Up ahead, dim beyond the smoke, a huge crash door began to slide shut.

"What the hell . . . ?"

The tech shivered. "Uh-oh," he said. "Trouble." Then his face changed. His lips drew back in a feral snarl. He began to laugh. Suddenly, without warning, his fingers curled into claws. His wild eyes focused on Jonathan. Screaming, he flung himself forward. *Pleb Psychosis*!

Jonathan swung the heavy barrel of the maser around and clubbed the tech across the face. Bone crunched and blood splashed. The tech dropped. Jonathan shot him twice before he hit the deck.

He looked down at the smoking corpse. Elsewhere in the huge space of the loading dock, other shrieks began to rise, a ghoulish symphony. Jonathan raised his head.

And everything had been going so *well* . . .

CHAPTER 14

1

Jim lurched halfway out of his chair. "What's going on?"

"Sit down!" Delta thundered. He glared at Jim, his lips working. "You must have thought you were pretty clever . . ." he said at last.

"I don't know what you're *talking* about," Jim said.

Delta smiled. The pupils of his eyes had shrunk to hard pinpoints. "Trojan horse," Delta said. "Did you actually think it would work?"

Jim shook his head. "Trojan . . ."

Delta cut him off with a savage shake of his head. Light glinted viciously off his silvery helmet. The cables rustled with his movement. He raised his right hand.

"In your DNA code. I see it now," he went on. His voice had become didactic, schoolteacherish: "You made a mistake. You thought the central computer system was the only one. And now you'll die for it."

"What?" Jim started from his seat again, then sank back as Delta pointed at him. "I said *sit down*. If you move again, I'll burn you on the spot!"

It had all changed again, too quickly. Jim's mind felt numb, useless. Full of chaotic noise. Nothing made sense. For a moment there, he'd felt a curious kind of kinship with the man who floated above him. And he hadn't done anything, not even said anything, had he? No . . . if he could only *think*. He put his palms to the sides of his head and squeezed, a gesture from his childhood.

Delta's voice floated down, quieter, colder, more focused. "Yes . . . now the analysis comes in. I should have waited. Are those your friends out there, Jim? That Pleb rabble infesting my outer halls?"

"I don't know," Jim said. "I don't know anything. What are you talking about?"

"Very nice. I could almost believe you, except for . . ." His voice trailed off as another avalanche of computerized information thundered into his skull.

"Except for *what*?" Jim wailed.

"It's inside you, like I said. Your DNA code. A very pretty job, by the way. Hmm . . ."

Jim stared up, confused and helpless.

"You know, maybe you don't know," Delta mused. "If you did . . ."

"Why won't you *tell* me?"

Delta opened his eyes. "The code, inside you. It builds nanotech. I didn't catch it at first, but now . . ." He sniffed, coughed once. "In me, too. Tiny machines, I'm infected. In the Comsat systems, in me, in you. But Jim, it's killing you. Still there, still working. You're breathing them out, sweating them out—my, you are sweating, aren't you? Heart rate through the roof. Maybe you don't know after all."

Delta's smile was thin and bitter. "Somebody else thinks the ends justify the means, Jim. They infected you with killer nanotech virus. It's eating you alive. We'll have to hurry."

Panicky adagios thrilled along Jim's nerves. His breath seemed to clog his throat and go no farther. Suddenly he felt dizzy. "Hurry?"

"Yes, yes, come on. Give it to me."

"Give you what?"

"The key code. I know you must have it. Carl must have given it to you. If you want to live more than another hour, tell me now, before it's too late. Come *on*, boy. *Tell me*!"

Jim could only stare up at him helplessly. He had not the remotest idea what Delta was raving about. And that meant, if Delta was telling the truth, that he was about to die.

"I don't know," he said dully. "I don't know."

Delta scratched his cheek idly. His fingertips painted livid red marks there, as if the flesh had grown soft, tender, easily bruised. He didn't seem to notice.

"Maybe you need some motivation," he said. "So you understand what's at risk."

His smile was knowing. Jim thought: Cat! But, no, he'd seen her, heading the other way when they'd traded. Could Delta have gotten her back somehow? He stiffened. Anything was possible.

Delta nodded. "How's your mom, Jim? Seen her around lately?" His smile changed. "Feeling motivated yet?"

2

Another time, not so long ago, Jim would have squirmed away from her, embarrassed. But now, huddled on the sofa next to Tabitha, his head buried against her shoulder, the smell of her hair in his nose, her arms warm and tight around him, he thought he would never want to move again. Wrapped in her comforting embrace, he felt about ten years old, and that was exactly what he wanted to feel: snug, protected, shielded against the harshness of the adult world.

"Mom . . ." he whispered.

She bent her cheek to him. "I know . . . be quiet, Jimmy. It's all right, it's okay. I'm here now. I won't let anything bad happen."

They both knew it was a lie, but it was a good lie. They both desperately needed to believe it. Across the large room, Delta still perched on his high throne. A console had grown up from its base: he played it like a crazed organist, his face stony, eyes slitted with concentration. Every once in a while he would look down at them, wait a moment, then go back to his work.

"Jimmy," Tabitha whispered. "Give him what he wants. Don't worry about being a tattletale. Just tell him."

He pushed his nose deeper into her shoulder blade. "Don't know," he mumbled. "I don't know what he wants."

She hugged him tighter. "It's okay." She waited a few beats, then said, "Tell me again, what he said. Maybe I can . . ."

He lifted his head slightly. She ruffled his hair and smiled into his bloodshot eyes. Deep inside, she felt a murderous rage. She wanted to *hurt* the man who'd done this to her boy.

"Oh, Mom . . ." He swallowed, coughed, swallowed again. He felt feverish and weak. Maybe Delta was right. Something was eating him up inside. Jonathan . . .

Yes, Jonathan would use him like this.

Something low and heavy rumbled, a muffled, distant sound. The deck vibrated slowly, subsided. Delta looked up again.

"I'm holding them, boy," he said. "You'd better make up your mind soon, though. You aren't in good shape."

Jim looked up at him, then looked away. Ugly purple blotches had appeared on the drumlike skin of Delta's face. In their centers were pockets of red, oozing rash. He was coughing almost continually now. Jim wondered if maybe he would get lucky, maybe Delta would die. But no, that didn't solve anything. If Delta died, Jim would quickly follow. Or so Delta said. Maybe he was lying?

But it hadn't felt like a lie.

"Jimmy . . . ?"

"Oh. Mom. He says I must have a code. He had video, a recording of Dad and me. When Dad was . . . dying."

Tabitha stroked his hair. "I know. Go on."

"Dad told me something, some numbers. Delta thought they were the key, a code that would unlock whatever is encoded in my DNA. But it didn't work. He controls a computer system . . . it's made up of linked human minds, Mom. The Plebs . . ."

He was babbling now, and she didn't understand one word in ten. But she let him go on, and held him tight, her own mind working furiously.

"He says my mom—my real mom—hid something in my DNA, and he wants to know what it is. He says if he has the key code, he can use his supercomputer—it's called a mind array, Mom—to decipher the code. That's what he wants, the key." He dropped his head again, seeking the warmth of her embrace. "But I don't know, I don't *have* it."

A siren burped into the silence of the room, ran up the scale, then cut off in mid-shriek.

"Quick, boy, time's running short," Delta said.

"It's okay, Jim. It'll be all right. We'll think of something . . ." She kissed his sweaty hair. "We always did, didn't we?"

She tried a weak smile, but he didn't see it. What a nightmare! She glared across the top of Jim's skull at Delta, wishing him dead. But though he seemed to be disintegrating before her very eyes, he was still alive. Wishing wouldn't make it so, not this time.

Jim made a soft, snuffling sound. She turned back to him.

"Remember the game?" she said. Maybe, if she could take his mind off this awful thing, calm him down . . .

He snorted again.

"'Tis always morning somewhere, Jim. Jim?"

He pulled away from her. There were tears on his face, but he managed a small smile. "Henry Wadsworth Longfellow," he said.

"Uh-huh . . . From?"

"'The Baron of Castine.'"

She shook her head. "Nope . . ."

"No, really," he said. "I'm sure."

She smiled, caught up in the momentary relief. "Too bad you don't have the book."

"But I do. It's in my pack somewhere. They took it away. . . ." He grinned wanly. "But I know I'm right, Mom. I can see the page in my mind. Section 110, upper right column. About . . . hmm . . . line two." He stopped. "Mom."

"What?" His body had gone tense against her.

"That's it," he whispered intensely. "That's *it*!"

"Jimmy, what—"

But Jim was rising from the sofa, his mouth open, one hand flapping wildly. "Delta! Where's my backpack?"

"What?" Delta sounded slightly dazed.

"My backpack, damn it! Where's my *backpack*?"

3

It was there. Even in his terrible weakness, he found it. But now he faced another, darker task: he knew the code. But even to save his own life, and his mother's, should he give it to Delta?

He recalled the horror of the Pleb Psychosis. If he gave Delta what he wanted, wouldn't he be helping the man to perpetuate that endless crime against humanity?

The ends, the means . . .

"Mom," he whispered.

She leaned close. "What would Dad want me to do?"

She stared at him, her compassion so strong he wanted to weep. "Your dad is dead, Jim," she said. "But he raised you to be a man. It's your decision now."

"Mom, I killed him."

She froze. Then she sighed. "I was afraid so," she said. "Everything happened so quickly, but I wondered."

He licked his lips. "It was an . . . accident. I was scared, and I just . . . pulled the trigger."

Gently, she wiped his sweating forehead. "And you blame yourself. You must, I know. But, Jim, you *can't.* It was an accident. Even your father . . ." She left the rest unspoken.

But he continued to lash himself, his eyes fevered with the past. "Yeah. Like it was an accident I disobeyed him and sent that application away. That's what started it. That's what killed him. I killed him twice, Mom. How can I ever live with that?"

She took his chin in her fingers and leaned close. In her eyes gleamed a steel he'd never seen before. "Because you must, Jim. Because your father would have understood, and he would have forgiven you. Do you understand *me*?"

He stared at her, uncomprehending. "Mom, I . . ."

Her voice quavered fiercely. "*I forgive you,* Jim. *Me. I forgive you, because he isn't here to do it himself. But I loved Carl Endicott more than anything in my life, and I forgive you!*"

She stopped, her lips shaking with the intensity of what she'd said.

And in that moment Jim felt a rush of understanding, even empathy for what Delta had done. In a high and perfect world, the ends could not justify the means. But humans were not high and perfect, not all the time. Sometimes, they were only human, and did human things. And all they could hope for was forgiveness.

It might be possible, someday, for him to forgive himself for what he'd done to his father. But if he now sacrificed his mother on the same altar of his own stubborn certainty, who could forgive him?

Had Delta felt the same way, long ago?

He turned his head slightly and spoke. "1992—217—4," he said. "Edition 1992, section 217, entry number four." He riffled through the ancient, yellowed pages. "Here," he said, pointing. She bent her head and read with him, a six-line entry. Together they spoke the final words. . . .

We are unlocking secrets billions of years old . . .

Then he said, "Delta?"

The older man said, "Yes, yes, I've already got it. Feeding it in . . . we'll see."

Jim looked back down. "Farouk el Baz said it. In *Skylab: Next Great Moment in Space.*" He paused. "It was a book code, Mom. One of the oldest codes there is—but you can't break it, unless you know the book."

Delta let out a short moan. Jim and Tabitha looked up. An expression of grim triumph was painting itself across Delta's disintegrating features.

"That's it," Delta grated. "It'll be a few minutes. I'm bringing the full power of the arrays to bear now."

Another explosion, this one sharper, clearer, closer, shook the big room. Tabitha gasped, and this time Jim hugged her. "Hang on, Mom. It's gonna be okay."

He turned back to stare at Delta, waiting. Delta's eyes were closed. The rash on his face had spread, so that now his features were nearly obscured by the dripping, oozing mass. But his eyes shone from the wreckage, still gleaming with fierce awareness.

"Well?" Jim said. "It that it? You getting what you wanted? Are we even now?" The words sounded strong, but his voice quavered. Delta eyed him.

"We'll see," he said.

4

Joey had a face like a horse, long and heavy-jawed, with a dusting of dirty blond stubble on his chin. His eyes were gray, sharp, watchful. He wore a dark brown shirt and leather pants with a chain belt. A gold necklace with a small Buddha pendant hung from his neck. A faint sheen of sweat slicked the acne scars on his forehead.

He was thin, but his thighs and butt were larger, out of proportion, and his arms seemed too short. Long, thin fingers, piano player's fingers, wrapped around the butt and stock of a laser rifle. He sat cross-legged, watching her, licking his lips regularly, like a metronome. Flick, flick. His teeth were yellow, and blackened along the gum line. A wirehead socket gleamed dully beneath greasy blond curls, behind his right ear.

Cat watched him. "Nervous?" she said.

He sucked in a short breath and shook his head. A rolling boom sounded from the direction of the entry gates that led deeper into Comsat One. He turned to look, then turned back.

"Sounds pretty hot in there," Cat said. "They might need every man they can get."

He stared at her. "Jonathan told me to watch you. So that's what I'm gonna do."

Of course. She'd never seen him before, but she knew him. Knew the type. Wireheads weren't real strong on independent thought. He would follow orders, a good soldier. He could have as easily, and happily, taken orders from Delta.

The world was full of people like him.

A raging wave of impatience swept her. She gritted her teeth. To have it end like this! She leaned back against the dirty tarps, trying to think. If she could get to Jim . . .

What then? She didn't know. But that wasn't the immediate problem. She couldn't do anything to help him sitting here. Maybe she couldn't do anything even if she could find him, but anything was better than this, better than worry and helplessness.

"Why don't you let me go?" she said, trying for as much reasonableness as she could manage. "I can't do anything now. It's too late. And Jonathan probably can use every gun he can find."

His eyes flickered, but he only tightened his lips and shook his head.

She nodded. "Well . . . guess I might as well get comfortable."

She was wearing a man's denim shirt. She smiled, and began to unfasten the top button. His eyes widened a bit. Good.

She let her fingers drop to the second button, leaned forward, still smiling.

He sighed faintly, his gaze riveted.

"Maybe we could do something to . . . pass the time. Aren't you bored?"

He licked his lips.

The second button popped open, and she caressed the third. "Really, Joey, what's the harm? Ain't nobody here but us chickens."

His pale face had taken on a pinkish tinge. She opened the third button, felt coolness on her sweat-slick skin. Joey uttered a soft moan and hitched himself up on his knees. His rifle dangled from his left hand, forgotten. Mesmerized by her peep show, he reached forward.

And she kicked him as hard as she could. She aimed for a spot exactly six inches below his belly button. He made a hard, gagging noise as all the air belched out of him. He doubled over, but by then she was already up and running.

5

Jonathan hacked a blue-uniformed marine across the throat, then shot him as he fell back. The roast-pork stench of burning human flesh hung thick in the air, mixed with the smell of fried insulation and the harsh, crackling odor of electrical equipment shorting out.

It wasn't going well, but not as badly as he'd feared. He checked the sketchy holographic map he'd stolen from Comsat's compromised central computers. He wasn't sure what was happening. There was no doubt they'd been successful with their Trojan horse. The central computers were no longer functioning at all: the virus encoded in Jim's DNA had destroyed them. But something else had taken over, some other computer—perhaps a backup system they hadn't known about, something shielded against what they'd hidden in the boy.

Still, if it was a backup system, it wasn't as strong or efficient as the main computers. There was resistance, but not overwhelming. And something was still going on in the Comsat's subsystems. Machines exploded for no reason. Some blast doors were shut, and they'd had to knock them down, but others hung inexplicably open. It was almost as if the backup system, whatever it was, had too many things on its cybertronic mind.

And there were other problems. He'd selected his people as carefully as he could, but some closet wireheaders must have sneaked through. Those were the ones succumbing to Pleb Psychosis, going suddenly berserk, screaming, turning their weapons on friend and foe alike, or even themselves.

If he'd needed any further proof that Delta and the Pleb Psychosis were somehow linked, he thought he had it. Of course, he wouldn't know finally until he had his strangler's fingers wrapped tightly around Delta's fat, quivering neck, but . . .

He inhaled sharply at that thought, then glanced around.

They were deep into the guts of the Comsat, not far from what the map said were the central offices. There was more armor there, no doubt, and the last-ditch defenses. It wouldn't be easy.

He motioned at one squad of three grimy soldiers, directing them to take the point. They ducked down and scurried forward.

No, not easy . . . but unless the Comsat's backup computers got a hell of a lot more efficient, they'd make it.

He swallowed a meaningless, bloody grin and plunged onward. From the shadows, behind him, Cat peeped around a smoldering chunk of nameless equipment, watching, waiting. After a moment, she followed.

6

Delta's tall room had remained curiously unaffected by all the carnage wrecking the rest of Comsat One. The dulled rumble of intermittent explosions penetrated its heavy shielding, and once or twice the lights flickered, but otherwise the atmosphere remained quiet and serene.

Jim and Tabitha huddled together on the sofa, the woman with her arm across the boy's shoulder, holding him as he coughed. He'd been coughing continuously, and now he was spitting up wads of cottony pink fluid. She glanced up at Delta, who had become a horror.

"Damn you, can't you *do* something?" she spit at him, her voice vibrating with tightly controlled rage.

He turned blindly in her direction. The rotting flesh of his face had turned the color of half-dried scabs, dark and crusty; in the cracks gleamed chips of white. She wondered if it was bone, if whatever was eating him would eventually strip him to a skeleton.

He opened his mouth, a loose black O, and spoke. His voice was garbled, vague and mumbling, as if part of his tongue was missing.

" . . . holding it," he said. "I have to . . . my own genetic codes . . . hormones . . ." He shook his head. Small dry flakes drifted up from the top of his skull. "Almost there . . . then Jim."

She subsided. The man was obviously fighting for his life, and though under any other circumstance her most fervent wish would have been for him to lose that fight, in this moment she was praying with every fiber of her soul that he would succeed.

Jim shuddered. His skin blared heat, like a small, soft furnace. A rope of saliva dangled from his chin. She wiped it off, then touched his forehead. He turned slightly. His eyes were wide, but the whites had turned the color of egg yolks, and the pupils didn't track on her.

"Jimmy . . ." She turned again. "Hurry up, damn you! He's dying . . ."

" . . . we all are . . ."

7

Delta sighed and banished the woman's irritating whine from his thoughts. As if he didn't have enough to do . . .

He had no idea what his physical appearance was like. He hadn't had a chance to look, though from the indicators he was monitoring, he doubted it was very good. No matter. Flesh could be repaired. First, though, he had to defeat the flesh eaters inside him, even though a part of his attention was occupied with the army of Plebs hacking and burning its way toward his inner citadel.

Maddening! He'd summoned reinforcements, and they were on the way, but like all such things, would no doubt arrive after the issue had been decided. This was a war of minutes, and it would take hours to lift any effective force from Earth and move it from the distribution center to his headquarters.

It was obvious they'd suspected the mind arrays, but they hadn't *known*, and that made all the difference. Plebs. A useless class, he was amazed they'd managed to cause him this much trouble already . . .

Not for much longer, though. He was deep inside himself, wired a thousand ways to the thing he and a dead woman had invented, the controller system and linkage generator for the mind array.

He loved the feeling of raw power when he jacked into the machines: a trillion trillion switches, self-creating, self-replicating, constantly orchestrating the feeds from a billion pulsating human minds. The system had been small, in the beginning, but he had built it to a point where it began to build on itself, and after that, it just kept on going. From a technological standpoint it was a landmark as big as the pyramids or the Great Wall of China, a human creation visible far down the reaches of the future, a turning point in human history.

His. Yes, really, it was. In the shaded corners of his soul he knew the inspiration had been hers. She—Kate—had made those first blinding leaps of intuition, but he'd taken them, refined them, smoothed off the rough edges, and made that first awkward, crude mechanism work. He couldn't have done it without her. He was not so great an egomaniac as to believe otherwise. But with that same calm pragmatism, he understood that she could never have carried through her first flashes to this magnificent cathedral of technology. For one thing, she hadn't been tough enough, bloody-minded enough, to make the choices that had to be made, the necessary choices.

But he knew all that already, and besides, for the first time in recent history he was under attack from what appeared to be a worthy opponent. In a way it was exhilarating. Almost as big a high as the arrays themselves . . .

And those—oh, God—it was like *being* God. He could never explain it, could barely wrap his own mind around it. Floating in the dark, sensing a billion whispering brains out there, filtered through the machines, responding to his every command. Sometimes like ice, sometimes in great roaring sheets of fire, and him playing them like the biggest church organ in the universe. . . .

It was addicting. He knew that some part of him was permanently out there, ghosting along in the silence, something that had, almost without his knowledge, gently separated from him over the years. He didn't care, in fact, welcomed the duality. The Janus face . . .

He sighed. Time to get to work. The code the boy had given him had unlocked everything necessary, and he already had his DNA pattern. Now it was only a matter of reading it, once again like God's own encyclopedia, except Kate had written these pages.

Messages. Memos from the past. He wondered if she'd known, if she'd imagined he would ever read these things. Her last will and testament.

Thrilled, he bent himself to the task, the good and pragmatic workman. And with one small part of his mind, he began to kill the invaders, both in his body and in his satellite. It didn't take much of his attention. It was like killing cockroaches . . .

8

"W*atch it!*" Jonathan howled. He ducked back as a fresh swarm of mobile laser-bots vomited from the dark passageway before him. He peered up over the smoldering wreckage of an office desk, part of the makeshift barricade they'd hastily shoved together to block the corridor, and snapped off a couple of quick shots. One of the little killer-bots sizzled, then vanished in a bright blue flash.

It had turned into a nightmare of smoke and heat and sudden, unexpected death. He jazzed his throat mike, hoping for something coherent, but all he could hear on his command frequencies was hopeless, panicked babble. They were losing. Somewhere, somehow, he'd made a terrible mistake, and soon, he supposed, he would pay the usual price for such things.

He crouched down, fumbled in his pack, found a fresh charge for his weapon, and snapped it in. Next to him a woman he hardly knew, thick, broad-shouldered, her wide, bovine face streaked with smoke and sweat. A line of congealed blood snaked across her smooth forehead, jinked down, and crossed her left eye, which bulged out, blind and staring.

She was breathing shallowly, probably in shock, but she still had a good grip on the big, old-fashioned slug gun in her right fist. "Mary . . ." he whispered hoarsely.

She didn't turn. Damn it, what was her name? He jabbed her in the shoulder. She jerked around, her good eye wide and rolling. Battle fatigue, mania, whatever . . . she might still have enough left to do some good. He pointed at the heavy bag he'd been carrying all along, now resting at his knee where he'd dropped it.

"Inside," he grunted. "One of the square ones."

She stared, then nodded and began to rummage. She pulled out a square gray package about six inches on a side, maybe an inch thick, and eyed him questioningly.

He nodded. "Over there, on that wall. Just slap it up, it's magnetic, it'll stick, then run like hell. I'll set it off."

She bobbed her head up and down, took a deep breath, and tensed. He slapped her on her shoulder and she took off, scrambling over the barricade, dodging and weaving. He peered over and watched, waited until she was leaping over a ruined pile of laser-bots, just where the controls for the next blast door ought to be. He squeezed the small detonator in his hands. She vanished in a blinding yellow fireball, but the explosion cleared the rest of the bots and jammed the blast door open permanently.

"Sorry, Mary," he muttered. "You know how it is . . ."

He would kill every last one of them if that's what it took to get his hands on Delta's flabby neck.

He glanced around one more time, then threw himself across the barricade. Only one more door, one more door to go . . .

CHAPTER 15

1

He understood how it worked. She had used the base pairs of the DNA—combinations of pairs of four nucleotides called adenine, guanine, cytosine, and thymine—to encode her message. In the structure of DNA, each "link" of the DNA was made up of these four, arranged in complementary pairs. The arrangement was ideal for the binary computer languages—a pair could be arranged in one way that meant "on," and an opposite that meant "off." It sounded complicated, but it was really very simple. And using this infinitely flexible method of encoding, messages of hundreds of billions of characters could be encoded in short spaces of the DNA molecule.

Delta sighed in appreciation as her handiwork unfolded before him in the whispering dark. He summoned his billion ghosts and put them to work. Then he waited, for how long he had no idea. Time itself was different when he melded himself into the mind arrays . . .

As he summoned more and more of the ghosts to the task, some of them, under intense pressure, collapsed. A part of his mind noted the failures, understanding that each failure represented the crushing of a single human mind into madness. All over the Terran System, and even as far away as Wolfbane, Plebs exploded into paroxysms of mindless violence.

He paid no attention. The ends, after all, justified the means . . . and this was important. Kate, his Kate, had left something behind, something so crucial she'd seen fit to encode it into her son's most basic building blocks: his DNA, the strands of life that made him what he was.

Idly, while the mind array did its work, he put a portion of the ghosts to work examining the structure of Jim's DNA itself. Ah, yes, Jim was definitely his mother's son. He knew Kate's genetic pattern as well as he knew his own, and the inheritance was obvious. Just as it was obvious that Carl Endicott had—

He stopped.

No, it wasn't obvious. He looked again. He didn't have a deep analysis of Carl's genetic code at hand—why should he? The man had been an employee, and then a traitor. But he could access the basic screening, and—

He gasped. No, the other inheritance was not from Carl Endicott. It was from . . .

His mind reeled. He drew back from the inescapable conclusion, shaken to his core. A truth he'd held unexamined for sixteen years trembled, then shattered in the spectral, humming darkness.

The unmistakable patterns he knew best of all, blended and mixed with Kate's. Mother and father together, their genetic history living on forever in their offspring's cells. So utterly normal. So devastating.

His world, the world he'd built over a decade and a half of bitterness and betrayal, teetered wildly.

And as he considered *that*—his mind open, naked, shocked with discovery—the ghosts finished their work and delivered their conclusions to him in one gigantic, rolling epiphany: Kate's secret.

Delta screamed.

2

The alarms had been shrieking in her ears for several minutes, but Steele had been busy. Encased in her armor, buoyed up with the strength of ten, she had given herself over to the slaughter, and now blood dripped from her mailed fists. Her battle maser was almost too hot to touch.

But now, for a moment, standing in a smoky corridor crossroads, she lifted her head and paused. Across the heads-up screen of her helmet, an ultimate alarm tripped in crimson letters, and a spot on a sketchy map blazed with a throbbing red dot.

"The inner blast doors," she muttered to herself.

The invaders had broken through the final defenses. How had it come to this? Delta himself was in danger!

She glanced down at the fallen Pleb who writhed beneath her left foot. Damn, her back hurt!

"Sorry, buddy, you lose," she told him, and pressed harder. Heard a sharp, bony crack, and the man went limp, his acne-scarred face suddenly smooth and peaceful.

A hand-lettered ID tag pinned to his shirt said only, "Joey."

"Sorry . . . Joey," she said again, not knowing why she said it. Then she turned and headed for Delta, and what—though she wasn't a superstitious woman at all—a premonition deep in her bones told her would be her final stand.

Well, she'd lived by it all her life, and had no qualms now about dying with it . . . why should she? She was a warrior woman. Her ancient decision, her fate . . .

Her sword.

3

He hung in darkness, surrounded by the glimmering light of his ghosts, his unknowing human slaves, as they chattered their irresistible messages endlessly, directly into his controlling mind.

His slaves. Some measurable percentage of them disintegrating even as he watched, their human minds burned out by the pressure of the flawed linkage, by the mind arrays he'd torn his whole life apart to save, years ago. The glorious creation upon whose altar he had sacrificed everything: love, family, hope, dreams. Upon which he'd placed everything of value, in order to preserve the larger good.

The altar whose iron name was *the ends justify the means.*

And every bit of that sacrifice now in stinking ruins, the dreadful sludge of that psychic burning defiling his nostrils. The charred remains of Kate, of the relationships he *could* have had, of the *future* that might have been his, and—worst of all!—

He'd been wrong.

The entire stinking sacrifice unnecessary and, most horrifying of all, perverse.

He should have waited, given her more time, *listened* to her. But no, he didn't do that, did he? He had his damnable ends to consider, to justify his equally damnable means, and so he had made his filthy sacrifice, and now he stared at that vile, smoking-ruin plain.

It was more than he could bear. And when her final message—not the revelation of science she'd achieved after he'd thrust her away—when those few simple words came drifting up, gentle as her remembered caresses—he wept.

After everything, even as the bloody end he'd made for her drew nigh, she'd found a way to leave her fatal benediction, encoded in the cells of her son. Had she known he would find it? *Hoped* he would?

"I still love you . . ."

"*No!*"

" . . . still love . . ."

"*NO!*"

"Love."

Delta changed. He had to. Once he had been something else, some *one* else, but he'd thought that man gone forever. Sacrificed as utterly as any smoking calf on the dark altar of necessity. Choices made, a life lived, the past unchanged and unchangeable. And now, whispering down the winds of years forgotten, a message unlooked for, unhoped for. A message of love.

She had loved *him*, even as he'd destroyed *her*.

Could he be forgiven?

Things broke apart. His carefully constructed center did not hold. Instead, the heart he'd believed hardened to everything but fear and duty shattered before the ultimate balm:

Love.

He'd murdered her for his means, and buried her beneath his ends, and even when he was done, she'd still loved him.

And so she resurrected a man who had once lived, but thought himself dead. Now that man strode forth, out of the dim halls of the past, once again understanding the joy of high purpose. He'd had his ends and means, but those ends no longer justified anything human.

Love is the resurrection.

And his sins were legion.

4

Tabitha raised her head. The monstrous, disintegrating thing on its throne tower was screaming. Bits of moist skin flew as it clawed at its sightless eyes.

She shuddered. What did it mean? Was Delta dying?

Jim moaned softly. He was drifting in and out of consciousness, alternating moments of clarity with longer stretches of delirium. The fevers were eating him up, and whatever devil things were hidden inside him were still doing their work. Even as she held him tighter his body convulsed into a long series of racking coughs.

She wiped away the pink drool, staring at Delta.

Her only hope—*Jim's* only hope.

"Don't die, damn you," she whispered. "Save my boy."

Jim began to cough again.

5

Delta's fleshy body was falling apart—he still hadn't unleashed the genetic therapies that would halt the molecular machines ripping him to pieces, he'd been too busy with the rest of it—but his mind was clear. And in its own way, that dry, familiar clarity was worse than madness, for he couldn't turn away from the truth.

In the end, his greatest failure had been one of imagination. He had not been able to see the possibilities. He had been blinded by the brilliance of their original discovery, seduced by the potential of the mind arrays, willing in his desperation to ignore their flaws.

Kate had not been, but he'd ignored her. Brushed her aside, though the heart of the discovery was hers. And so he had sinned, and his first sin was pride. Followed shortly by vanity, and finally by murder on a personal, then a vast, scale.

He checked her results a third time, but nothing had changed. He could find no flaw in her work. She had broken through, had trusted her own imagination, her own brilliance, and . . . gone beyond.

So while he clutched the fruit of her first, broken discovery to him, defending it against her doubts, she had kept on. And succeeded.

It was all tied together, the linkage, the Pleb Psychosis, the power of the arrays themselves. She had solved it finally, in another of those breakthroughs that come only every generation or so: the linkages were wrong. It was those imperfect linkages that placed unbearable pressure on individual human minds, and destroyed some percentage of them with each use of the array.

Her new programs fixed all that. These arrays would not destroy their individual parts. And as a consequence of that, of the efficiency of the new links and controller programs, her mind arrays would be a hundred—a thousand!—times more powerful than anything he'd ever dreamed of.

It was conceivable that every member of the human race might be linked seamlessly, even unconsciously, into a computer so powerful that the most secret writings of the universe itself might finally be read.

And he had thrown it away. If he'd waited only a few more months, trusted her a little better, *imagined the possibilities* . . .

But he hadn't. Sixteen years. What could humanity have done with sixteen years of Kate's improved mind arrays? He shuddered. His imagination, so weak then, now roared in his mind: anything. Everything! The possibilities were endless.

No fears of alien technology. In one leap, Kate had moved beyond any alien science he'd ever heard of. If computer power was the key to modern science, she'd built a machine to unlock every door. In sixteen years, mankind might have . . .

But no. Instead, humanity had wallowed, barely keeping pace, while he cemented his power and imposed his xenophobic will on government, on the future itself. He'd walled man away from the universe, weak and fearful, clinging to his pitiful, flawed discoveries.

And then he'd killed her.

He shuddered again. What if she'd been slower, or he'd been quicker? She might never have come to this—or, worse, left no record of it.

She hadn't had much time. And she'd been fearful. She hid it in plain sight, though, in the one thing besides the arrays she'd created. The most precious thing she'd made.

Ah, tiger. Burning bright. Thy fearful symmetry . . .

Jim. The secret made flesh. The hope of humanity, embodied and embedded in the cells of one sixteen-year-old boy.

Jim . . .

Delta, filled with fear and trembling, came awake. And found chaos.

6

Jim thought: *I don't feel good.*

He raised his head and blinked. Everything blurry. He blinked again, and slowly, his vision sharpened. "Mom?"

Her lips were on his ear. "Hang on, Jimmy . . ."

He felt very light-headed. He turned, and saw her face, her eyes, so concerned. Worried about him.

He tried to grin. "It's okay, Mom. Everything will be okay." He didn't know if that was true—in fact, he doubted that it was—but he had to say something. The look on her face was just too awful.

"Mom?"

"Shh, Jimmy. Rest, be quiet. Save your strength."

He raised his eyes, trying to remember. The long trip, the Comsat. Delta.

He looked up, and saw him, slumped in his throne chair, high above, like some ancient dreadful king.

Part of Delta's face had simply melted. What showed through was half a skull, white teeth grinning. And the rest of him, beneath his clothing, had become almost shapeless, as if skin had sloughed off and puddled in the baggy creases of his suit.

It was inconceivable that he could still live, and Jim felt his guts clutch up at the sight: *last hope*, he thought bitterly. *And now he's dead—*

Delta's one remaining eye suddenly opened, glittered. Tabitha gasped. The tall doors at the far end of the room slammed open, and Cat came running through, an overheated laser pistol in her hand.

"Jim!"

He raised one hand, waved weakly. "Over here . . ."

She glanced back over her shoulder, then rushed to him. "Thank God!"

Tabitha flung herself across Jim protectively. "Stay back!" she snarled.

Cat gestured with the pistol. "I'm Cat. Who are you?"

"My mom," Jim muttered. It took him a moment to remember that Tabitha would not know Cat. The two women in his life. For some reason he found that funny, and giggled.

"Mom, she's a friend. It's okay." He felt Tabitha relax, then slide back from him.

Cat said, "You're his mom?"

Tabitha nodded.

"We don't have much time. We've got to get you out of here. The Comsat's breaking apart. I don't know how much longer we have—but we've got to hurry." She reached forward and grabbed Jim's hand, to drag him upright, but Tabitha jerked him back.

"No!"

"What do you mean, no? Are you crazy, lady?"

Frantic, Tabitha began to babble. "No, there's something inside him, it's killing him, that man up there, he's the only one who can save him—"

Cat shook her head. "What?"

Jim said, "It's true, Cat. Jonathan put something inside me, something to kill Delta with. But it's killing me, too . . ." He tried a grin, but it vanished as he doubled over in another coughing spell.

Cat stared down. "Jesus . . ."

Delta said, "Probably won't help at the moment. Get him over here. Bring him to me." His voice was soft, rotten, corroded. Hard to understand.

Cat whirled, bringing up her pistol.

"Don't," Delta said. "Not if you want to save him. I told you, bring him to me."

A soft whining sound filled the room. Delta's tall throne began to descend. He raised one hand, beckoning. Naked bone showed through the knuckles. Delta didn't seem to notice.

Cat turned back to Tabitha. "Bring him?"

Tabitha nodded. She already had an arm underneath Jim's back, pushing him up. "It's the only hope we've got. Help me."

Together, grunting and straining, the two women half carried Jim across the room, to where Delta waited like a dying god for sacrifice.

A soft voice, barely audible over the din beyond the shattered doors, said, "Don't bother, Cat. They're dead meat, both of them."

7

Cat turned. "Jonathan."

He stood framed in the doors, smoke billowing out around him. His expression was calm, mild, his gaze bleary as he nodded and stepped on into the room.

"The kid looks in bad shape," he said, moving forward. He moved to go around them, toward Delta, whose throne had dropped back down and was now only a large chair. Delta sat, a rotting ruin, his bald head still crowned by the silvery helmet that connected him to the mind arrays.

"Hello, old man," Jonathan said gently. "I've been looking forward to meeting you."

"Jonathan, no!" She let go of Jim and moved to block his path. "If you kill him, Jim will die!"

Jonathan paused. A puzzled expression drifted across his pudding features. "Yeah? And so?"

Cat shook her head. "Damn it, can't you see? He's dying, Delta's dying. But that thing you put in Jim, he can stop it. He said he would."

"And you believe him? Of course he's dying. I killed him. But I want to feel it, understand? His neck in my hands." Jonathan shook his head. "Cat. Get out of my way."

"No, I won't let you do this. Jim's innocent, he doesn't deserve this."

"Huh. I'd laugh if you weren't making me sick. So he's innocent. How many other innocents has that bastard behind you put down? You forgot about them?" He took a deep breath. "I'm done with your crap, Cat. Out of my way."

Jim, swaying as he leaned against Tabitha, lurched away from her, all his weight behind the blow he aimed at the back of Jonathan's head. He'd trained in martial arts academies for years. He was young, his reflexes superb. And Jonathan was facing away from him, concentrating on Cat.

His attack never came within a foot of Jonathan's unkempt hair.

Jonathan hunched as Jim moved, ducking and turning, his right foot coming up, blocking the blow, deflecting it. And as Jim turned with it, Jonathan's small hand flashed out, once, twice. Jim shrieked once and dropped, clutching his right shoulder with his left hand.

Jonathan looked down on him, an expression of mild interest on his face. "The puppy has claws. Well, sort of." He grinned apologetically, then swung back around to face Cat.

"What? You, too?" He shrugged. "It doesn't make any difference to me, Cat, but you really ought to make up your mind whose side you're on."

She dropped into a fighter's crouch. "You're as bad as Delta is," she breathed. "Killers, both of you."

He nodded. "It took you this long to figure it out? Of course I am, Cat. That's how I made it this far, into this room. I'm a killer. He killed your parents, among others, and now I'm gonna kill him. Takes a monster to kill a monster. Plain and simple, right?"

She shook her head. "No. He has to fix Jim, first."

"Ah. I see. True love." Jonathan sighed. "Well, I wish I had time for this, but, sorry. I don't."

He launched himself at her. She barely fended off his first blow, but his follow-up wheel kick numbed her thigh and turned her around. She stuck her right hand up and he batted it away, coming across her forehead with the heel of his left hand.

She staggered, a roaring in her ears, momentarily blinded. She came back, shaking her head, and saw him grinning at her, his right fist poised for a final blow.

"Say bye-bye, Cat," he murmured.

"Hey, cheese face," the rough, smoke-hacked voice said. "Why don't you pick on somebody bigger than you?"

Jonathan's eyes jerked hard right. "You!"

"That's right, wonder boy," Commander Steele said. "Me."

8

Jim faded out then, but only for a moment, as Tabitha dragged him back, out of the way and wrestled him up onto the couch. The pain was a fountain of bright sparks running from his shoulder to his brain.

Tabitha tried to shield him, but he groaned, "No . . . let me see."

Steele's helmet was gone. Her black hair hung stringy from her head, framing her waxen face. Her smeared lipstick was a brilliant splotch of color, giving her features an artificial, doll-like cast. As she moved toward Jonathan, her battle armor gave off tiny humming sounds.

Jonathan squared off, facing her, as Cat fell back, gasping for breath. He put his hands out. "I'm augmented," he said.

Steele nodded. "Got yourself some pretty, hyped-up artificial muscles, have you? Well, I always wondered . . ."

"What's that?" Jonathan said.

"Which way was better. The armor, or your stuff. I guess we're gonna find out."

Jonathan smiled. "Guess we are."

They both moved at the same time.

"My backpack," Jim whispered.

"What?" Tabitha said.

"My backpack. On the floor there. Get it for me."

From his vantage point, it looked like ballet. Jim knew what he was watching. He'd trained for years. But these two were experts. Even so, it took only instants.

They came together, hands and feet moving in blurs. Jim heard the sound of flesh meeting flesh, harsh grunts, the whir of Steele's armor. Apart then, circling, appraising. A blue welt under Steele's right eye, another bleeding gash on Jonathan's forehead. One more moment of appraisal, then abrupt, fierce movement.

When they separated again, both were badly damaged. Steele's right arm dangled useless at her side. Jonathan, trying to circle, limped badly. Jim could hear the crackling of damaged knee cartilage with every halting step he took.

Steele shook hair out of her eyes. Blood sprayed from her nose with the motion. She inhaled harshly, and launched herself a third time.

This time, they both went down. Jim leaned forward, his breath fiery in his throat, his vision suddenly blurring again. He had his backpack in his lap, working it open, his shoulder a slab, a glacier of agony. He felt inside, forgot what he was doing, looked up.

Jonathan, slowly coming to his knees, his bland features a mask of blood. He raised his good arm, hand curved into a killing axe, lips split in a slash of white triumph.

"Yeah," he grunted. "Now we know . . ."

Jim fingers found the cool, hard shape, curled around it, dragged it out of the pack in one jerky motion, his shoulder screaming. He bit his lip, tasted blood, and raised his arm. The torn muscles in his shoulder grated in protest, and the pain cleared his vision for a moment. He froze then, his damaged shoulder quivering. It was all he could do to hold it steady. . . .

Can I do it? Can I do this terrible thing? Some deep part of him whispered that he could, but it would change him forever.

His belly heaved with bile and terror. Out of the corner of his eye he saw Tabitha's face, wide-eyed, fear and hope and repulsion warring on her features. He sucked in a breath that tasted of burned iron and blood, and looked back at Jonathan.

At his killing hand, blurring toward Steele's throat.

He pulled the trigger on the S&R .75.

The big rocket-propelled slug took Jonathan on the side and obliterated everything above his shoulder blades. A gray-specked, chunky fountain of blood burst from his headless trunk. The power of the tiny rocket was so great that his corpse barely moved. It hung, a puppet suddenly without strings, and then it dropped straight down. The fingers on Jonathan's right hand twitched, like shrimp cooking and shrinking.

Steele hitched herself up on her side and eyed Jonathan's remains. Her face was spattered with bits and pieces of him. She examined the carnage with mild interest, then glanced over at Jim.

"So, now what?" she said.

Jim coughed, and then began to vomit.

Those dead fingers, twitching.

Oh my God, he thought. *Oh my God oh my God . . .*

9

Delta had watched it all through his one remaining eye. Much of his brain was gone by now—he'd waited too long to tend to his own damage. But that was all right, he told himself. Some part of his iron will yet remained, and, deep inside his soul, he was still willing to believe that the ends must justify the means.

Even if the means included his own death. Only a part of him monitored the outside world, through his rapidly atrophying physical senses, but in the cool, thunderous dark of the cyberworld, where he lived with his billion ghosts, all was well.

He wondered about that for a moment, once again feeling that curious sense of *otherness*, almost as if there were two of him, separate and yet somehow the same, a single wholeness.

"Bring him . . ." he whispered.

Jim lolled weakly, drool and vomit trailing down his chin. He was mostly deadweight as Tabitha and Cat wrestled him back to Delta.

"That helmet," Delta said, pointing to a twin of his own now evident in the base of his chair. "Put it on." His one eye rolled.

"Then leave me alone. I'll take care of it."

Tabitha and Cat finished, then stepped back, staring at each other.

She loves him, Tabitha thought. It was a strange idea. There was a whole new Jim, created since her captivity, she knew nothing about. She wondered how much he had changed.

Enough to be able to kill, evidently.

The two women eyed each other. "Pray . . ." Tabitha said.

Cat nodded.

Behind them, Steele coughed again and sat up. "Damn, that stings," she said.

CHAPTER 16

1

In his measureless, echoing cyberworld, Delta spread Jim's DNA out like a book and went to work. It wasn't really that hard, not when he knew what he was doing. He had no illusions about his own skills: he was an excellent technician, and he had a billion busy little helpers.

Once again he quivered with delight as he examined the perfection of the thing Kate had created, written in the boy's deep cellular record. He took a nip here, a tuck there—his own little genetic graffiti . . .

The nanotech time bomb the Plebs had put there was a nice piece of work, though nothing of a level to compare with Kate's messages.

He unwound those diabolic codes, and replaced them with new instructions—healing machines—then watched as this fresh army spread itself rapidly to the rest of the boy, unlocking the old, dangerous codes, dissipating them.

Finally, almost as an afterthought, he examined the damage to the boy's shoulder. Torn muscles, lacerated tendons. Those repairs would take longer, but he started them anyway. A little bonus. He wondered if Jim would even notice.

Probably not . . .

And finally, he was done. Kate's secret still remained. It was his secret, too, but he wouldn't be able to keep it for long. What he'd done for Jim was no longer possible for himself. His time, at long last, was coming to an end, him and the flawed, deadly thing he'd built on the ashes of nearly forgotten dreams.

Well, in a way, it was a relief. And fitting, as well. In the end, all debts must be paid, and his debts were monstrous. The chip of his own life would hardly tip that hideous scale.

He sighed. Withdraw now, get the boy up, and out. He could hold the Comsat together a little while yet, but no longer than that. It was all slipping out of his hands, falling to the boy now, the hope, the secrets, the future.

He felt curiously uplifted with the realization. For him, it was over, or soon would be. And in that lifting he felt relieved at last, the weight of his own twisted duty finally falling away.

I tried, he consoled himself. *I was wrong, but I did try.*

Maybe the boy would do better. He hoped so.

He unlinked the two of them, let Jim fall away, gentle as a leaf drifting in the dark, receding, dwindling . . . gone.

Now he was alone, if he could be alone with a billion fading voices—and in the distance, he sensed it, growing closer, coming for him.

The other.

He stretched his invisible arms in supplication, and greeting.

Time now.

2

Jim awoke as from a dream. That same sensation, opening his eyes and seeing familiar things, somehow strange. And his mind stuffed with fading memories, recollections of things that could not have been.

Faces now, Tabitha, eyes concerned, and Cat, lines of wrinkled pain on her clear, young features, peering over Tabitha's shoulder.

"Jim . . . ?" Tabitha said.

He stared up at her, thinking about it, feeling himself inside his skin. Something heavy, on his head . . .

He grinned. "Hi, Mom," he said.

She burst into tears.

3

They were bunched at a door that had been hidden in the wall beyond Delta's desk, the three of them, still touching each other unconsciously, as if seeking collective assurance they were all whole, all there. All still surviving.

Jim moved his right arm. Still painful, but much better than he remembered. Or did he remember? So much was blurring now, fading away . . .

Steele limped over. "It's back down that corridor. A small ship, a private lock. It was his bolt-hole, if everything else went to hell." Another explosion shook the room. Small flakes of metallic paint drifted down from the ceiling. "And it sure is," Steele went on. "Going to hell."

Cat stared at her. "Aren't you coming?"

Steele shook her head. "Nope."

Jim eyed her coldly. He still had the heavy pistol in his hand. "You were the reason . . ." he whispered, hating her.

Steele stared at him. "Yes, I would have killed your father. You did it by mistake, but if I could have, I would have killed him. It was my job, kid. And maybe even a little personal, too. I always wondered which of us was better . . ."

She glanced down at his pistol, shrugged, turned and walked away. "Use it, if you want," she said. "I don't care anymore."

Jim raised the pistol, but only for a moment. There had been enough killing, at least by his hand.

Steele said, "I'll just stay right here." She looked at Delta, then turned back to face them. She noted that Jim's pistol was still at his side, and nodded.

"Why?" Cat said.

"Oh, you know. Because . . ." Steele said. "You better get going. I don't think this wreck is gonna hold together much longer."

She tipped them a crooked, red-smeared grin and turned away. The last they saw of her, she was limping toward the moldering pile that had once been a man. As she approached him, a coffin-like apparatus rose from the floor as she bent over to scoop him up, into her steel arms.

As he realized he no longer wished to kill her, Jim felt another weight rise from him, and for the first time understood the crushing burden of vengeance—not only on the object, but on the bearer as well. Hate corroded every vessel. It was something he would keep in mind.

He put away the heavy gun. Let her die by some other hand. His was empty now.

"Why's she staying?" Jim asked softly, as they hurried down the corridor.

Both women glanced at each other, then away. Cat said it.

"Because she loves him."

"Oh," Jim said. And wondered if he would ever really understand anything, anything at all.

4

Now even the billion voices had gone, and only the *other* remained. He heard it whispering to him in the dark, speaking secrets, promises.

Offering forgiveness. He wanted that, forgiveness, but was afraid. To just let go like that? So hard . . .

He could sense the world, the real world breaking up. Somewhere far away from him, across some divide he'd never seen before, the great Comsat was shuddering, its spine broken, its electronic nerves feeding on themselves, the pressures building.

Let that go, too, let that great weight rise up, away. And then the other spoke, an echo of himself: *Let go.*

He sighed.

Let go . . .

So hard . . . so easy.

Flying now, flying away, and the light growing, growing brighter around him.

He opened his eyes. "Steele?"

She was there, too. In the light.

Smiling . . .

5

It was a small scout craft. The controls were unfamiliar, but not impossible. Jim had flown simulated missions in cybertrainers in school, ships not unlike this one.

He took them straight out, very fast, pushing the muscular little engine to its limit. It was only in holovids that pilots hung around when something as big as Comsat blew up. In real life you ran, as far and as fast as you could, unless you wanted to go space-dancing with a wall of white-hot debris.

The shock wave caught him unawares, an onrushing tsunami of hard radiation, and he looked up at the view monitors. They had gone dark, like smoked glass, protecting the eye against the light to follow.

Even so, it was spectacular. The first white blossom, opening and shrinking, and then the second: an endless volcano of pure light, breaking and spreading, eclipsing even the sun itself.

Like . . . fireworks, he thought, awed. The biggest fireworks ever made.

And so they were, which was only fitting. Delta had built the biggest computers and housed them in the largest construction ever built by human hands. And in the passing of those two, the light of their death would fall on planets a million years distant, a million years in the future—for in the universe, light itself is the longest memorial . . .

He heard a strange, choking sound, and looked behind him. Both Cat and Tabitha were crying softly. It took him a moment to realize he was, too.

Something great had passed away. It seemed only fitting to shed a few tears.

After a while he took a plot and changed their course. The North American Skysnake was probably badly damaged, but there were others.

He aimed for one, and they went.

In the dark, the great flare guttered, and went out.

It was over.

6

OLFBANE

Tabitha said, "I think I'm going to sell the mountain place, Jim. I don't . . . I just couldn't—"

He looked up. Cat was sprawled on the floor of their living room, her nose in a holovid.

"Sure, Mom," he said. "I understand. I don't have any memories of that place but bad ones, anyway."

In fact, his memory had been more than strange of late. A lot of what had happened—the bad parts, at least—had faded until it was like a scary dream, something brushed away in the morning light. Yet there were scars, callused places inside him, inside his soul, that would never be the same again. Sometimes, staring out his window at the familiar scenes, everything looked weird, strange—frightening.

And he felt, every once in a while, that something was almost on the tip of his mental tongue, something trying to speak. To tell him something he already knew, if he could only remember.

Tabitha told him it was stress, and it would fade, but he wondered. Cat was more direct, and her therapy more enjoyable, but even with her he sensed the strangeness and a growing distance.

People thrown together by storms, changed and changed again, and now, with the storms subsiding, lives to pick up. He wondered if he would be in the life Cat eventually chose.

Somehow, he doubted it, and somehow, he thought it didn't matter, and that in the end he would be grateful for what he had.

The only real nightmares he still suffered were of Jonathan's fingers, twitching like blind worms, dead. He shivered as he thought of that.

"Sell the place, Mom. Really," he said. He flashed on the cabin, on fire spitting from the darkness. Let that one fade, too.

He settled back against the sofa, half-drowsy. He'd been sleeping a lot since their return. Then, for some reason, as he drifted halfway between sleep and waking, he remembered the message he'd found on his mail system when they returned home. Crisp and straightforward, typically military. From the Space Academy.

"*Dear Applicant:*

We will be happy to process your application. Unfortunately, there is an error. The match between Carl Endicott's genotype and your own is incorrect. Please supply the correct genotype as soon as possible, so that we may continue with the application procedure.

Sincerely,

Office of the Commandant"

So Carl was not his real father, and without knowing who *was*, he couldn't get into the Academy. He had not even the glimmering of an answer, but somehow, this didn't disturb him.

For there *was* an answer, somewhere, and he would find it. In the meantime, as for the rest of it . . .

Once again, whispering in the shadows of his mind, he heard it, Carl Endicott's voice: *I love you more than life itself . . . you believe that, don't you?*

"Yes, Dad," he murmured to himself. "I do. And I love you, too."

Not everything was blood. Sometimes, it was only love. And sometimes, love had to be enough.

EPILOGUE

A whole quadrant surrounding the disaster had been blocked off by ConFleet, but it was a vast area of space, not easily policed.

The alien shadowcraft, protected by technologies only vaguely understood by the scientists of the fleet, had no trouble penetrating into the heart of that region, where the debris from the death of Comsat still whirled in dangerous maelstroms.

The little vessel crept along, picking, choosing, tasting, sampling. Inside, a certain cold watchfulness . . .

Not knowing, only guessing. But possible, possible. And if it was true—

On the third day one of the grappling nets hauled in a piece of charred wreckage about the size of a small refrigerator. It took another day for the analysis to bear fruit, but when it did—

Oh, what a harvest.

A fragment hovered, cradled in a magneto-gravitic beam, bathed in harsh, blue-white light.

The claw was scaled, one of five at the end of a slick, smooth, brown tentacle. Gently, the claw touched the remnant.

So much!

The voice, deep, breathy, like the scrape of dry leather over wet stone, murmuring to itself, soft with triumph—

"Ahhhhh . . ."

The boy.

Find the boy.

BIBLIOGRAPHY

Some good all-around texts explaining most of the concepts of genetics, cell structure, DNA, and chromosomes used in *Delta Search* are:

Amazing Schemes Within Your Genes, by Frances R. Balkwill and Mic Rolph (Illustrator), Library Binding, published by Carolrhoda Books, October 1993. ISBN: 0876148046.

Genetics & Human Health: A Journey Within, by Faith Hickman Brynie, Library Binding, published by Millbrook Press, 1995. ISBN: 1562945459.

Genetics (Breakthrough), by Tony Hooper, Library Binding, published by Raintree/Steck Vaughn, 1993. ISBN: 0811423328.

Signs of Life: The Language and Meanings of DNA, by Robert Pollack, published by Houghton Mifflin Company, 1994. ISBN: 0395644984.

We now live in a time when not only paper and print are sources of information, so I am including references to data available in other mediums, such as CD-ROM and the World Wide Web.

In *The Microsoft Bookshelf* version of *The Concise Columbia Encyclopedia*, Columbia University Press, Copyright © 1995 by Columbia University Press, use the "find" function to reference:

Genetics
Genetic Engineering
Biotechnology
Pharming
Molecular Biology

On the World Wide Web[1], current resources are:

Primer on Molecular Genetics
Type: world wide web
Audience: biomedical researchers, science educators, biotechnologists, biologists
Access: http://www.gdb.org/Dan/DOE/intro.html

Embracing Change with All Four Arms
Type: world wide web
Audience: anti-genetics engineers
Access:
http://ccme-mac4.bsd.uchicago.edu/JCV/JGeneTech. html

Embracing Change with All Four Arms is the title of a paper defending the field of genetic engineering. It examines the various arguments against gene research and offers counterarguments and reasons that many commonly held fears are unfounded. Also linked to this paper is the Genome Project (a research program to map DNA sequences) and a primer on genetic engineering and its possible benefits to humans.

---

[1]Caution: WWW sites change with great frequency. You may also use one of the WWW search engines like *Yahoo!* or *Alta Vista* to search on genetics, biotechnology, or the like; all references here are taken from the *Microsoft Bookshelf Internet Directory 96–97* edited by Kevin Savetz.

The basic text on nanotechnology is:

Drexler, Eric. *Engines of Creation.* Anchor Books, 1987. ISBN: 0385199732.

An excellent nanotechnology site on the World Wide Web (found by using Alta Vista to search on "nanotechnology") is:
http://alpha.genebee.msu.su/nanotech/ntmiracle.html

Here you will find a good basic overview of nanotechnology, as well as many links to other sites dealing with the subject.